NYXIA
UPRISING

NYXIA UPRISING

THE NYXIA TRIAD

— Book 3 —

SCOTT REINTGEN

CROWN 👑 NEW YORK

Text copyright © 2019 by Scott Reintgen
Jacket art copyright © 2019 by Getty Images/Sunny

All rights reserved. Published in the United States by Crown Books for
Young Readers, an imprint of Random House Children's Books,
a division of Penguin Random House LLC, New York.

Crown and the colophon are registered trademarks of
Penguin Random House LLC.

Visit us on the Web! GetUnderlined.com

Educators and librarians, for a variety of teaching tools, visit us at
RHTeachersLibrarians.com

Library of Congress Cataloging-in-Publication Data
Names: Reintgen, Scott, author.
Title: Nyxia uprising / Scott Reintgen.
Description: First edition. | New York : Crown, [2019] |
Series: The nyxia triad ; book 3 | Summary: "Emmett and the
Genesis team must join forces with a surprising set of allies if
they're ever to make it home alive" —Provided by publisher.
Identifiers: LCCN 2018049016 | ISBN 978-0-399-55687-6 (hardback) |
ISBN 978-0-399-55689-0 (ebook)
Subjects: | CYAC: Conduct of life—Fiction. | Mines and mineral resources—
Fiction. | Life on other planets—Fiction. | Science fiction.
Classification: LCC PZ7.1.R4554 Nyz 2019 | DDC [Fic]—dc23

Printed in the United States of America
10 9 8 7 6 5 4 3 2 1
First Edition

TO MY SON, HENRY.

Sometimes we forget that magic is real. You are my precious reminder. Your smile is the bright lamppost at the edge of Narnia. Each laugh is a lettered invitation to Hogwarts. When I scoop you up into my arms, it is magic that makes us dragons soaring on wide-swept wings. Consider this a promise, sweet boy, to always help you see the magic you've shown me.

Love, Dad

PART I

SURVIVAL

CHAPTER 1

THE KING

Longwei Yu

18 days 12 hours 11 minutes

Babel's king bleeds.

For a moment, I think I've lost the trail. But I double back and find his blood painted across moonlit leaves. A great streak of scarlet marks the body of a swollen trunk. If I squinted any longer, I might have been able to convince myself the mark looked like the Chinese characters for *dying*.

I need this king alive.

Moonlight dominates the clearing. A creek angles west. It forks, and just there, I see where Defoe must have gone. There are no footprints, not in this ghostly place, but it's the most reasonable decision. A massive tree has been exposed at the roots. They curl above and around a hollow. It's the kind of burrow a deer might sleep in. I watch the shadows for several minutes.

No movement.

I follow the creek forward. The trees sway, their branches and leaves grasping at the light of the nearest moon. It almost feels as if the entire forest is flinching away from where Defoe is hidden. Fifty meters. I lift both hands innocently into the air. My eyes trace over the landscape, through the shadows. I'm not eager to die just because some creature has picked up our scent.

Twenty-five meters. I pause, hands still raised, awaiting an invitation. The shadows are too deep to see anything. Breathing. I can hear breathing. One shallow breath after another.

Reaching up, I tap the light on my shoulder. A beam flashes out—like a third moon—and highlights the make-shift cavern. Defoe is there. His eyes take in the sight of me before closing in pain. I can feel him grasping, the subtle trace of nyxia in the air. Clearly, he's far too weak to do much with the substance. I have a choice to make. The consequences will echo.

The first choice ends here and now. How painfully simple it would be to finish him. One of Babel's greatest threats, erased. It would eliminate any opportunity for him to hurt the others.

It would also eliminate any opportunity to infiltrate Babel. Show up on their doorstep without him and I become a prisoner. The other choice: Save him. Rescue. Subvert. Wait.

When I strike, I want to make sure I hit an artery. My two choices and their consequences play out in less than a breath. "Mr. Defoe." I make my voice calm. "I came to help you."

He wheezes. It's almost a laugh. It is clear what he thinks of me.

"Longwei—of course you did. . . ."

I watch as he leans his head back. Hidden at his hip, an explosive. Identical to the one he used on the battlefield. The same device that nearly ripped my friends apart with a single blast. Defoe lifts the device so I can see it more clearly.

"I thought—well, never mind what I thought." A cough shakes his body. "Take this. Replace my fingers on the pin and get rid of it. Three-second charge. Throw it as far as you can."

His arm shakes, but I am steady. I replace his fingers quickly, device secured, and turn. Twenty paces bring me back to the edge of the creek. With a deep breath, I throw the grenade as far as I can. Moonlight dances across its spiraling surface; then the grenade falls below the tree line and vanishes briefly from sight. A second passes before an explosion tears the darkness in two.

Bright and loud. A pair of birds take to the air. Something massive stirs deeper in the forest. I move back to Defoe's side. "I can't—stop the bleeding," he gasps. "The nyxia won't take."

I kneel so that my shoulder light is centered on the curled, covered stump of his arm. He has a soiled towel wrapped around it. Ineffective. I set down my own pack and start digging.

A new bandage, gauze, a plastic bag.

"I need to unwrap your current bandage."

Defoe nods once. I pinch the gauze between two fingers, carefully avoiding the blood, and lift one corner. The folds unravel. Defoe doesn't protest as the material rips and snags.

The wound exposes the bloody interior of his arm. Babel's king. How human he seems now. For too long I thought him a god. Seeing him this way will help in all that is to come.

I pack the gauze in tight around the exposed areas before wrapping the bandage tightly. Layer after layer. I use a piece of nyxia to seal it to his arm. Defoe lets out a groan as I pull the plastic bag over the entire wrapping, cinching it on his forearm, closing everything within.

"It needs to be iced," I say.

"It needs a lot more than ice," he replies. "I haven't slept. I've forced myself to keep moving. I need you to seal us in here. Keep us safe. Do you know how to do the manipulation?"

In answer, I reach for my nyxia. The substance pulses. A firm thought casts it out like a curtain, big enough to drape over the entrance of the hollow. "Like this?"

"Adjust it," Defoe gasps back. "So we can see out, but nothing can see in."

The change takes a few attempts. Defoe worms his way deeper into the hollow so there's room for me. I reach up, tucking the top of the nyxian drape between a set of exposed roots. I test it with a tug and it holds. The fabric stretches as I adjust the flaps and enclose us. There are gaps to let oxygen in, but we're hidden from prying eyes now. Defoe turns his back to me, injured arm balanced delicately on his hip.

"Sleep. I need sleep."

For the second time, I consider killing him.

The moment slips by like a long, slithering snake. Understanding shivers down my spine. I can feel the goose bumps run down my neck and arms. I know what keeping him alive will mean. Someone will die. A friend of mine, perhaps. Defoe is formidable. He can turn the tides in a single battle with ease. His intelligence will also give Babel the upper hand in the coming days.

Who will die because I let him live? What will the cost be?

I force myself to swallow those fears. I chase the dark thoughts away and remember that it's wise to lose a battle if it means we can win the war.

Unbidden, my eyes roam up to the distant moons. Glacius looks like an unpolished pearl; Magness like a bloodshot eye. The two moons appear hammer-struck into the sky. It's hard to remember they are moving, spinning, spiraling. I know their paths are drawing them inevitably toward one another. I keep the thought quiet—almost afraid Defoe might hear it if I think about it for too long. But no matter how much I try to bury it, the truth is impossible to ignore.

This world is coming to an end.

At dawn, we march through the forest and onto an open plain. The first continent was marked by creeks and rivers. This one is dotted instead with old ruins. Stone buildings long abandoned, the patterns they carved into the hills all but faded.

For all his faults, I admire Defoe's sense of efficiency. He breathes and walks and uses every ounce of what he has left to move toward safety. He speaks rarely and I follow his lead.

Our silence is interrupted once: a loud, droning beep. It's sharp and ear-piercing. Defoe stares down at his watch as the noise winds to a more bearable volume. I glance over in time to see four blue lights, arranged like cardinal directions. The northern one flickers and vanishes.

Defoe considers the watch long after it goes silent. His expression is telling, dark.

It takes us seven hours and forty-eight minutes to find a roaming unit of Babel marines. They emerge from the cover of the nearest hill like ghosts dressed in black. Their weapons are drawn and raised until they realize it's Defoe. In a breath their original directive is abandoned. They transform into escorts. We're directed to an elevated ruin just south of the location.

There's enough light to see a sprawl of vehicles packed into the abandoned courtyard. Everything bears Babel's signature designs: nyxian, sleek, deadly. Even injured, Defoe straightens his shoulders and marches into camp like a king. I am less revered. One of the marines stops me. I'm briefly frisked, my weapons removed. I take a deep breath and wonder if my chance to strike just slipped through my fingers.

But Defoe waits. Once my weapons have been removed, he signals for me to join him. I might be defanged, but I'm still in the right position. A marine leads us around an armored truck and directly to a team of techies. Holoscreens display satellite imagery, live-feed camera shots, and landscape views. Defoe doesn't hesitate. "Give me a full status update."

There's confusion as the techies turn to take in the scene.

Every eye settles on the bleeding stump I treated the night before. In the day's failing light, it looks like a poor excuse for medical treatment. One of his men arrives at the same conclusion.

"Mr. Defoe," he says. "We need to treat your arm. You're bleeding, sir."

He glances at his bandages. "In a minute. I want a status update. Now."

One of the other techies takes the lead. I note he has the same glove that Kit Gander wore. When he swipes a finger through the air, one of the smaller screens migrates to the central monitor. The image resolves into a massive map of Magnia. We all watch as the empty outlines of continents begin to populate. Lines—like the migratory patterns of birds—color the screen.

"Blue lines are likely escape routes for each ring," the techie explains. "Our teams are working through the wreckage of Sevenset. The reported casualties are far lower than expected, sir. After discovering the first deep-sea tunnel, our crews ran scans as directed. We have a general idea of where the evacuees would have gone, but there's still no explanation for how they evacuated so quickly. The amount of time between when we disabled the defenses and launched the attack was less than five minutes."

"And each ring has its own evacuation tunnel?" Defoe asks.

"There are hundreds of tunnels, sir," the techie answers. "But there do appear to be tunnels specifically designated for leaving Sevenset. They're all buried far more deeply than the rest."

"Seven exit points that connect to four different continents." Defoe considers that. I can see him trying to figure out where they went wrong, how the strike could have come too slow. I'm thankful that he doesn't look at me. "The facility we destroyed to the north was designed for aircraft warfare. The designs were pedestrian compared to our tech, but it was the clear destination for the group leaving the Sanctum. Are there matching bases near the other exit points?"

The techie shakes his head. "We have no visuals."

Those words draw Defoe's attention more sharply. He doesn't look surprised. Rather, it's a confirmation of something he already suspected. He glances down at the missing light on his watch.

"When were the last satellite images sent from the Tower Space Station?"

"Four or five hours ago?" The head techie frowns. "We weren't sure what to make of it. Command was directing us away from the crews that escaped our initial attack. But every single soldier on this mission knows the Adamite leadership was our primary objective. We hesitated to pull troops until we had confirmation from you."

Defoe nods. "Did you receive any distress signals?"

The techies exchange glances. "None, sir."

"Send a request for verbal confirmation. Ask for a Code Four Update."

There's a brief pause. "You suspect casualties?"

"Just send it."

The room grows tense as the techies scramble to complete the request. I listen as they carefully pronounce each word. The message vaults through atmospheres, corrects for orbiting patterns, and glows green upon delivery. Everyone takes their cues from Mr. Defoe. Silence is held sacred until a response appears in front of the central techie. He leans forward, squinting, and reads.

"All-clear response. No casualties."

Defoe clinches his good fist. "So the Tower Space Station is compromised."

The entire group stares back at him. Only the lead techie manages to find his voice.

"But they're reporting no casualties. . . ."

He holds up his watch. Three of the lights are still glowing blue. The fourth light is gone. Defoe decides to pull back the curtains and explain the mystery. "And yet this tells me that David Requin is dead. Combine that information with their desire to redirect you from our priority target, and we can make the reasonable assumption. Let's keep lines open, but treat all communication with them as tainted. I'd like to start gathering as much intelligence on the ground as possible. Falsify any reports you send back to them. Let's go ahead and get working on action plans for recovering the space station."

When the others don't move, Defoe raises an eyebrow. The look transforms hesitation into action. The techies busy themselves, and a handful of marines retreat to discuss strategies.

Defoe looks deep in thought. "Wait. The *Genesis 14*. When is it scheduled to arrive?"

"Any day now, sir."

"And can we communicate directly with them?"

The techie shakes his head. "We didn't diversify our

outbound communications from the planet. All our messages have to go through the Tower Space Station."

Defoe looks briefly disappointed by that. "Get to work. Action items to me within the hour. I'm going to have this arm treated, and by the time I'm finished, I want a debriefing session with strategies for every outcome."

I stand there—a forgotten shadow—as the others begin to work. Defoe pulls one of the techies aside. He speaks, and it's clear that he's forgotten I'm there. Either he's forgotten, or he truly trusts me. As the camp spirals into chaos, Defoe offers me a single insight into his next plan.

He says, "Activate the Prodigal."

CHAPTER 2

EXPLORERS AND SURVIVORS

Morning Rodriguez
15 days 08 hours 12 minutes

We are the first human explorers of this world. The first and the last.

No one will find our footsteps. No one will see the hills we see now. This world is about to come to an end. Our group can't stop looking up. Both moons hang in the sky. Glacius is almost full, but the angles and light have narrowed Magness down to a curving blade that's edged by a single, fiery streak. It's an ax waiting to fall on the exposed neck of the planet.

Fifteen days. The moons will collide in just fifteen days.

"Base ahead," the call echoes down the lines. "Base ahead."

I glance at Emmett. When he thinks no one's watching, his shoulders always slump now. The weight of all of this. That's one of the fundamental differences I've learned between the two of us. Emmett draws his strength from what has happened. I draw mine from what comes next. One isn't better than the other, but it does mean we come to each problem from different angles.

A quick survey shows the whole group is heavy shoulders and empty hearts. I haven't seen many smiles since we started marching. The threat finally feels real, because this time Babel wrote the words in blood: Jaime, Omar, Loche, Brett, Bilal, Kaya. Emmett whispers their names in his sleep. I'm glad that he does. Babel wants to erase those names, but we're fighting for a different end to their story. We want a history where their names are remembered and the people who killed them are brought to justice. I'm not sure how we're going to pull it off, but we will, we have to.

A second shout works its way down the lines.

"Units Three, Seven, and Eight on patrol!"

No surprise Genesis isn't involved. The Imago leadership intentionally keeps us out of the action. We haven't seen Babel troops in days, but the Imago don't want to lose their lifeline to Earth. We're the ones who promised to represent them. They'll do anything to keep us safe.

Or maybe they're worried we'll explore other options.

The crew looks happy to take a seat in the shade of the run-down compound. Jacquelyn and Speaker disappear inside, followed by the Daughters and a handful of guards. We pass a few canteens around, heaving sighs as we sprawl in the swaying grass. I imagine Feoria painting this scene— using the same colors she used for our portraits. A landscape dotted with young soldiers marching into a war they never asked to fight.

"What are we doing?" Katsu complains. "What the hell are we doing out here?"

I don't think he's actually looking for an answer, but Parvin offers one. The two of them have been digging under each other's skin the whole march. "They're running scans for activity in the launch stations. You know that, Katsu."

He lets out a laugh. "Can't wait to see the video footage of all those Imago waving down at us as they launch into space and leave us here to die."

And now he's digging under my skin. "No one's gonna die."

Katsu doesn't even look at me. He just leans back and waves up at the sky.

"You up there, Anton?" he calls. "If you can hear me, send down a pair of sunglasses. I'd like to at least watch the world end in style. You guys heard Jacquelyn talking about what will happen after the moons hit, right? We don't even get the badass one-shot meteor that just vaporizes everything. It's a bunch of *little* meteors. Boring stuff at first. But the bigger pieces will cause chain earthquakes, so that's cool. Maybe a few continent-consuming fires. And she said all that debris will eventually choke out the atmosphere. I always thought air quality was bad in Tokyo, but this?" He looks back up into the sky. "Anton! Send down oxygen masks too!"

I shoot a look over at Emmett. His whole face unlocks, like he's realizing for the first time that Katsu is under *his* command. I raise an eyebrow that would make mi abuelita proud and he finally intervenes. "Cool it, Katsu."

Katsu looks over at Emmett. I watch as he takes in the group and realizes it's not the right time for his standard comedy routine. He finally shuts his mouth, and I take advantage of the silence. Leading is all about momentum. Time to rally the crew.

"One way or another," I say, "we're going home."

No one responds. For the first time, I'm promising something I'm not sure I can deliver. Azima slips off to talk with Beckway. I'm not the only one who has noticed the two of them marching together. It has the taste of a doomed romance. I glance back and catch Parvin watching them. Noor sets a comforting hand on her best friend's shoulder. Omar died right after he told Parvin how much he liked her. Our days might be numbered down here, but I still hate Babel for taking those final weeks from them.

The thought drags my attention back to Emmett. He's leaned against the building with his eyes closed. The soldier's marching beard suits him. It frames perfect lips and softens the carved jaw. This damn boy. The boy who let me listen to his favorite song. The boy who tackled me into the water. I want to take this boy back to Earth so bad it hurts. I want to meet his mom and eat burgers and dance at parties. . . .

I let out a sigh. We have to survive today before I can think about tomorrow.

It takes an hour for Jacquelyn to resurface. She makes a line for our group.

"We've got news," she says. "You'll all want to be inside for this one."

At some point, I learned to read a voice. Life with mi abuelita taught me that much. How she used to come back from the hospital and say everything with mother was fine. Just fine. Those two words had a little piece of everything in them. Hope that it really might be fine. Fear that it never could be. Anger that we were going to lose her too. A quiet determination to beat an endless cycle. Jacquelyn's voice splits the same way.

I can hear doubt and love and fear and hope. It takes us all a few seconds to stand up, shake the dust, and trudge toward the entrance. I fall in beside Emmett. Our shoulders touch briefly as we both set our eyes on the next obstacle. Our romance isn't about kissing and holding hands now. It's about carving a path home, together.

On our left, the *Genesis 13* crew is huddled together. Guards circle, even though they're all chained up. Emmett's gone over and talked to them a few times. He's got the biggest heart I've ever seen. I can't force myself to extend an olive branch. The sight of the survivors takes me back to the first time we met outside the repository building. All the blood spilled there.

I'm not the only one who notices them.

"I feel bad for them," Alex mutters.

Katsu shakes his head. "If Jaime missed that head butt on Defoe, we'd be the ones marching in chains. If you ask me, we're wasting time dragging them across this godforsaken continent."

"Good thing no one is asking you," Parvin cuts back.

The crew goes silent after that. I realize some of them agree with Katsu. It's the first potential divide. The first small step away from *we* to words like *us versus them*.

Jacquelyn guides us inside and surprise echoes through our ranks. Outside, the building looked abandoned: faded stones and warped railings. But two steps inside pulls back the curtain. There are Imago guards manning a handful of technological consoles. Analytics roll down the screens alongside complicated maps of the entire planet.

"We gutted these old shelters," Jacquelyn explains. "Built a few fallout bases just in case our plans didn't work as intended. It wasn't easy to keep the construction off of Babel's radars."

I resist pointing out that the reason we're here is that they didn't keep their *real* base off Babel's radars. We still have no idea what gave us away. Maybe Babel just got lucky.

She leads us into a wider room. There's a table full of Imago generals, all waiting on us. Feoria stands. A casual sweep of the queen's hand brings a digital screen to life. The images resolve into a map as we take our seats. My mind skips back to the first time we saw a map of this new world. David Requin—Jacquelyn's uncle—walked us into a lie that would change our lives forever. He did it with a damn smile on his face too.

"We will not waste your time," Feoria begins. "We have enough data to make decisions about what we do next. Babel presented you with partial truths. Time is too precious for us to make the same mistakes they did. We want you to know everything that we know."

She waves her hand again. Eight circles appear on the map. The locations don't have a clear pattern. Some hover on the coasts of their continents. Others are nestled in valleys between mountain chains. Most of the circles are lit green, but one glows red. I can't help noting that the red location is the closest one to us. Feoria points to it.

"Our launch station. Destroyed. As you know, there are

seven other launch stations and each was designed to accommodate an individual ring."

As she speaks, the seven remaining circles flicker with movement. Color drains until each one is left looking like a pie chart. Percentages appear on the screen—written in their numerical system but converted so we can understand them too.

"Jacquelyn and Erone installed movement tracking in each base. It was the quickest and most effective way to gauge the activity at each individual base without sending messages that Babel could intercept. She can explain the system better than I can."

Jacquelyn steps neatly into the conversation. "The data reports movement back from every room inside each base. Let's use Launch Bay 5 as an example. That location shows seventy-three percent movement. That means our sensors have detected movement in over three-fourths of the building. We can conclude that the survivors of the Fifth Ring have reached the destination and are preparing for our prearranged launch date."

I consider the numbers with fresh eyes. Two of the bases are over 75 percent. Several others hover closer to the halfway mark. But my attention eventually gets drawn to the launch station that's sitting in the southeast corner of the map. It's an ominous black circle. The number next to it reads zero.

Emmett asks the question on everyone's mind. "So they haven't reached the base?"

"Exactly," Feoria answers. "Our best guess is that they encountered Babel. Jacquelyn's censors make it clear, however, that no one occupies the base. The Second Ring had one of the shortest evacuation routes too. They should have arrived by now."

Our crew exchanges dark glances. Feoria takes a moment to let the weight of the news sink in before she continues. "We believe this makes our next move quite clear."

"We head to Launch Bay 2," I say.

Feoria confirms my guess. "We were afraid to march toward an occupied launch station. Not only because Babel might be tracking and hunting us, but we also feared what would happen when we arrived. Think about how much we have asked our people to do. Only sixty people from each ring were chosen to launch into space. Such a small number of intended survivors.

"So what would happen if we arrived at one of the stations—a station we promised would be theirs to use—and demanded more sacrifice? I know our people. If their queens came knocking in the final hour, they would have set their lives aside for us and the Remnant. But I could not demand that at this point. I could not stand to take away what little we have given them."

"But the station is empty," Katsu points out. "Problem solved."

Every Imago glares at him. It takes all my restraint to not throw a hatchet in his direction.

"Put the pieces together, Katsu," I say. "That station isn't supposed to be empty. Something horrible must have happened."

"But—yeah—oh . . ." Katsu stares at the screen. "Sorry, I was just thinking . . ."

"About survival," Feoria finishes for him. "So are we. We are all wise enough to hold more than one thing in our hearts and heads. I do not know what happened to the Second Ring. My heart breaks for my people. But that same heart can hope for us. The moons will not care who comes and goes. The moons will not wait for us to make up our minds either. We have to start marching."

Parvin looks around at the rest of the group. Our group's been gravitating toward her leadership in these situations. She sums up our position simply. "So we march."

Feoria nods. "But we must do so wisely. Speaker?"

Our original escort takes his feet. Speaker is the first Imago we ever encountered. At this point, I would count him as a friend. His nyxian implant curls around one eye like a bull's-eye. I note the cruel mace that tosses against his hip with dark promise. He didn't used to wear it so openly. Babel's attack changed that. His voice is so quiet that we all have to lean forward to hear him.

"We suspect most of Babel's forces are near Sevenset. That makes the northern route to Launch Bay 2 the safest one," he explains. An outline of the route appears on the screen. "There are harbors along the western half of Settler's Run—our current continent. Several are outfitted with the ships we would need to make the passage. It would be unwise for our entire group to get too far away from the coastline. We would sail north and circle the eastern shoulder of the Ironsides."

A slight glow highlights the planned route. The imaginary ships slip neatly through a narrow pass between two larger continents before rounding the northern border of the land Speaker referred to as the Ironsides. The whole continent looks like a wilderness of mountain chains and hidden valleys. Our suggested route is roundabout—like going around the southern tip of Africa—but I think it's fair to assume that they know their world better than we do. The projected ships make landfall hundreds of kilometers to the south.

"Our primary expedition lands in the Veering Bay. Then we march over land. Jacquelyn believes we have fifteen days before the moons collide. This route will require nearly half of that timeline, so long as there aren't complications."

I'm still sorting through the plan when Parvin objects. I was busy looking at the big picture, but she caught the smaller detail I missed.

"Primary expedition? I assume that means there is a secondary one?"

Speaker glances at Feoria. The queen frowns before offering her silent approval. Of course there's something else. The Imago are almost as fond of fine print as Babel.

"We believe a small, secondary expedition is the wisest option," he says. "To the north, Jacquelyn has a ship called the *Colossus*. It is equipped with supplies for a group of four. It was originally created to traverse the frozen seas to the north. That is the most direct route."

A line cuts through the pole and directly to the smallest continent on the map: Risend. The route shows the smaller crew stopping at a supply base there before heading directly to Launch Bay 2. I can't help frowning. It sounds like the smartest strategy. Why the hesitation?

Speaker explains. "Dividing our forces gives us a better

chance of survival. We will outfit the *Colossus* with two of our soldiers." He pauses meaningfully. "And two of yours."

"No." The word is out of Emmett's mouth about two seconds before it echoes from mine. Parvin frowns at us like we're not being diplomatic enough, but this is a hard no. Emmett speaks for both of us. "We're not splitting up, Speak."

"Have you forgotten our arrangement?" Feoria replies. "We agreed to work together. We promised to prioritize your safety, but the whole point of that agreement was to deliver both you and the Remnant safely back to Earth. This decision accomplishes both of those things."

I'm about to squash all of that, but Parvin is quicker than me for once.

"Let them explain it," she says. "Let's hear them out."

Jacquelyn takes the opening. "The *Colossus* is traveling the safest route. Babel won't be watching territory it thinks no one can cross. Sending a second crew gives us a piece on the game board they don't know about. And surely you realize the primary route will be dangerous. We are moving in a large group. Babel will pursue us. There is no guarantee we survive. The volunteers that we send will act as insurance."

"Insurance?" Emmett repeats the word. "You serious?"

"What happens if we fail?" Jacquelyn replies. "If our group is defeated? What if none of us ever launches back up into space? The Imago who *do* launch at the other stations will have no one at their side. Saving our species will be far more difficult without you as our emissaries."

A heavy silence follows. We all want to be stubborn and stick together and ignore the logic of their plan. Speaker adds his voice again. "Strategically speaking, a smaller group has the best chance of reaching Launch Bay 2 alive. We cannot risk staying together."

Parvin nods. I know she likes this plan. It's the most rational decision. But at this point, I'm struggling with the potential pain of having Emmett ripped from my side by a snap of Imago fingers. Our group has already been thrown around and treated like a piece on everyone else's game board. We don't need to go through all of that *again*.

"I don't like it," I repeat. "This isn't happening."

Parvin shakes her head. Aboard the *Genesis 12,* she would have just nodded along with me, followed my plan. But now she's confident enough to disagree. "That's not your call, Morning. Feoria is right. We agreed to a partnership. Babel landed the first blow in the fight, but that doesn't change the promises we made. Do you want to be just like Babel? Making promises and breaking them at the slightest change in the wind? That's not who we are."

My cheeks flush. Up and down our table, Parvin's argument appears to be winning out. She fights to keep the momentum. "Business partners can make requests of each other." Parvin gestures to the Imago. "You want two of us to go? Then two of us will go. But when we make a request like this, it better be treated with just as much respect and weight."

"You have our word," Feoria agrees.

Parvin looks up and down our ranks. "Okay. Does anyone *want* to go?"

Silence. We all have reasons to stay. I slip my hand into Emmett's under the table. He squeezes back as the wait stretches. After nearly a minute of silence, Parvin makes a frustrated noise. She digs through her knapsack. We all watch as she pulls out a journal, flips it to a blank page, and rips out a sheet. Only when she starts tearing off smaller pieces do I realize where this is heading. She passes the pieces around.

"Write your name down," she instructs. And then she digs back in her knapsack again and removes a pretty junky-looking Dodgers baseball cap. "When you're done, put it in the hat."

I'm frustrated and angry and terrified, but it takes less than a thought to manipulate my ring into a pen. I furiously write down each letter of my name and fold the little slip to shove it inside the outstretched hat. Emmett does the same thing. He writes carefully, in big looping letters, and I realize he's just as scared as I am. This is the kind of game that I always lose. If there's some element of skill or control, I can win. But if it relies on luck? I never stand a chance.

Parvin counts the little slips before shaking them up. She holds the hat out in Azima's direction, and this is a game that even she can't make fun. Her face is grim as she reaches into the hat and pulls the first name. I try to remember how I folded mine—did it look like that one? Could it have been that crumpled? The first fear is followed by the second. What did Emmett's slip look like?

"You've got to be kidding me." Azima tosses the slip back onto the table and tightens her jaw. "Of course I'd pick my own name. The worst luck in the world . . ."

The rest of our crew lets out a breath before remembering two names will be chosen. Azima reaches in again, clearly annoyed, and unfolds the second slip. A shiver runs down my spine. Some current through the air that has my stomach twisting into knots. The dreadful seconds pass before Azima looks up and offers an apologetic smile. Her eyes skip over me and settle on the only person I didn't want her to choose.

"Emmett," she announces. "It's Emmett."

CHAPTER 3

GOODBYE

Emmett Atwater
15 days 06 hours 14 minutes

Man. Ain't that some shit.

I almost smile—like my name got chosen for the lottery or something. We always did drawings at school. People would come in and offer a hundred bucks on a gift card or something. Never had my name pulled for one of those. But this? Of course.

Of *course.*

Morning's got my hand in a death grip, and I realize she's holding it to stop herself from hitting someone. I give her hand a squeeze before nodding to Speaker. "When do we leave?"

"Tonight," he replies. "You will have a full escort of Imago guards. Emmett and Azima, please remain seated as the others file out. I would like to go over the general plan with you."

The others take his words as a dismissal. Katsu's been acting like an annoying little brother the entire march, but he slaps a hand on my shoulder as he goes. Alex leans down and hugs my neck. Jazzy kisses my cheek. They're all treating it like I've been sentenced to death or something. It takes a few minutes for the room to clear out. Azima collapses into a chair, half muttering to herself.

Morning doesn't move, doesn't even let go of my hand.

Only one other Imago stays in the room with Speaker. I've gotten used to seeing the Imago women on our march. They're taller than the men, with slightly narrowed features. This particular Imago is noticeably young. Even sitting with perfect posture and arms crossed, she doesn't look any older than twelve. She sports a pair of thick leather gloves, a high-collared military jacket, and dark eye shadow. It's about as close to Goth as the Imago get.

"This is Greenlaw," Speaker announces. "She tested off the charts in military tactics and political reasoning. The Remnant voted unanimously for her to join our mission, such is the respect she commands among them. Our current queens have already passed on their seal. She is to be our new leader in the new world."

I can't help stating the obvious. "Isn't she, like, twelve?"

"Nineteen," Greenlaw snipes back. "How old were you when you launched into space?"

It's a fair point. "Sure, I launched into space, but it's not like I was sent to represent all of humanity or something. I'm just saying—it's kind of a lot of responsibility, isn't it?"

"Do my shoulders look bent?" She offers the slightest smile. "I have trained for this moment since birth. My record in school is without blemish. Whatever comes, I am ready."

Morning whispers, "I like her."

I smile. Of course she does. Speaker clears his throat.

"We should discuss the basics of the mission."

For the first time, my shoulders relax. I realize it's done. I'm going. Morning and I will separate and that's the way it will be. She seems to have arrived at the same conclusion. She listens intently as Speaker walks us through the general timeline. Greenlaw asks a few probing questions and it's not hard to see why she was chosen. She is the pristine representation of who they are as a people. She asks both big and small questions. How will what happens echo around the world? Across the universe? Morning asks a few questions too. Azima and I sit in uncomfortable silence.

The plan has us reaching Launch Bay 2 a few days before the rest of the group. Our function will be to act as scouts. Figure out if Babel's in the area. Be on the lookout for slings as well. Anything that could threaten the potential launch. Our first task, though, is to reactivate a defunct satellite disruption device located at a base on the more southern continent. It should provide blackout coverage to almost that entire hemisphere. If Babel's monitoring the region of the Ironsides where Launch Bay 2 is located, we'll make it that much harder to track us.

"Take a few hours to say your goodbyes," Speaker concludes. "We leave tonight."

Greenlaw politely excuses herself from the room. Azima trails the girl. Between them and Speak, I'm actually feeling decent about my odds of surviving. Morning directs me back out of the room. The rest of our crew is gone, probably bunking somewhere inside the base.

"Come on. Let's find a room."

She leads me through the base. There are Imago every-where, so the hallways are packed until we go down a few staircases and into a quieter section. I'm surprised how deep the whole building goes. Morning's voice is quiet as she says, "It's actually a good plan."

"Not bad," I say. "But there's a quote about that. Some-thing about mice and men, right?"

"Steinbeck," Morning confirms. "Our class was reading his book right before Babel came to recruit me. Our teacher paired our class with these kids from Apex High School. Kind of feels like it happened to someone else. My part-ner was this girl named Anna Roberds. I'll never forget the name because I kept trying to call her Roberts the whole time. We always cracked up about it. The two of us had to do the whole project together. I was out in California. She was in North Carolina. The teachers wanted us to discuss how easy it was to communicate coast to coast. Compare our lives to the people in the book."

I'm nodding. It sounds like a classic teacher idea.

"And? What was the conclusion?"

"It sucks to be poor," Morning replies with a smile. "Kind of why we're here, isn't it?"

We keep walking. I'm not sure if Morning actually knows where we're going, or if it's just a walk to clear our heads. It feels selfish almost. The past few weeks, we've been acting like leaders. Everything has been about the group. It's been so hard to convince them to stand shoulder to shoulder with all the gaps Babel's left in our ranks. But that's our best chance of going home.

The idea of home makes me think of Moms and Pops.

"I hope my family is still getting checks," I say. "Bad enough Babel's screwing us over. If they're messing with my parents, I'm going to do more than just burn it all down. It'll be a strike-their-name-from-the-history-books kind of deal."

"Too much publicity," Morning points out. "I could kiss whoever wrote the Babel Files article. It's one thing to break your promises out here where no one can see it happen. But it's a whole other thing to mess with people while the whole country is watching. It's the one silver lining I've held on to in all of this. Imagining my family getting checks. Life getting easier for them. Finally breaking even on mi abuelita's health care bills. At least we earned them that much."

"You could kiss the person who wrote the Babel Files?" I raise an eyebrow. "And here I was thinking we were going steady or whatever. . . ."

Morning smacks my arm. "Desperate."

But the next second, she hooks her arm back in mine and leads us both into an empty side room. I can't help but smile as she closes the door behind us. It's not the time or the place, but here we are, in an abandoned room at the end of the world. There are a few busted chairs around the place and a single globe of light dangling from the ceiling. My eyes drink in the details of this girl—this woman—that I've fallen for on an alien planet. There's the familiar braid and my favorite freckle and those collarbones peeking just past her suit collar.

Morning takes one look at me and laughs.

"I didn't bring you here to make out. Wipe that grin off your face. We've got work to do."

I frown. "Work?"

"Like I'm going to let you march off into the wild without every trick I have. Take out some nyxia. We have enough time to practice the most important manipulations."

"Seriously? No kissing?"

She actually reaches out and bops me on the forehead. "Get your nyxia. Now."

About twenty seconds after I've fumbled a piece out of my knapsack, Morning has transformed into a first-class instructor. She walks me through some manipulations I never could have imagined. Some are easier than others. She shows me the doorway trick she used in her duel with Jerricho. Another highlight is the manipulation she and Anton came up with for getting him safely into space. It's a desperate measure, but at this point, everything is a desperate measure.

I'm still working out how to create a third doorway in her teleportation trick, when a polite knock interrupts us. I'm not sure how Speaker knew where we were, but he glances inside long enough to say, "The escort is gathering at ground level."

A second later and he's gone and it's just us again. Morning stands about two feet too far away. It's not hard to remember the first time we talked aboard the Tower Space Station. It was all so awkward. The gap on the scoreboard. The divide of being on opposite teams. We had good reasons to keep our distance, but in the end, those reasons didn't matter. I've had reasons to fight since the beginning. I wanted to win a new life for myself and my family.

But when Babel showed their hand, the goal became survival. I want to go home. I want to cook out on weekends with Moms and Pops. I want to shoot hoops with PJ and the boys. All that would have been reason enough to fight. Fuel for every battle to come, but I'm not just fighting for what I left behind. I have a future worth fighting for too. Morning and I deserve to go home. We deserve to kick back and watch movies together. Go out on dates and laugh about nothing at all.

Babel will burn before they take that from me.

I take a step forward and she presses one hand against my chest. It's enough to leave me breathless. The same hand sneaks up and grabs my collar, pulls me closer. Her voice is quiet.

"This is not our last kiss."

She presses her lips to mine.

"And neither is this one."

She kisses me again.

"Or this one."

When she pulls away, it's a miracle I'm still standing. A fierceness flashes in her eyes, and I hope she sees the same thing in mine. There are promises I want to make. Big and wild dreams I want to share with her. All we have to do is fight. All we have to do is survive.

Do that and there's a whole world waiting just for us.

It's the kind of dream I never say out loud. It's always felt too risky, too dangerous. When have dreams this big ever come true for a kid like me? I usually don't speak them out loud because I'm afraid of them. But not this time. I take her hand and start leading her back through the base.

"So when you meet the fam," I say, "you'll have to get past Pops first. He's all about plans. It's his thing. Wants to know where people are heading. So he'll ask about college. What kind of job do you want? All that. Just weather the storm, and he'll come around eventually.

"Moms, though? Moms will love you because I love you. Pretty much that simple. It doesn't hurt to tell her how good the cooking is, though. She's *real* proud of the little sea salt she sprinkles on chocolate chip cookies. She likes the little touches. So make sure you point out a few of those."

We take the first staircase. Morning has gone quiet. A glance shows she's crying. It's not a bad thing, though. There's no defeat in it. These are hopeful tears. So I keep talking.

"Uncle Larry's the weird one." A few Imago pass us in the hallway. The entrance is crowded with our escort. "He's kind of a close talker. Awkward hugs. All that. Don't worry, though, I'll keep an eye out for you and won't let you get trapped in a convo for too long. You'll meet PJ and the boys too. No real advice there. It's kind of a sink-or-float deal with them. You're on your own."

Morning's grip on my hand tightens. Speaker is waiting. Azima glances our way before looking quickly back in the other direction. The rest of our crew has gathered out front. Morning turns back to face me. Maybe she doesn't want them to see her tears. Or maybe she wants it to be just the two of us for a few more seconds.

"I can't wait," she whispers. And then fiercer: "Stay *alive*. Get to the station. You promised to take me out for a nice space launch. Don't forget that. Meet me in the middle, okay?"

I kiss her forehead. "Meet you in the middle."

She wipes away the tears and leads us out. The whole Genesis crew crowds forward. It's a little awkward, trying to say a goodbye that we all hope isn't really goodbye. Alex bumps both fists and calls me brother. Jazzy wraps me in a massive hug that you only get from sisters—or people who've transformed into sisters. The last one to come forward is Katsu. He puts an arm around my shoulder and pulls me off to one side. His face looks more serious than I've ever seen it.

"If you make it back," he says, "and we don't, promise you'll do something for me?"

I eye him. "Anything, man."

He takes a deep breath. "Will you tell everyone I was really popular out here? You know, like the Imago's favorite. There's this girl who wouldn't date me in middle school. I kind of want her to feel like she missed out. . . ."

"What's wrong with you?"

He laughs obnoxiously. "Don't act like you don't love me. Be safe, man. I'll make sure to keep everyone in order here. No worries with Captain Katsu at the helm."

"I'm sure you will."

Speaker gives the signal, and our escort forms up ranks. I slide back Morning's way and steal a final hug from her. I always forget how strong she is. Bones crushed and lungs emptied, I start the long walk north. Azima's striding ahead with Greenlaw beside her. The smell of Morning stays with me until we reach the first tree line. I glance back long enough to catch her eye one more time.

That final look says a thousand things.

This is not goodbye.

That was not our last kiss.

Survive.

Meet me in the middle.

And then the forest swallows the sight of her.

CHAPTER 4

ALONE

Emmett Atwater
15 days 03 hours 46 minutes

Layered in new gear, we march through the northernmost valley. Our chosen trail dumps us into the cover of a forest that runs nearly all the way to the coast. A breeze shakes through the trees, but it's still warm. I can feel my suit adjusting to the temperature to keep me cool as we walk. Jacquelyn has us outfitted in gear that's just as sophisticated as anything Babel gave us. Some of the elements are so similar that I can only guess who copied who: Babel or the Imago?

Speaker hands us devices that look just like scouters. Azima notes the similarity as she slides the device on above one ear. I slide my own lens down in front of my left eye and start blinking through settings. There's a screen that tracks our progress along the designated route to the coast. I toggle through until the whole thing flickers into *KillCall*-style night vision. The world takes on bold outlines in the dark.

I find myself walking a familiar rhythm. It's the same careful stride I learned on the streets of Detroit. The same walk I needed aboard the *Genesis 11,* the same walk I've needed my whole life. It's a signal to the world that I know it's dangerous, that I'm ready for whatever will come.

Our armed guard has me feeling like a celebrity, the same way we always felt walking through the rings of Sevenset. Speaker informs us that they're less concerned about an attack from Babel than they are with the wildlife that frequents our current continent—Settler's Run. He never explains the name, but every abandoned ruin is a big enough clue. This land was once full of people. Even the forest trails lead us past long-faded forts. I can't help thinking this is how their whole world will look before long.

Maybe it's an old habit, but Speaker whispers as we walk, pointing out certain plants and tracks in the packed mud. He doesn't seem to mind teaching us about a world that's on the verge of extinction. "We directed Babel toward Grimgarden for your landing," he explains. "It's the safest of our five continents. Very few primes. Most of the symbiotic predators there avoid the Imago—and by extension, humans. They wanted the path of least resistance for your journey to Sevenset."

I nod at that. We know now that Babel's primary goal was never safe mining practices. It wasn't even about getting their hands on more nyxia. Those were backup plans and bonuses that went hand in hand with their *real* goal. Get us into the city. Disable the defenses. Destroy the Imago. Everything else—the training, the simulations, the instructions—were just opening moves in the endgame Babel was playing.

We were made to compete. We were forced to fight. I

spent so much time sizing everyone else up that I never really saw the actual reasons behind what they were doing. The truth is that both the Imago *and* Babel gambled on us. And I'm still not sure who won.

"Final clearing ahead."

The announcement comes from Greenlaw. A glance back shows her striding purposefully inside the protection of our armed guard. Her eyes are focused on the scouter readouts. It's not hard to see why she was chosen. She walks like she's already a queen. Guess it helps to have an official seal in your back pocket that *says* you're the queen.

Our escort pauses at the edge of the clearing. Rolling hills sit between us and the cliffs that are marked clearly on the maps. I lose count of the abandoned farms and silos that populate the silent landscape. My scouter brings up a single glowing dot in the distance, slightly to the west.

"What is that?" I ask. "The marker?"

Speaker answers in a whisper. "A person."

"Just one?"

"Oddly enough, yes."

He gives another signal and the whole group reaches for weapons. Speaker removes his mace carefully. Greenlaw's gloves *blur*. I wait for them to take shape, maybe boxing claws like mine, but they stay in that strange state of between. I raise an eyebrow as we move forward.

There's a pattern to our progress. Two scouts swing wide. Four crouch their way directly ahead of us. Speaker gestures for us to fall in as the entire group closes on the distant target.

My eyes trace the dark plain. We pass abandoned sheds

and long-faded wells. Over one hill after the next, skirting the piles of rusting machinery as we go. It almost looks like any farm town back on Earth, and at the same time, it looks completely alien. The tools are different shapes. The farm structures designed for different purposes. About halfway across, I spot the fire.

Flames flicker against the gathered shadows. Our scouts surround the location. A single figure hunches there, nursing some kind of spitted meat. Again I'm struck by the familiarity of the scene: a man tending food at a lonely fire. It could be happening anywhere on Earth. Except I've never seen anyone on Earth spit something like what he's cooking.

It's a massive insect. Glittered wings are slowly singeing their way to black. A honeycombed eye stares out, and it takes a few seconds to realize that it's not one large eye, but hundreds of smaller ones. It gives off the satisfying campfire crackle, but the smell isn't exactly ringing any bells for me.

"Come now," the Imago says, back still to us. "I heard you long before you entered this clearing. Join me—if you like. The fire is warm. The food is passable."

It's the first time I've ever heard a man's age in his voice. He sounds ancient. Speaker makes a show of putting his weapon away. Greenlaw shimmies her wrists, and the nyxia settles back into those thick leather gloves. The rest of our group follows suit.

Speaker and the others have mentioned Imago living outside of Sevenset, but I always imagined reclusive mountain villages, not hermits roasting bugs bigger than my head. The entire group circles to face the man, but Speaker still keeps a cautious distance.

Time has weathered the stranger in every way. Not just in the slight wrinkles around his mouth or the quiet hunch of shoulders, but even in the look he gives us. Someone younger would tense up as strangers circled their home. It's incredibly clear he couldn't care less about us.

"You live here?" Speaker asks.

The man smiles and his teeth are surprisingly white. "Most days."

"When did you leave Sevenset?"

He lifts his hand in answer. The entire group sees the puckered scars where two left fingers used to be. "Released with honors," he grunts. "Over twelve years ago now."

I realize he must have served with the Seventh. That earns slightly more respectful stances from some of our guard. Speaker considers the man, and his conflict is clear. It takes a second for me to put all the pieces together. Twelve years is a long time, and definitely before the Imago knew about the collision course of their two moons. No one's told him the world is coming to an end. But we can't take him with us. There aren't exactly extra seats at the launch station.

Speaker makes the decision. "We did not mean to intrude," he says. "Stay warm, friend."

He turns to lead us on, and the man's calm exterior finally breaks. Desperation bleeds into his expression. He was trying to act like he wasn't afraid. It's pretty clear that he's less afraid of us killing him than he is of being left alone again.

"News from the city? Any scrap will do."

Speaker turns back. A shiver races down my spine. It's

such an intimate moment. Maybe the last time the hermit will ever speak to another person before the world comes to an end.

"The queens are well," Speaker says. "The moons are bright."

It has the sound of a standard phrase, something said in passing. Speaker's voice catches at the end of it, and he turns again. The guards follow, but I can't move from the spot. The man must have heard the little shake in Speaker's voice too because confusion spreads across his face. I stand there knowing the rest of his life will be spent wondering what he wasn't worthy of hearing.

It's too much.

"The moons are going to collide," I say. "The world is ending."

His eyes drink me in. For the first time, he sees I don't belong there, that I'm not an Imago. Silently, he reaches out and rotates the spit. "It was always going to end, though, wasn't it?" he asks.

Speaker and the others are waiting for me to follow, but I can't help thinking of Morning. The rest of our Genesis crew. We're bracing for the end of the world, but at least we're doing it together. "You shouldn't be alone," I say. "When it happens, you shouldn't be alone."

That brings a smile to the man's face. His fingers trace a little mark that runs down the right side of his neck, and I realize it's the standard nyxian implant every Imago has. "We are never alone. I wish you all the best, stranger. If the world is ending, you are in good company."

His eyes fix back on the task at hand. I watch him work

the meat away from the spit, and Azima has to pull me on after the others. Speaker was worried about wild animals interrupting our flight to the north. The hermit was never a threat, but I don't think I'll ever escape the mental image of him sitting at his lonely fire as the moons collide.

Our maps mark the cove as five hundred meters away, but every passing minute seems to weigh an hour. The scent of the sea grows thicker. It's followed by the sound of swells, waves lashing against stone. A veil of thinning trees breaks. We look down on a thrashing sea. The Imago keep moving, but the sight of it pulls Azima and me up short. The cove curls around the rocky shoulders of a distant island. The whole thing is brightened by the grasping moonlight.

"Back home I never saw the ocean," I say. "Just lakes."

A huge swell slaps the wall below us. Foam spews up, reaching for the moons.

"Come," Azima says. "Let's go. Home is waiting."

The idea of *home* steels something inside me.

The two of us exchange a glance, and we don't need to say the words aloud. Our plan is to leave this world behind. It's heartbreaking, but we know that home is waiting in the star-bright distance. With the weight of both worlds on our shoulders, we follow the Imago down the stone shoreline and take the first step on our long journey home.

CHAPTER 5

THE *COLOSSUS*

Emmett Atwater

15 days 01 hour 08 minutes

The *Colossus* rises from the deep.

Moonlight shines across its silver hull. The ship is the same size as the ones we normally use, but the modifications are obvious. The nose rounds into the form of a massive iron fist. A series of drills undergird the front section, and they look ready to pulverize. We watch as the remaining guards raise buried ropes and heave, drawing the ship closer to shore.

Speaker piles equipment into a rowboat and gestures for us to join him. Azima flashes that familiar grin. She bumps my shoulder before marching into the water. "We're like explorers!"

I have a hard time sharing her enthusiasm. Greenlaw follows with a smile. I splash in after them—thankful for the upgraded boots—and I help Speaker shove our rowboat out into the water. Once the bottom slides free, Speaker and

I climb inside. Greenlaw takes the nyxian oars, and I can't help noticing the way the material reacts to her touch. The blades at the end of each oar transform into a more complex design. As Greenlaw lowers them into the water, the blades start to spin like propellers. We dart forward immediately.

"Whoa," Azima says, eyes wide. "How did you do that?"

Greenlaw grins. "It's the gloves. They're my own design. I use them for everything."

I nod over to her. "Is it something you can teach us?"

"Of course," she says confidently. "This trick will take you eight years to master."

I have to force myself not to remind her that we have about fifteen days left on this planet. She guides us over slight swells and toward the looming form of the *Colossus*. When we're in range, I rise on unsteady feet and help spin the hatch wheel. Our crew throws a few bags of equipment inside. Back on shore, the Imago are raising a second hidden ship.

This one is identical to the training ships we always used. The makeshift crew takes up stations and gets their engine humming before easing gently in our direction. We climb aboard and abandon the little rowboat. "Let's get moving," Speaker says, sealing the hatch shut.

He takes the front-facing captain's chair, and we take flanking seats around him. Holoscreens provide live footage from cameras attached to the exterior of the ship. It's almost like staring out through windows that aren't really there.

At the sound of Speaker's voice, the entire dashboard lights up. "*Colossus,* this is your captain," he says. "Please extend auxiliary power and chain of command to the other members of the ship. Announce your names, please."

We take turns enunciating in clear voices. The computer registers our names as valid passcodes. Speaker leans over the controls and has the ship moving after a few minutes. To our right, the Imago passenger ship glides out too. Midnight waves surround us. A slight shudder announces our impending immersion. Water rises along the exterior walls, and all I can think about is that lonely Imago and the end of the world. I decide to change the subject.

"Speak, why the second ship?"

Our companion ship revs their engines before vanishing with a quick burst of speed.

"We are taking all precautions," Speaker answers. "If Babel is monitoring our movements, we hope the other ship catches their eye. It's a diversion. We will veil our radar signature for a few hours. By the time we surface, we hope to be outside the zones Babel is monitoring. You can use our extended journey to review schematics of the first destination. Or sleep. Who wants to go first?"

I shake my head. "Not sure I'll be able to sleep right now."

"I'd rather study," Azima agrees, then laughs. "Never thought I'd say that."

Speaker rises. "I'll take the first shift. Greenlaw, try not to get us all killed."

The younger Imago makes a gesture I've never seen—a quick slap of one hand into the palm of the other. I'm not sure what it means, but Speaker's grin widens as he offers her the captain seat. He crosses the room, and I'm wondering where he's planning on taking a nap. The answer comes from a tug of a lever on the far wall. Four stacked military cots release, all connected by rope ladders. He takes the bottom bunk and wrestles his way beneath prepackaged blankets.

"Greenlaw," I say, turning back. "Those gloves. How do they work?"

She smiles at the question. "So eager to learn. Where do I begin? I suppose with the basics. Speaker is older. Most of his generation use primal manipulation. It's all about possession. One person and his or her ability to change the nyxia's form. My style is called forged manipulation."

"Like your creatures?" I ask. "Primes and forged?"

"Exactly. Primes operate on their own. The forged combine forces to help one another. My goal is to manipulate your manipulation. You provide the foundation. I add the boom."

Azima leans in curiously. "Why doesn't everyone use it?"

Greenlaw shrugs. "It requires a very intimate trust. The Remnant uses it because we've trained together for the last five years. I think we all took to forged manipulations because we knew we were going to a new world, and that we would have only each other."

"And us," Azima points out. "You have us too."

That earns another smile from Greenlaw. "Want me to show you how it works?"

I look around the room. There's not a ton of room inside our cockpit, but Azima can't resist the offered demonstration. Greenlaw asks her to manipulate a favorite weapon. Azima's thought shapes the material easily into her favorite spear.

"Go through a few strikes. Your normal style."

Azima uses all the available space. She spins and ducks and stabs. Greenlaw watches her movements carefully before nodding. "All right. I'm going to reach for your nyxia. It will be your instinct to *resist*. It's likely what you were taught. Fight that instinct. Feel my reach. Recognize it as a friend giving you a helpful push in a new direction."

I watch Azima take her stance again. The air shivers as Greenlaw attempts the first forged manipulation. Azima flinches before laughing out loud.

"Sorry! Do it again! I'm ready this time."

An invisible reach brushes through the air again, and this time I see Azima's eyes narrow with satisfaction. She works through the same movements as before. Sliding a back foot, bringing the spear around to block an imaginary strike, and then planting her back leg. As she thrusts the spear forward, Greenlaw throws both hands out with perfect timing.

And three blades spring out from the tip of Azima's weapon. She lets out a gasp when each of them lodges dangerously into the interior walls of the ship. There's a second of raised eyebrows and dropped jaws before Azima grins back. "How *cool* is that?"

Greenlaw smiles. "If you can learn to stay open to me, we'll have a lot of fun together."

There's a slight rumble from the bunks. Speaker doesn't bother unburying himself, but his voice echoes sternly through the piled covers. "No projectiles inside the ship, please."

The three of us exchange grins.

"Come on," Greenlaw says. "I'll pull up the base schematics for you to study."

It takes a few seconds for her to get a secondary screen loaded up. She focuses on driving as Azima and I dive down into research. There's an unspoken focus. I'm not sure if it's the threat of the moons hanging overhead or a sliver of hope for home, but we want this. We have to succeed.

Babel built this competitive edge in us, or maybe they grew it out of what was already there. Either way, I realize there's also a part of me that's eager for revenge. I want Babel's plans to go up in flames. Azima's curiosity helps. She points out things I miss on the maps, and she's careful to read every footnote the architect left on the original blueprints.

Our mission outline has us landing on the southwestern shore of a continent called Risend. It's the smallest continent, and the only note we have about it claims that it's where Babel first landed all those years ago. Our route moves inland for about fifteen kilometers before reaching a series of finger-thin ravines that mark the entire map.

Azima taps a dark X on the screen: Ravine Shelter.

It stretches over one of the canyons. Blueprints show a tower on either side, connected by seven habitable bridges. The upper three crossings connect directly to the exteriors of both towers, but the lower four feed through the sides of the ravine and into buried sections of each tower.

"This note here." Azima points. "It says 'Use the grappling hooks.' "

I nod. "Saw that earlier."

"What on earth is a grappling hook?"

"You shoot them," I say, a little unsure myself. "And they hook on to stuff?"

Azima's eyes narrow knowingly. "Ahh. Like Batman?"

"Just call me Bruce Wayne."

She laughs at that and pushes up from her seat. "Enough studying. I can't even see straight. I'm going to get some sleep, Emmett. Wake me up when it's time to hit something, fathom?"

"I fathom."

For a while, I play the part of useless copilot. Speaker eventually relieves me, falling easily into conversation with the younger Imago. I retreat to the bunks and fall asleep. I'm not sure how long I'm out, but there's a point when the entire ship starts shaking with vibration.

I feel like I'm back inside my drill in the mine, diving down for more nyxia until an arctic morning hisses and snaps at the windows. We're back along the surface, and the ship's iron fist of a nose is punching through what looks like an endless sea of ice. I can hear the front drills spinning as they grind the scattering shards and propel us gradually forward. As the ship approaches more unbroken ice, Speaker activates something just like the pulse punches of Babel's drills.

They smash and weaken the frozen ice before the great belly of our ship crashes into the breaking pieces with real force. The idea of more sleep vanishes. A tap on the shoulder relieves Greenlaw. She heads for the bunks as I take one of the copilot seats. Speaker fights the terrain for another half hour. Eventually, he shows me the controls and takes a break to rub blistered hands.

I know this is a job I can do. My hands remember the motions, and can handle the wear and tear. It's just like riding the drill. Speaker stands at my shoulder for a while, but he sees I know my stuff and eventually leans back and closes his eyes. Somehow, Azima sleeps through the whole thing.

Destruction is the right kind of therapy. I doubt Vandy would approve, but something floods through me, offers my broken soul a sweet relief. I start to revel in how easy it is to destroy the frozen ocean that's between us and our goal. It helps me remember the promises I made to Morning, and the promises I made outside of the garden where we buried our friends.

Meet you in the middle. But along the way, Babel will burn.

That's my song now. I'm coming for them, and I'll take everything that I can. The thought fills me with fire. The boat raises up before crashing down. The drills spin and coil.

All that ice grinds to nothing behind us.

CHAPTER 6

RAVINE SHELTER

Emmett Atwater

13 days 20 hours 37 minutes

Speaker takes over when we're just fifty kilometers from landfall.

Azima calls me back to the bunks, and I let the rhythm rock me into a kind-of sleep. The lack of movement wakes me back up as soon as we're anchored. In silence, the four of us suit up for the next phase.

Our exosuits have every imaginable gadget. Stealth fibers to keep us off Babel's radars. Temperature control that adjusts to the slight chill in the air. Pockets of nyxia layered into the joints of the suit to be used as needed. There's even a little place along the utility belt where my boxing claws hook in. All it takes is a snap and a twist and I can raise my hands, ready for a fight. Azima's spear works the same way.

Beside us, Speaker inspects his mace before strapping it to his back. Greenlaw tucks away a few daggers before checking her gloves again. She catches me looking and raises an eyebrow. "What?"

"I just remembered what Feoria said. You're the future queen or whatever, right? I guess I'm just surprised Speak is going to let you fight if it comes to that."

Greenlaw returns a confused smile. "Is that how things work in your world? You only have to fight if you choose to fight? In our world, the fight comes to you whether you ask for it or not. Everhounds can pick up a scent three forests over. Arabellas feel the vibrations of *every* footstep. Not to mention your kind have been in the sky since before I was born. I am always ready, because I know the fight will come, whether I want it to or not."

She marches forward without another word.

Azima smiles before following. "I really like her."

"Beware queens," Speaker says to me, almost laughing. "They have a habit of conquering."

We all start inland, and he briefs us as we march.

"You've reviewed the schematics," he says. "Let me update you on mission directives. First, I have the latest readouts from the base. There is movement inside. We are not sure who the occupants are. It is pretty minimal, and it is recent. It could be Babel. Or it could be nesting eradakan. We will only know once we are inside."

"I'm sure whatever is there will have fangs and poisoned claws and all that," Azima adds.

Speaker shakes his head. "Freiza birds use poison, but they don't migrate this far south."

Azima looks back at me and rolls her eyes. This place seems like it's just one nightmare after the next. I can't believe Babel ever imagined they'd be able to conquer this world. It's far wilder than they ever knew. Even if they had succeeded—removed the Imago—it's not hard imagining a few more lost colonies finding their way into the history books.

"Be prepared for anything," Speaker continues. "We are entering the base from *below*. If it is Babel, our arrival will be a fine surprise. Our goal is to neutralize the site and access the towers. Each one is equipped with Jacquelyn's jamming devices. The science is beyond me, but they create a signal that will disrupt Babel's satellite imagery. Specifically, they won't be able to monitor any regions around Launch Bay 2. It is impossible to fully hide from Babel, but we believe this will clear a path for us."

Azima and I nod. So we're not sure who's home, but we'll knock at the door with a heavy fist. I can hear a little thrill in Speaker's voice. The same thrill is in our quick steps and eager hands. We can taste blood in the air. I'd guess all of us are eager to take a shot at Babel.

The conversation revolves around a nervous string of facts. Risend, Speaker reminds us, is where Babel first landed. It wasn't a heavily populated region, and Babel had mined over 90 percent of the island before the first Imago envoy reached them. Before it all went south. Azima and I exchange a meaningful glance. We've seen the footage that day. It was a massacre.

"I was there," Speaker says.

"But that's not possible. . . ." I trail off because of course he could have been there. It was twenty-seven years ago. Longer than I've been alive, but a short stretch of time for their kind.

"Babel came in arrogance," Speaker explains. "There were two villages on Risend. Outsiders. Like the man we saw by the fire. Or the groups that eventually came to be known as slings. That doesn't change the fact that they were *our* people. Babel ambushed the villages. The Imago were left dead. We answered in kind. Sometimes I wonder if we made a mistake that day. Taking blood for blood. I wonder if that mentality led to where we are now. Fighting each other instead of cooperating peacefully."

We walk in silence. I'm thankful when Azima puts words to what I'm thinking.

"You can't believe that," she says. "Speaker, the same thing happened in our world. In the country I lived in— and all the countries around it—people with power came and took whatever the hell they wanted to take. They break the bodies they want to break. They destroy things. They rename them. And then they pretend it was *always* theirs. Babel would have done the same."

Speaker considers her words before nodding, an affectation he's picked up from us.

"You are right. And the moons have made it meaningless. It will not matter who controls the land when they collide. It is no longer a question of being conquered. There is only the need to survive and advance. Either we leave this world or we die."

His words and our footsteps are the only sounds. He's right. Babel woke up the morning after Sevenset fell and probably thought they'd won. This world belonged to them now. I wonder how long it will take them to realize what they've inherited. And I hope we're gone when the moons do crash into each other. I know that's the moment when people will *really* start to panic.

I've seen those movies before. There aren't any rules in fallen worlds.

Our crew covers the kilometers easily. Risend is cold, but it's got nothing on winter in Detroit. Once we're down in the ravines, the wind starts to pick up. Azima's smart enough to remove her bracelet and jam it inside her knapsack. Nothing bright to catch the eyes of potential Babel snipers. We flank a dried riverbed through the snaking canyons. Damp spots suck at our boots. Birds wheel in the sky. All brief glimpses of a world I'll never really know.

Speaker pauses a few kilometers out. I'm surprised to see him remove what looks like a rifle from his knapsack. I find myself staring as he screws a nyxian cylinder over the barrel. He eyes the distant birds before offering the rifle to Greenlaw.

"Top marks in your class, no?" he asks with a smile. "Let us see it."

Greenlaw takes the rifle, adjusts a few levers, and raises it. Now that I know how her gloves work, I can see the manipulation in action. The material hardens until it's like she's holding the weapon in a steady, iron-like grip. The gun looks massive compared to her, but there's nothing uncomfortable about how she finds the target, exhales once, and fires.

We know she pulled the trigger, because the recoil works back through her shoulders, and one of the birds falls in an unnatural spiral. The others scatter to the west. I flinched back a little, expecting a boom, but no sound ever came. Not even a whisper. I watch as Greenlaw unscrews the nyxian cylinder and tosses it to Speaker.

"How was that?" she asks.

He smiles. "Living up to your reputation."

She carefully stows the rifle back in our equipment bag as Speaker eyes the vanishing flock of birds. "Dirks," he reminds us. "Prophetic creatures. They know when there will be blood. Eating the dead gives them a sense of who will die next. Their presence is a clear warning."

"Warning?" Azima asks, eyeing the empty sky. "What warning?"

Greenlaw answers. "Something unfriendly is in the shelter. The birds promise blood."

Those words bring a new tension to the air. We walk braced for bullets, our eyes on every blowing branch. My mind traces back to the rifle shot, though. The video game player in me can't help asking. "It was so quiet," I say. "You used a silencer?"

Speaker digs out the cylinder. "All the sound channels into this. The rifle shot is stored inside it now. I can use it later if needed. Always nice to have a diversion."

I nod at that. "And you used a gun. I didn't know the Imago had guns."

"We have used long-ranged weapons for centuries. Honestly, they are a little old-fashioned. The weapons that Babel uses are almost relics to us. They were rendered ineffective in some of the cross-continent wars we waged two hundred years ago. For good reason too. Activate the nyxia on your shoulder. It's a preset defense every Imago child would know."

I reach across my chest and set a finger on the nyxia. It's been a while since I really needed to manipulate anything. Thankfully, there's not too much rust in my mental reach. The substance activates, but instead of having to push an image forward, there's already one waiting for me. It reminds me of the preset designs Babel installed in their boats. Bilal and the other crewmates who were sitting at the defensive stations could shape the nyxia however they wanted. But there were preset designs engineered into their station too, which made it easier to react to changes in a fight. The same kind of image is in the nyxia implanted into my shoulder. All it needs is a shove.

The form manifests. A translucent shield circles the air in front of me and pulses with static discharge. It looks just like the one I used in my fight against Roathy up in space. Another thought has the substance retreating back into the designed recess on my shoulder.

"That defense will activate quicker than your instincts can," Speaker says. "Most of our buildings are outfitted the same way. Our expertise has always been in defensive capability. You haven't even seen our tactical battle grids yet. They are as striking and beautiful as any work of art."

"I always wondered about that," I reply. "I didn't get why Babel's missiles weren't a bigger factor. If they had all the normal weaponry, I figured they could have won a long time ago."

Speaker shrugs. "Why bring guns when you really need a knife?"

I smile, knowing he just debunked a century's worth

of action movies. The belly of the ravine constricts as we march, choking with discarded rocks and dying trees. Our path reaches a crook we all remember from studying the maps. On cue, the entire party looks up.

Both towers still stand, but with the slumped shoulders of old and weathered stone. It's hard to tell if the buildings were ever beautiful. The bridges, though, are awe-inspiring. They latch one tower to the other, like faded bindings that the passing decades couldn't bend.

Azima notes the detail that the rest of us miss. "Only six bridges."

We eye the towers and see she's right. The seventh and lowest bridge has fallen. We don't have an angle on the valley directly below it, but I can make out the gaping wounds at the buried base of each tower. The collapsed bridge has left the lowest floors open to the elements.

Speaker wonders aloud. "Jacquelyn's sensors indicate movement. The dirks predict blood. It could be an animal. Or Babel. Or slings. We need to be ready for every possibility."

The terrain masks our approach. We walk along the paths where the brush is thickest. Speaker has us crawling on hands and knees when necessary. Eventually, our positions on the scouter line up with the pinged location of Ravine Shelter. A pile of scattered stones marks the spot. The corpse of the fallen bridge has been slowly buried by time and rain. Speaker positions us in an opening, and we stare up at the black belly of the sixth bridge.

Speaker lowers his voice to a whisper. "A few quick

signals. A double-clenched fist means *keep going.* A hand held wide and flat means *wait.* A single finger circling means *spread out and search.*"

We nod to him before he pulls out the rifle and fits it with a different scope. Adjusting the sights, he aims and fires. There's a sharp click as something dark vaults through the sky. We watch it smack against the bottom of the bridge and stick. He turns back to us.

"In thirty seconds, that will block outgoing transmissions," he explains. "Ready?"

The three of us nod. Azima whispers something about Batman as we remove the grappling guns from the main bag. Speaker shows us where and how to aim, pointing out a target ten meters left of the gaping hole in the western tower. He models attaching his hip harness to the back of the gun before giving us the count. "One, two, three . . ."

Azima and I both fire. Speaker's eyes widen, and he shoots his gun a second after ours. Greenlaw throws us the strangest look in the world as she does the same.

"Who shoots on three?" she whispers. "You *always* shoot on four. . . ."

I can't help grinning Azima's way as the hooks dig loudly into stone. We copy Speaker, giving our ropes a few testing tugs. "Secure the first tower," he says. "Eliminate any threatening targets. We'll work across to the second tower after that. After we will activate the base's radar jammers and leave as quickly as possible."

He pulls the trigger of his grappling hook a second time. The switch has him spinning slowly skyward. Greenlaw has a wild grin on her face as she launches up after him.

"You're next, Batman," Azima says.

I pull on the trigger and feel the tug on my gun first. It works down through my arms and finally all the way to my hips. The ascent is awkward as hell. We spin up through the grasping branches, and I realize this is the most vulnerable moment. If a bird of prey is eyeing this canyon, I'm betting we'll look like a choice meal. Same goes for a Babel sniper.

My body tenses, but the shot never comes. The retracting mechanism clicks, and we're left swinging three meters beneath the bridge, about two meters from the gaping entryway. I try not to look down, try not to think about the fact that we're hundreds of meters in the air. The only room we can see of the tower's interior is marked by decay. Time has gutted the place. Speaker swings himself until he has enough momentum to grab hold of a half-hanging metal bar. He levers himself forward and lands safely in the room.

Secured, he unclips himself and gestures for us to do the same. Greenlaw is the first one to swing over. She's athletic, though, and watching her clasp hands with Speaker just reminds me that she's probably trained for stuff like this her entire life. Speaker pulls Azima in next, and then me. We all crouch by the doorway as wind continues whipping through the exposed room.

Speaker counts to four and enters.

A stone stairwell leads up. Azima twists her spear free and resets her grip. I slide my hands into my boxing claws. We follow Speaker through the first hallway: nothing.

He raises a fist and double-clenches it. *Keep going.*

We pause at the next door. Even opened gently, there's an obvious groan. The four of us sweep inside, remembering that each level of the tower has four separate rooms that wrap around the central staircase. Tension and adrenaline pulse as I duck into the second room. Azima enters the third. But all of them are empty. Speaker leads us through each level with meticulous care. He keeps one hand free for doors and hand signals, the other clenched around the grip of his mace. But there aren't any signs of life.

On the fifth floor, Speaker opens the main door. My breath catches. He takes one step and his entire body goes rigid. There's a Babel marine standing about a handshake away.

And everything happens in less than a breath.

CHAPTER 7

LIFE AND DEATH

———

Emmett Atwater
13 days 18 hours 31 minutes

The Babel marine's eyes widen. He's balancing a plastic food ration in both hands. A single second ticks away. The man drops the tray. Speaker ghosts forward. His mace bites diagonally across a gaping jaw. There's a muffled gurgle as blood splatters black fatigues. The man spins and his body slumps. Death comes quickly.

I realize I'm not even breathing. We all listen for other noises. Speaker locks eyes with Greenlaw and his order for her is clear: *hold the door.* He orders Azima and me to *spread out and search* with him. We glide silently from room to room. I try to ignore the fact that there's a dead body on the floor, that there's blood slowly spreading.

My fists tighten inside my gloves. The next room is empty. So is the next. There are messy bunks and discarded clothes, but no more soldiers. Greenlaw steps aside, and we start up the next flight of stairs. This time we hear the noises before we see the soldiers.

I'm not sure what I expected. Sounds of torture? Radioed missile codes? I've always imagined Babel as hundreds of Defoes roaming around and doing whatever the hell they wanted. Instead, the sounds we hear through the door are the most normal damn thing I could have imagined hearing: a card game.

One soldier raises the bet. Another folds. Someone laughs about how Johnson is *always* folding. There's a creak as someone shifts in their seat. Two other soldiers call, and the next card gets turned over. I hear the whole thing like I'm in the room, watching over someone's shoulder. A familiar game being played out in another world.

Speaker unclips a device from his waist. He signals for the rest of us to *wait*. We all know what is about to happen. That new anthem beats in my chest. Babel will burn. This is what I've wanted the whole time. A chance at revenge. For Jaime and Kaya and Bilal and the rest. I try to cling to the fact that these are the same soldiers who dropped bombs on Sevenset. The same ones who fired on Omar and would kill us if given the chance.

They are soldiers.

This is war.

All of them are guilty. Aren't they?

Speaker shoulders through the door, and the images come in absurd fast-forward. Seven marines sit around a table, lounging like they're in Johnson's basement. Every face turns, and it's clear they're expecting the dead guy who's going cold a floor below us.

The sight of us on their doorstep erases every smile.

A dull thud sounds as Speaker tosses an apple-sized object onto the table. It skids across the table, through piled coins and fluttering bills, and stops dead on a pair of nines. Speaker summons the nyxian shield from his shoulder and shapes it across the doorway. He layers the protection with a second barrier and braces his arms against them. Seven guns turn and fire.

An explosion shakes the entire building. For a second, I forget to peel off and check the other rooms, because bright flames fill the quarantined space. It's over before any of them even have a chance to scream. I wanted to feel this moment, but I thought it'd feel good. The destruction of Babel bodies. An answer for all our lost friends.

The good vibes never come.

Speaker leaves one of his shields up, letting the fire run its course. He signals for us to keep moving, and I'm thankful there's enough smoke in the room to hide the horror inside.

"They know we are here," Speaker calls. "Eyes open around every corner."

We clear the first tower, but gunfire greets us on the upper bridge. Speaker glances around the corner before dodging back. "Three on the bridge. Emmett on my left. Azima on my right. Greenlaw, follow me center. If you feel inclined to use those gloves, I would not object."

His shoulder shield activates. We mimic him and let our shields blossom into the air. When the defense fully solidifies, we round the corner. Gunfire echoes uselessly. A hundred paces and we're halfway to the three waiting guards. Speaker was right. They brought guns to a knife fight.

All of them drop weapons and scramble for belted blades, but Greenlaw has her own tricks. I feel her subtle touch as she reaches for our shields. All four of them pulse forward. There's a bright flare of light, and the Babel soldiers stumble back like they've been blinded by a flashbang.

My target strikes out at random, his legs unsteady. I bring my right smashing down on his wrist, and the blow sends his blade clattering away. It's a pitiful moment. A man who has always been a predator becomes my prey. I circle, and my anger sings.

I bring an ungodly hook across his temple. He falls to the ground like a string-cut puppet. Azima's target is bleeding from neck and knees. Greenlaw steps forward and finishes him with a flawless knife thrust. Speaker stands alone. His marine is gone, and his mace is bloody. I stare over in confusion until I notice the windowed gaps along the bridge. Big enough for a man to fly through.

"Sweep down across the bridges," he orders. "There may be one or two left. Stay together."

"What about you?" Azima asks breathlessly.

He points through an eastern-facing window. A lone marine is making a run for it. He's weighed down by extra gear and rations, and his head jerks back in terror every few steps. Speaker patiently begins unloading his rifle. "I am a fine shot too. Clear the lower bridges."

Blood pulses in my neck as we sweep into the second tower. Their crow's nest is filled with abandoned radio equipment, a few long-range weapons. Azima and I are about to duck back out of the room, when we hear the undercurrent. Our eyes trail the noise back to its source: military headsets. "It's a broadcast," I say. "Greenlaw, keep an eye on the door."

She bristles slightly at being ordered, but eventually turns to the entrance, eyes alert. Azima snatches up the nearest set and tosses it to me. She puts on her own, and a familiar voice curls to life.

I shiver a little, because it's like Marcus Defoe is in the room with us, speaking with that flawless delivery. "This announcement is for all Genesis 11 and Genesis 12 survivors. We're offering a final chance at redemption. The first four members who report back to a Babel facility will be groomed for a return journey to Earth. We are only offering this to the first four returning employees. You can report to Foundry, Myriad, or Ophelia Stations. Surrender to one of our roaming units is also acceptable. I repeat: we will only offer this to the first four volunteers."

The message cuts for a second and then loops back through. I exchange an uncomfortable glance with Azima. Babel's extending a peace offering. Clearly they're intending for us to get the message, but we haven't heard any of their broadcasts since we started marching.

It sounds like one final effort to lure us away from the Imago, or to cause division in our own ranks. There are a few survivors who might actually consider defecting. It would cause a headache at best, a full rebellion at the worst. And like most of Babel's promises, it sounds far too good to be true. Azima slams her headphones down after a few seconds.

"Promising more false gold," she says. "Let's keep moving."

We signal the all clear. Greenlaw pauses us in the entryway.

"I want you two to sweep down this tower," she says. "I

will sweep the original tower again. The schematics made it clear that the bridges can be accessed from both directions. We cannot risk any soldiers doubling back and getting in behind us. Meet me on each bridge. Clear them that way."

"Are you sure we should split up?" Azima asks.

"It is the wisest tactic," Greenlaw answers. "Go."

Her quick exit doesn't give us much time to argue. Azima throws me a look before leading the descent. The next few bridges are identical to the first. No signs of Babel soldiers either. The designs change a little as we work our way underground, though. I remember the schematics looked strange on these levels, and now I can finally see why. One side of the bridge is lined with scouting windows that overlook the ravine. The other side has been converted into old-school prison units with bars running from ceiling to floor.

Greenlaw appears on the opposite end of each bridge, gesturing silent all clears to us.

Overhead, the crack of a rifle sounds. Followed by a second. It's not hard to imagine the Babel soldier stumbling as Speaker shoulders his weapon.

No wonder the dirks were coming here. Death feels like it's following us around at this point. In space, across Magnia, everywhere. On the last bridge, we're greeted by gunfire. I flinch back, but our shields are faster. Three shots deflect against the summoned black.

Azima lifts her spear. We march in step. The final bridge is lined with jail cells like the others. Old-fashioned bars that are long-rusted. One door hangs open in the distance. The soldier stands with his gun set to a prisoner's head. My feet stutter to a stop. The sight stuns me.

It's Roathy.

He's a little worn, but I'd recognize his face anywhere. The last few months, it's a face that slipped in and out of my dreams. Those same features twisted with anger as he raged against the injustice of being left behind in space. Later I found out why he was so desperate. It wasn't about the money or winning Babel's prize. It was about Isadora and the child they were expecting.

Morning guessed that Roathy was dead. She thought Babel might have executed him. But clearly they didn't. Instead, they kept him as a prisoner and a bargaining chip. It makes sense. Babel has always been smart about not wasting too many pieces on their game board.

"Emmett." Azima's whisper is a hiss. "What do we do?"

I'm not sure. I can barely think straight. Roathy looks at us like two ghosts that have come back to haunt him. The marine feels like a random backdrop as we continue forward, shield raised and ready. The solider has a knife-thin beard. He looks like he's in his late twenties or early thirties. His hand is steady on the grip of his pistol.

"Come any closer," he warns, "and I kill him."

Roathy actually laughs. The two of us have a history. We come with baggage. This random guard has no idea how badly he's misplaying his hand. Roathy and I share a smile, and I realize this might be the first time we've ever had an inside joke.

"You think I'm kidding?" the marine says. "Stay back."

We keep closing the gap. Roathy grins wickedly. I'm not sure what he thinks is happening or if he knows why they brought him down to Magnia. I can feel Azima keeping the pace. We're about twenty steps away now. The marine's eyes flicker between us. He's gripping his weapon a little tighter, because he knows the moment is coming.

Of course, he's not watching what's behind him.

A flicker of movement appears over his left shoulder. I lift both hands patiently into the air. It's a pretend surrender. The guard smiles, because he doesn't see Greenlaw snaking forward.

"Put the gun down," I offer. "Just let him go, all right?"

"Like hell," the guard mutters. Something in his expression dies. He points the gun at my forehead. My shield is up, but at this range? Every instinct has me bracing for the blow. Two explosions drown the room. Beneath the ringing that follows, I can hear the marine scream.

Greenlaw's blade slips into his back. His knees buckle. The gun tumbles away. It looks like a clean kill until the marine grabs her forearm. She stumbles forward, and that's all it takes for him to jab a belt knife into her thigh. The future Imago queen screams.

Azima gets there first. Her right boot cracks into the marine's jaw. The force of the blow snaps his head back against the cement. She jams her other foot down on the hand that's holding the knife, and the marine screams. Another kick sends the weapon spinning away. Azima slides past him to tend to Greenlaw.

I replace her, standing over him and watching as he chokes on his own blood. Roathy stands to one side. He watches the scene with a curious expression, like he's walked into a new world and he's trying to figure out what the rules are. Azima already has a cloth pressed to Greenlaw's wound. She looks furious with herself for making such a dangerous mistake.

"Please," the marine begs now. "Just take them. You can have them."

I frown. The words don't make any sense. "Them?"

He looks back to a second cell, eyes rolling as the pain doubles. I glance over at Roathy, and he nods a confirmation. It's not some last-second trick. There really is another prisoner.

Skirting the fallen soldier, I look inside. A figure sits in one corner. He looks up and smiles at me in a way that Roathy never would. The sight of him is a miracle. It is an impossibility. My whole world trembles. I slump against the bars, as broken by the sight of him living and breathing as I was by the thought of him dead and gone.

The name breathes through my lips.

"Bilal?"

CHAPTER 8

NEW RECRUITS

Morning Rodriguez

12 days 02 hours 12 minutes

For the first time in days, we make land.

It's a mercy too. Katsu was starting to run back through the same jokes. A few more days and I think Parvin would have thrown him overboard in his sleep. Our caravan of ships dock in an old way station. It's a bare-bones harbor that the Imago clearly abandoned decades ago. This place wasn't exactly on Jacquelyn's radar either, so there aren't any bells or whistles in the buildings. Instead, our crew makes camp in a town square that's more wild grass than stone.

I stand just outside the circle of remaining Genesis survivors. Jazzy sits behind Ida, patiently braiding the girl's bright white hair. It's nice to see Ida interact with *anyone* besides Isadora. Jazzy's telling a story as her fingers work, something about falling off a pageant stage.

Alex sits behind them. His eyes always drift *up,* like if he looks long enough, Anton will write him a message in the stars. Even the smallest sign of life would do. *I'm here. I'm safe. I miss you all.*

Noor's right in the middle of everyone, snoring like a freight train. Girl can sleep just about anywhere. One time she fell asleep during the mining simulations. The Babel techs said they'd never had that happen before. A few meters away, Katsu sits cross-legged. He's trying to lob chunks of bread into Noor's gaping mouth. I shake my head. Little brothers are so annoying.

This is the family I inherited. Katsu is Emmett's brother, which makes him my brother too. Thinking about Emmett splits my heart into a million pieces. He's out there somewhere. He's not here at my side, where he should be, where I can keep him safe.

"You are such a mother hen."

The voice comes from behind. A little chill runs the length of my spine. I'm getting too soft. Letting anyone sneak up on me is a bad idea, but especially Isadora. I start to turn a dark look in her direction, but then I notice how she's standing. Her stomach is round enough now to be uncomfortable. She always sets a proud hand there, like nothing in the world could please her more.

"I care about them," I reply sharply. "Got a problem with that?"

She smiles. "Of course not. You have your children. I have mine. You have your love. I have mine. I've told you before, we have *a lot* more in common than you want to admit."

Those words scrape and scratch. I am *not* like her. I'm trying to think of something cruel to say, when she takes a step closer. She claps a firm hand on my shoulder before I can flinch away.

"You're scared. Our men are *strong,* though. Not as strong as us. You're made of iron. I'm the same. We're the ones who walk through burning buildings and come out the other side breathing fire. But the two of them are strong enough. Roathy will find me. I'll find him. Fear does *nothing.* Don't spend time on it. Fight instead. Lead. When all of this ends, we'll kiss our men and go home and live like queens."

She nods once and slips back into camp. I find myself nodding with her. Somewhere along the way, I stopped believing we would make it. I watch as Isadora settles into her nook of camp. She sleeps on her side these days. The baby's made sleeping on her back impossible. I realize she can't afford to stop believing all of this will work. She's believing it for more than just herself. And so am I.

"Morning?" Parvin appears at my side. I remember Jacquelyn snagged her right as we made camp. Something about logistics. "We have a few new recruits."

Over one shoulder, three shadows wait. The Genesis 13 survivors.

It's a surprise. "Feoria let them go?"

Parvin nods. "We had a trial."

My eyes widen. "A trial? Seriously?"

"That's why Jacquelyn grabbed me. Don't worry. I argued for them. The Imago were going to have them Gripped. My argument won out."

Aboard the *Genesis 12,* Parvin was the perfect teammate and soldier. Always waited for my command and executed the task. Now she's taking her own initiative. I want to feel a surge of pride for how my friend has grown, but that same initiative is the reason Emmett isn't with me. Right now it tastes more bitter than it does sweet. I glance from her to the former prisoners.

"'Lo, Genesis 13." I wave them forward. "Let's get a look at you."

All three approach hesitantly. I realize the only time they've really seen me is on the battlefield. Their last memory of me is as the girl who took Marcus Defoe's hand from him. Each of them wears a Babel-provided uniform. The names are printed in pristine, unfading letters.

Gio's slightly lighter skinned than Emmett. Kid is tall, but most of the height is courtesy of an unruly flat-top. Silver rings pierce his left eyebrow. He's not exactly handsome, but definitely memorable. Victoria barely reaches his shoulders. Her hair tosses in a bowl cut, dyed with fading purple streaks. She'd look like a little kid if not for the piercing blue eyes. Beatty's the last one. It's hard not to see a little Jaime in him. The same pale skin, the same dark hair. He stands confidently too. He doesn't look like a boy who was just escorted across continents in handcuffs.

"I'm Morning. We're the Genesis 11 and 12 crews. If you're going to march with us, there are a few ground rules we need to get out of the way first. . . ."

I pause long enough to gauge reactions. Victoria looks overwhelmed. Gio's nodding along like he's already on the team, but a smirk crawls over Beatty's face. It digs under my skin.

"Something funny?"

Beatty shrugs. "All of this is funny. Your whole captain

routine. This whole march. We watched the live feed from our ship. Sevenset has fallen. Babel wins. What's the point of all this?"

For the first time, I hear the British accent. It shows just how little I know about them. We've marched across one continent and sailed around another, but I have no idea who they are or where they're from. His comment flashes its own ignorance. For a second, I weigh the risks of letting them into what we know. We can't afford to lose the advantage of surprise, but I also know we can't just keep them in the dark. If they see who Babel *really* is, they'll know we're the only people they can trust. It's time to swap stories.

"Let's start at the beginning." I point to the sky. "See those two moons? In twelve days, they're going to collide. . . ."

It takes about five minutes to catch them up. Beatty's smirk vanishes. Each new revelation strikes like lightning. I take great care to point all the anger and blame in Babel's direction. If we're going to fight our way back into space, we need them to know who the real enemy is.

"We're going home," I say firmly. "Shoulder to shoulder. Fathom?"

The three of them stare back. Gio raises an eyebrow. "Fathom? What's that?"

"It's—you'll figure it out. Get some sleep. We'll introduce you in the morning."

As they file past, Parvin catches my eye. She lowers her voice to less than a whisper.

"We need to make sure we don't promise them anything we can't give them."

I frown. "Meaning what?"

"They didn't get Gripped, but there was still a punishment. Feoria isn't extending them the same priority status as us. They'll be treated like the non-Remnant Imago survivors."

The truth shakes through me. "Seriously? There are hundreds of us, Parvin. Launch Bay 2 has only sixty seats. We can't leave them to die down here."

"I did my best," Parvin replies. "Their names will go into the lottery with the rest. What would you have said that I didn't? Genesis 13 tried to kill the Imago—and us—just a few weeks ago. They're lucky the Imago spared them at all."

"Lucky." I repeat the word, unbelieving. "It's a delayed death sentence."

"You keep forgetting we're in a partnership. The Imago built the spaceships. They're our way home. We don't have any right to force their hand on this, and you know it. Without them, we'd just be stuck down here. Besides, are you going to give up *your* spot? Emmett's?"

I'm surprised how deep the question cuts. It just about knocks the breath from my lungs.

"Didn't think so," she whispers. "So why should they sacrifice a cousin or a brother or a queen for one of the Genesis 13 survivors? The best we can do is hope they're chosen in the lottery."

Both of us watch as the former prisoners join our camp. They hover at the outskirts like nervous freshmen at a new school. Anger still hums through me. "It's not fair."

"It never is."

"I bet Genesis 13 thinks they're just the last ones who get to launch. They don't know there are limited seats at Launch Bay 2."

"And they need to keep thinking that," Parvin replies. "Tell them the truth and we have no idea how they will react. Desperate people do desperate things."

I shake my head. "It makes me feel horrible."

Parvin surprises me by taking a step closer. She sets both hands on my shoulders and locks eyes with me. "It should. I'd be worried if this was *easy*. It means you're still in there. That big heart that's always had room for all of us in it. Get some sleep. We march at dawn."

She joins the others. They're kind words, but I'm having a hard time making them feel *true*. I stand there and think about Emmett. About the hell we're both going to survive in the coming days. He's out there somewhere. I know he's doing everything in his power to reach Launch Bay 2. I remind myself that that is the only goal that really matters.

Get to the launch station. Keep everyone alive. Go home.

"Meet you in the middle," I whisper. "Be safe, Emmett."

In the sky, the two moons keep their distance for now. It almost looks like they're giving us a little extra time. Just a few more days or hours or seconds.

Enough time to find our way home.

CHAPTER 9

THE WIZARD BEHIND
THE CURTAIN

Anton Stepanov
12 days 02 hours 03 minutes

We take our places before the massive black walls. It's hard not to smile.

It's just such a divine moment. I've stood here before. This is where we learned about the *Genesis 11*. Babel carved out such a dramatic moment for us. Requin and Defoe exchanged their smiles. It was such a fun little secret for them. A planned surprise that they knew would break us one more time. But now? Now I'm the wizard behind the curtain.

Aguilar stands on my right. I'm still not sure how we would have done any of this without her. I could have unleashed Erone on the command deck and bloodied up the place, sure, but Aguilar is the one who allowed us to take control of the ship without taking heads from shoulders.

She designed a false flaw in the outgoing encryption software to handle most of the heavy lifting. Instead of allowing messages to the incoming *Genesis 14* or down to the Babel command centers on-planet, her program rerouted all back-door communications to her own private server. It's all be-yond me, but from there, Aguilar traced the breaches back and ferreted out two treasonous techies. The only failure on our record is the disappearance of Bilal and Roathy. All the relief I felt when I found out Bilal was alive *vanished* the second Aguilar told me prison units had been emptied be-fore we took control of the bridge. She's 99 percent certain they're down on Magnia.

I'm afraid we lost them again.

At least we control the station. For the past few weeks, I've approved all messages between ships. Aguilar edits them to sound like Babel's space communication protocol. For a while, I was questioning why she was so dedicated, but she explained her situation clearly enough.

"Thirteen years," Aguilar said. "I signed up for three, but once they had me out here, that didn't matter. Not really. Some of the techies come and go, but the good ones haven't seen home in a decade. If you push back, they offer you more money. If you say no to the cash, they threaten your family. If you don't have any family to threaten, they kill you. I'm ready to go home and I've got a better chance with you in charge."

Aguilar's story is sad. So is mine. But our stories fall short of what Babel did to Erone. The Adamite stands on my left. He's been training down in the Rabbit Room. Running, fighting, manipulating. A few weeks and he's a spectacle again. Muscles layered over muscles, a head and a half taller than me, with the deadly broadsword strapped to his back.

For all his physical restoration, it's clear to me that Erone will not recover.

Over the past few days, he's slipped deeper into madness. He talks to shadows. He cries out in the night. His moods shift unpredictably. But I need him. He's a threat Babel understands. As we prepare to meet new enemies, I have to risk having him at my side. The black walls rumble. It sounds like the engine of a plane, revolving until the ground vibrates beneath their power.

"Remember that they have been lied to, Erone," I warn him. "Like us. They were tricked like us. We have no idea what Babel told them. Killing anyone is a last resort."

Erone lets out a breath. "As you say."

The walls separate enough to walk forward. I lead the two of them across the fifteen meters that divide the Tower Space Station from the freshly docked *Genesis 14*. Aguilar has been feeding them standard update messages for weeks. They have no idea Requin is dead. Their leader—Katherine Ford—thinks he's coming to greet the new crew.

It's a pleasure to flash my nastiest smile in his place.

The crew is lined up the way *Genesis 11* was. Ten teenagers front the group.

A dark-skinned girl with an almost golden 'fro. Two boys on her left sport matching topknots—though one is Japanese and the other looks Baltic. One pair stands side by side, and I do a double take. They're identical twins. A quick scan shows similar features in sets across the room. God in heaven. Seriously? Did Babel really recruit *siblings* for this mission? The group looks like we did: broad-shouldered and half-broken. Babel's games have carved them into more, skinned them into less. I can see hope in every eye. That's how we must have looked too.

No one's scraped through the first layer of Babel's promises.

Time to help them with the fine print.

The medics wait behind them. I see looks of surprise. The contestants had no idea what to expect, no idea what waited behind the wall. The medics all know an Adamite shouldn't be strolling into the room. Aguilar might look normal, but I'm a surprise too. Near the back of the room, two marines start forward. I spy their leader standing dramatically off to the right. I'm guessing she just gave a booming speech about the future and what's next and manifest destiny. Katherine Ford is recognizable. The red hair, the sharp glare.

She figures it out first. "Breach. We have an Adamite out of containment. Breach."

Too bad her warning doesn't make it past Aguilar's headset. The marines are halfway to us when Erone makes his own move. His sword is off his back and at Ford's neck in a breath. I'm honestly stunned when the blade stops. It's an unusual display of restraint for him.

The marines pause, guns raised, uncertain now. Ford is a cold stone. Like all the Babel commanders. She stares back defiantly, and I can't help but grin as I hold out both arms in welcome.

"You finally made it. Welcome! You've arrived at the Tower Space Station. I'm sure Ms. Ford here has informed you that this is Babel's base of operations for missions on Magnia."

"Former base of operations," Aguilar corrects.

"Former." I repeat the word and nod. "That's true. Their *former* base of operations. Erone and I had some issues with Babel's old chain of command. We're in charge now. So if you don't want to be floated out and fossilized in space, set all your weapons and nyxia on the ground, now."

Awkward silence follows. Some of the contestants look back to their medics for guidance. A few look pissed off, like they're seeing the grand prizes that Babel offered them slip down the river.

Sighing, I nod to Ford. "Instruct your trainees to comply with my order. Otherwise, it will be Erone's distinct privilege to remove that intelligent head from your shoulders."

Ford eyes the room. I know she's calculating every angle. What are the odds they can take us? Her own death is a mathematical certainty in every scenario, but she's not cut from the same cloth as Requin or Defoe. None of this was ever about her. I've read her file. It's about the advancement of a legacy. It's about reaching across the universe and accomplishing the impossible. She's not above sacrificing herself, but I'm hoping she sees it would be a waste. They're not prepared for a battle. Erone would rip through their ranks in minutes.

After a second, Ford gambles on staying alive.

"You heard him," she says. "Remove your nyxia. Guns too."

I spy a range of reactions—stubborn, curious, fearful—as the room bends to obey her command. The Japanese kid with the topknot grins at me before sliding some nasty little knives onto the ground. I like him already. Most of them store their nyxia the way we did—as rings or bracelets or necklaces. A little pile gathers by their feet. I slide it all back toward Aguilar and start the obligatory second round. If any of them are like me, I know they'll try to keep *something*.

"Hands up," I order. "No one moves, no one talks."

Pockets and ankles and belts. I find little goodies on just about everyone. The Japanese kid grins again when I pull three more knives from all the places I'd have hidden them. One of the identical twins had a coin hidden behind one ear like a full-flung magician. When I reach the girl with the 'fro, she purses her lips and raises both eyebrows like this is the most boring part of her day.

And then she snakes forward.

I twist to the right, but she's lightning. One arm slides under my own. An opposite hand locks the hold around my shoulder and neck. She squeezes tight, and a noise chokes out of me. I catch a flash of Aguilar's panicked face. Erone tilts his head like a curious cat.

I'm freaking out, because I know the Imago is about two seconds away from bringing a storm down on all of them. The girl's technique is flawless. Legs braced, grip tightening. It's so precise, but well-trained fighters never expect someone to play dirty. Her height makes the move a little easier. I stomp down, plant both feet, and launch my head back into her chin.

Light explodes across my vision. The pain is staggering, but she lets me go. I put three steps between us and have a dagger raised by the time the room blinks back into view. No one moves. The girl has a bloody lip and an angry glare waiting for me, but the rest of the crew stares over my shoulder. It takes a second to figure out they're looking at Erone.

He strides away from Katherine Ford. The woman's lips are parted in a strangled sigh. Her eyes stare strangely past us. Erone's bulk doesn't hide the sight of blood gushing down her suit. He readies his sword for the next offender, but surrender comes immediately. Damn it, Erone.

Hands go up. Some of them beg for mercy. The whole group scrambles to get rid of their nyxia, as if it's made of poison. Erone's chest rises and falls, rises and falls. He lifts his sword.

"Erone." My voice is sharp. "It's done. No more."

He glances over like hearing his own name has called him out of some other world. Slowly, he lowers the sword. The room takes a collective breath. Only the brave girl with the 'fro can't calm down. She's hyperventilating—both hands trembling. No one moves to help her. They're afraid to be associated with her now. She's the one who brought the angel of death to life.

I watch as the shock sets in. Of course. They've been fighting in simulations this whole time. No real blood. No real deaths. The only consequences so far have been how far they move up and down the scoreboard. This is their first taste of war, and it's breaking them.

Sighing, I make the order. "Babel personnel to the right. Recruits to the left."

A glance shows Ford has gone still. Erone made a mistake. He disobeyed the one order I gave him, but his stunt makes the rest of it easy. We order the remaining marines and astronauts out of the bowels of *Genesis 14*. Some of them round the corner ready for a gunfight.

But then they see Ford's body, our captives. It snuffs out the rebellion pretty quickly. Each of them sets down weapons and files into place. Aguilar matches the numbers to the ship's digital manifest. Once the count is right, we escort them into the Tower Space Station.

Three separate rooms. One for the marines, one for the medics, and another for the contestants. Aguilar's programmed the cells. They'll have food and water, but their only possible escape is through the bone-thick windows and out into space. None of them are that desperate.

Eventually, Erone leaves. Bored or restless, he heads back to the command center. Aguilar sends orders to follow the refueling protocol. Our skeleton crew is still working on *Genesis 13*, so it will take time to have the fourth ship readied. But when they finish, we'll have four ways home.

I start back through the ship's ghostly hallways with Aguilar at my side.

"Erone is becoming an issue," she notes.

"I'm working on it. We still need him."

And we do need him. Some of Vandemeer's recruits are loyal to us. But fear keeps the rest of our current techies and astronauts from rebelling. Erone is like a fire. We need enough of him to keep things warm, but not so much of him that everything goes up in flames.

"Any luck contacting Morning?" I ask.

Aguilar shakes her head. "Without a proper link, it's almost impossible. She would have to be in one of Babel's bases to make it work. Until then, there's no chance of contact."

Our unsolvable riddle. We control space. The ships belong to us, but no one on our side actually knows we're winning. It's also been hard to interpret the satellite data we've been getting. There are only a few things we know with 100 percent certainty. Babel attacked Sevenset. I've seen the footage. A single report came back suggesting the kill count was very low. Erone confirmed the Imago plan to abandon Sevenset and launch into space. We were shocked.

After that, we know the Genesis crews escaped the city and we know Babel attacked them at the exit points. And that's about the point where we took control. A few reports came back suggesting Defoe might be dead, but I didn't buy those for a second. Ever since then, the reports from the ground have been a mess. Aguilar suspects they've figured us out, but it's hard to say for sure.

Our options are limited too. We have a handful of escape pods left. Do we risk sending someone down to Magnia? Aguilar's suggested a few potential locations, but there's no guarantee that the person we send down would ever find the Genesis crews. And who do we send down?

Erone can't be trusted. Aguilar refuses. I thought about going, but it's not hard to see the consequences of that. Aguilar has been invaluable, but I get the feeling that she'd head home in a heartbeat if she could. And she's brilliant, so I know it wouldn't be hard for her to organize a crew on one of the ships and fly back to Earth. Entire worlds depend on my decisions.

There's a truth to choke on.

"Let's keep working on it," I say. "I'm going to check on Erone."

Aguilar nods once before taking the opposite tunnel. She wisely moved the command center out of the central hub and to a backup console. She explained it was the best way to track the activity of the less trustworthy techies, said it was like monitoring a small town versus analyzing an entire continent. While Aguilar rules over the techies, Erone broods. He always sits in the old command center, staring down at his home planet. I'd rather have him there than prowling the rooms we use as prison cells, picking unlucky victims to be put to the sword for random reasons.

"Anton." The voice comes from an adjacent hall. "Hey, Anton!"

Vandemeer. The Dutchman looks healthy, even if he's short a few fingers. Babel figured out his role after I broke Erone free. I found him locked away, half-starving. We went there looking for Bilal, but Vandemeer could only confirm they'd been taken away days before. Since then, he's been in charge of organizing crews for our eventual escape.

"How are we looking, Vandemeer?"

"*Genesis 11* and *12* are fully prepped. Have been for a while. We finished up with *13*. I've designated it as our emergency vessel. It's docked near the prison wards. Still working on loyal astronauts. We have enough to man two of the ships right now. But most of them feel honor-bound to their contracts and to Babel. They don't think we have any real evidence against the company."

Evidence. Like his missing fingers? Like the vids of Sevenset? It's enough to make me sick. Resistance to truth is so frustrating. Some people can't see anything but the money. I know it's even harder for the true scientists and explorers. Babel is the ultimate vessel for doing what's never been done before. It must be hard to believe their benefactors are brutal murderers.

"Keep up the good work," I say. "I'll catch up with you at dinner."

Vandemeer heads on to the next task. The remaining checkpoints slide open for me. I follow the familiar trail I took the day we unseated Requin from his throne. There are rows of empty data centers circling the room. I find Erone waiting in his normal chair . . .

. . . and my whole body goes still. He's seated. The guilty sword has been set aside. Both hands are pressed to his temples, and his face is pinched in a grimace. He remains perfectly motionless as I walk to the center of the room. There's no sign that he heard me enter at all.

"Erone?"

His eyes open. He looks unfocused, like he's staring at me through fog. An odd smile appears on his face. "Anton? It was you all this time?"

Danger echoes in his voice. There's a promise, a warning. I stare back at him, unsure how to answer. What does he mean? Was it me all this time? Erone lifts one arm, but it drags strangely before falling limp. What the hell is happening to him? He looks around at the empty command center like he's never seen it before.

"Where is everyone?" he asks. "Where are the others?"

I shake my head. "In the new command center. Are you all right, Erone?"

His eyes take in the empty room again. "Katherine Ford is dead."

I'm not sure if it's a question or a statement, but I nod.

"That's what I wanted to talk to you about." He's framed by the backdrop of space. I can see Magnia resting on one of his shoulders. It almost makes him look like Atlas. "I understand why you did it, but we're getting to the more complicated part. We have no idea what happens next. We can't just kill people who are valuable. We could have used Ford to barter with them. Understand?"

Erone blinks twice. He takes his feet, and for a second, I'm convinced he's going to reach for his sword. His eyes dance around the room. I've never seen him look so unsteady.

"Oh, Anton, the game is only beginning. . . ."

He takes one step, and his eyes roll. I leap forward, but I'm too late to catch him. There's a loud crash as Erone passes out. His strange words echo.

And then an alarm shrieks overhead.

CHAPTER 10

MY GREATEST WEAPON

Longwei Yu

12 days 02 hours 05 minutes

Silence has always been my greatest weapon. It served me well aboard the *Genesis 11.* Stay quiet long enough and people forget you're there. Every day I used my silence to learn more about my competitors. Now I use it to learn more about Babel.

A pair of techies hover over the motionless form of Marcus Defoe. I sit in the opposite corner and listen to their conversation. Like fools, the two of them speak the details that Defoe has always been too careful to share with me.

"No way he connects," one says. "The Prodigal wasn't designed to work at this distance."

The other shakes her head. "Their tech always works. It's a nyxian-based link. He activated the Prodigal before launching down. All he had to do was plug in. I guarantee it's working."

"No way. My guess is he's getting a bunch of white noise."

"How much you want to bet?"

Defoe twitches slightly. The two of them eye him for a second before exchanging shrugs. He's lying down on one of their military gurneys. A series of cords attach to his temples, the back of his head, even up through his nostrils. All of it connects back to one of Babel's mobile command consoles. A medic stands nearby, monitoring vitals, but Defoe breathes in a steady and predictable rhythm. Even this doesn't raise his heart rate.

"Creepy as hell if it works," one techie says. "I always thought—"

A sharp gasp from Defoe cuts the sentence in two. He comes struggling back to us, his nostrils flaring angrily against the intrusive wires. The medic shoves forward and starts unstrapping each cord with delicate care. Defoe blinks a few times, exhales deeply, and sits up.

"I didn't have full control," he says. "But it worked. I was . . . present."

"Distance," the skeptical techie confirms. "At this distance . . ."

"But it *did* work," the other chimes in. "What kind of access did you have?"

Defoe looks almost childlike. It's the face of an explorer who has entered new territory and can't wait to report back. Like the others in the room, he's forgotten I'm here.

"Some movement," he says. "Full vision and hearing, but not much else. I do think distance weakened the link. When I tried to walk, the connection severed. Proximity will help."

The skeptical techie nods. "I thought the Prodigal was locked up?"

"He escaped. Or someone released him," Defoe answers. He stands and stretches like he's woken up from the longest nap of his life. "It's perfect. We've lost control of the ship, but he's in command. Regrettably, Katherine Ford is dead. The command center is empty. Erone is there. So is Anton Stepanov."

And now Defoe remembers my presence. His glare sears its way across the room, and for the first time since rescuing him, there's suspicion in it. I keep my features carefully neutral. This is where my time aboard the ship needs to work in my favor. Emmett and I discussed this. What would Babel believe and expect of my loyalties? Defoe monitored my competition. He knows—or thinks he knows—that there is nothing but hatred between myself and the other Genesis members.

I knit both eyebrows together. "Anton left us."

"To go where?" Defoe asks carefully.

"He went to Sevenset. Morning said he had better plans."

Defoe shakes his head. "That's the story she fed Requin. You're telling me you didn't know *anything* else? How could Anton even get back up to space?"

He'll eventually figure out how. The pieces of the puzzle will lead him back to Foundry. Defoe will trace Anton's disappearance to that day, and he'll know that the only aircraft that launched back into space were the shipping vessels full of nyxia. I decide to offer him something profoundly foolish. Nothing removes suspicion like inaccuracy.

"The Adamites sent him," I guess, letting my eyes widen with feigned realization. "He went to Sevenset, and they arranged to send him back up into space. The person you mentioned—Erone—the two of them must have launched together."

Defoe scowls at my pretended cluelessness. It's hard to stay suspicious of a fool.

"Erone was already in space. Besides, the Adamites don't have the technology. Anton must have infiltrated one of our ships." His eyes drill back in my direction. "Is there anything else you haven't mentioned?"

I've spent so many sleepless hours combing back through the details. What do I say? What do I not say? I take a moment to weigh everything I have learned. Babel lost contact with one of their southern bases. Defoe deployed units from Myriad Station to investigate. I also know that a crew on the western front is gathering surveillance footage of one of the Imago launch stations.

Every new detail is another piece in Defoe's puzzle. It will not be long before he figures out that this world is coming to an end. The moons have to collide eventually.

I know I need Defoe to figure it out too. I want the Imago to have the upper hand and to launch first. I want my friends to make it to the Tower Space Station without getting gunned down, but if Babel never pieces together that the moons are on a collision course, I'll die down here with them. Some small part of me says the noble thing is to keep them here. Distract them. I think it's what Emmett would do if he were in my place. Give himself up so that others could live.

Defoe snaps his fingers. "Longwei. I asked you a question. Is there anything else?"

"I'm thinking. . . ." About which pieces of the puzzle to give him, which pieces to keep hidden. "There was a map. It was in one of the rooms we often passed. There were marked locations on it. I didn't realize they were important. I'm wondering if . . . these stations . . ."

Excitement steals through Defoe's expression. He crosses over to the nearest console and brings up a digital map. A swipe of his hand clears out the previous markings.

"Show us."

I take a deep breath and bring up my memory of the map. This is the first moment where I put myself in danger. It is the first moment where I protect my friends. An image of the location sits in the back of my head. I know that Defoe knows the location of the supply station he destroyed. Another sat on the westernmost continent. Is that the one they're already spying on?

I tap the screen. A circle glows there. "This was our target."

Carefully, I align my memory of the map with what's in front of me. I trace the coast of the western continent before tapping the map again. It's just a guess. Another circle appears.

"I remember this location too."

Defoe confirms nothing for me. His look urges me to continue. I do not let my hand tremble. And now I lead their troops to the *wrong* locations. It will be the only way to give my friends and the Imago a chance to survive. I carefully assess the map and start marking the wrong locations. One hundred kilometers south. On the wrong coastlines. In the wrong valleys. I bite my lip and shake my head, erasing one to adjust it slightly to the north. I give all the appearance of being meticulous. When I finally look up, Defoe stands like a conqueror. His doubts have vanished.

"Get these locations to the other generals," he says. "Don't let any of this feed back to the Tower Space Station. Let's reorient our attack strategies. Any word from Gadhavi?"

It takes a minute for a marine to return with news.

"We have a trail. Our team is in position. Commander Gadhavi thinks the traces are a match with what we saw leaving the coast. He suspects that all the remaining Genesis crews are there. Our two units are an hour north of their position. Awaiting your command."

Defoe offers a satisfied smile. "Strike as soon as possible."

I have to hide the fear that thunders through me. My plan worked. Defoe will slowly lead Babel's forces to all the wrong locations, but it might not be enough to save my friends. It will help the Imago. Babel's military units will head to the wrong areas. The survivors will launch from their stations without issue. But now the soldiers are claiming to have tracked Emmett and the others. I take a deep breath. My mind is racing. How do I throw them off the scent? Images of Emmett and Katsu and the others flash through my mind. Are they about to die?

Am I to blame?

"Remember," Defoe says. "We need Genesis survivors."

The marine salutes before marching away. Survivors. They need survivors. The slightest relief breathes through me. Our whole camp buzzes to life. Defoe considers the news before turning back to the techies. "Bring the device. Longwei, you're coming with us."

I'm so used to following Defoe's commands that my body moves before my mind can process what he's saying. Defoe leads us through the swirling activity of the camp.

"Are we joining the attack, sir?"

"That eager to prove yourself? There's plenty of time for that. No, we're returning to space." This time, I can't hide my surprise. Defoe takes note. "Temporarily. You just gave us a foothold in the battle down here. It's time to use our last inroad and take back the station as well. Our units down here can hold their own. I need you with me."

"Of course, sir."

"I want to know *everything*. Any detail you remember from Sevenset. Even if you weren't included in certain conversations, what was said in passing might be enough to provide more clues. Understand? I need to know *everything*."

I nod. "Yes, sir."

"The flight will—"

"Mr. Defoe." Another techie rushes out of the makeshift command center. "We're just getting word from our reconnaissance team stationed outside of the Adamite base. Three separate distress signals. The station is active."

Defoe's eyes narrow. "So they're launching an attack. Where are they heading?"

The techie shakes his head. "Up. The ships launched *up*. Our team reports that they're leaving the atmosphere. Sir, the Adamites are launching into *space*."

Just below all his carefully groomed features, I finally see fear. Defoe stares at the man for a second and then transforms back into a fearless leader. His voice echoes through the camp.

"Gun them down. Activate every silo. I want our squads mobilizing toward the labeled launch stations. Feed them Longwei's coordinates for the other launch locations *now*. Anything that moves into the sky is a target. Tell Gadhavi's crew to redirect. I want half his crew to track the group. I want the other half searching for the anticipated launch station. Reports on the hour. Let's move."

I take quiet pleasure in knowing they'll move to the wrong locations. By the time they reach them, I will be in space with Defoe. I say a quiet prayer for my friends. *Launch. Survive. Meet me in the stars.* In all the chaos, I carefully follow Defoe to the nearest ship. My eyes dance up. The moons are overhead. Is it my imagination, or are they closer now than ever?

The sight is swallowed as we duck into a cockpit.

There's a moment where Defoe considers me. The engines are roaring. He reaches back and hands me the sword that was initially confiscated. I stow it at my feet and nod back to him as the ship starts to rumble all around us.

I am the only quiet thing.

And silence is my greatest weapon.

CHAPTER 11

ALARMS

Anton Stepanov
12 days 01 hour 58 minutes

I take time to check Erone's vitals before shoving back through the maze of rooms and tunnels and hallways. It's hard to leave him there—in such a vulnerable state—but our converted Babel employees are too afraid of him to risk entering this room anyway. I just hope when he wakes up he's back to normal. I've got bigger problems to handle right now.

Alarms are still screaming through the station, and I can't help feeling like Erone's episode is the beginning of something far worse. I feel like he's been slipping away from us, but this time was different somehow. Something in his voice was just wrong.

Aguilar pings my headset. "I'm rerouting you, Anton. Activate your scouter."

The nyxian headpiece slides neatly over one eye. A series of readouts skip across my vision before Aguilar accesses the data remotely. There's a pause, and then my new route flashes to life. A red streak shows where I need to walk. I keep one hand over the hilt of my knife just in case something nasty rounds the corner. "What the hell's happening?" I hiss through the comm.

"One of our prisoner groups escaped containment. Follow the route."

An ETA flashes in the corner of my vision. I'm about a minute away. A few techies appear at the end of another tunnel. I spy red bandannas tied around forearms. That was Vandemeer's idea. Something to mark the loyal members of our rebellion at a glance. I'm not sure what they're working on, but Aguilar's route has me rounding another corner and moving the opposite direction.

The ship actually trembles.

"What the hell . . ."

I turn a final corner and find Aguilar barking orders. A pair of marines flank a battered entryway. It's one of the containment rooms, but I can't remember which set of prisoners was inside this one. Whoever it was, they tested the hell out of the frame. There's a nasty-looking set of dents that have bent the whole thing inward, but somehow it held.

"Triple-check those knots," Aguilar orders the marines. "Your suits are green-lit. Let's get this room sealed. Do not harm anyone who's still inside. Disarm and subdue if necessary, got it?"

Both guards have thick black ropes wrapped around their waists. Aguilar pauses long enough to glance back at me. "There's a breach. It's the *Genesis 14* crew."

I take my place at her side as she manipulates nyxia. She doesn't have the same handle on it that I do, but she's good enough now to create a barrier. The translucent material stretches until we're cut off completely from the two marines. At her signal, they forge ahead. The door swings open, and there's an immediate suction. Both guards float forward, feet lifting briefly from the ground. The knots hold, though, and the two of them duck inside.

"God in heaven," I whisper. In the distance, there's a gaping hole where glass should be. The empty cold of space sucks at the shattered edges. My mouth hangs open at the thought of someone being stupid enough to break out that way. "They're all dead."

Both marines are working to reseal the room. Aguilar shakes her head.

"They broke it intentionally, Anton," she replies. "You really think they did this without having some kind of plan? If they're anything like you and the other recruits, they're smart. I'm guessing we'll get another breach report soon. They're somewhere on the exterior of the ship. Eventually they'll have to break back in. We'll keep an eye on all the loading bays."

There's another suction sound. The two marines touch back down and signal an all clear to us. At the same time, the alarms overhead stop shrieking. Aguilar pulls her nyxian shield back into a bracelet before marching on to inspect the damage. One of the marines gestures to a table in the far corner. A lonely stool fronts the high top. "There used to be two chairs," he says.

"Unbelievable," Aguilar whispers. She taps her scouter, and I hear the static snap of her voice as it punches back through the comm system. "I need eyes on all our exterior cameras. Any signs of movement should be reported back to me immediately. Copy?"

A second passes. "Copy that."

Aguilar turns back. "They had more nyxia."

"No kidding," I say. "What do we do now?"

I'm about to tell her what happened with Erone, but realize that's not something that should be said in front of two random marines. I have no idea what they'd do without that threat looming in the backdrop. Aguilar opens her mouth to give an order, when new alarms shriek to life.

Pulsing booms spaced out by a few seconds.

It's a different alarm.

"What is that one for?" I ask.

Aguilar's eyes go wide. "An object broke the lower atmospheric zone."

"Meaning what?"

Her eyes trace the shattered glass, the empty room.

"Someone is launching into space."

CHAPTER 12

DOVER BEACH

Morning Rodriguez
11 days 22 hours 18 minutes

Our Imago escorts insist these are the valleys. The big mountains, according to them, all sit in the northern half of the continent. That doesn't offer our crew a whole lot of comfort as we forge our way up one hill after another.

"You know," Katsu complains. "After you go up a few hills, usually you go back *down* a few of them. Maybe I missed a geography lesson or something. Or maybe it's a spiritual thing. Maybe this is the afterlife and we're all slowly making the ascent to heaven."

Parvin rolls her eyes. "Check the readouts. We're coming up on the descent."

"That's another thing," Katsu says. "These readouts. Great technology, right? Do you think the Imago ever considered inventing cars? Or planes? Why aren't we snapping our fingers and teleporting to Launch Bay 2? I thought the Imago were the more intelligent species or whatever."

On the far right of our group, Beckway clears his throat

awkwardly. He's wearing his hair in the usual topknot. "I am walking right here, Katsu. You know that, right?"

Katsu glances over. "Beckway! Didn't see you there. But now that you're here, why the *hell* are we walking? Are you testing our viability as a species or something?"

I see a few smiles flicker across a few faces. Katsu might be annoying, but our group needs to laugh a little. The Genesis 13 members have all taken to him too. I thought our team would extend an olive branch, but it's been slow going. Our brightest memory of them is the furious fighting that happened around the repository. We lost friends that day. So did they.

"We are quite capable of traveling quickly," Beckway answers. "You have seen our boats, have you not? You've also seen the nyxian carriers we use to travel overland."

That catches my attention. The spiraling black spheres we saw when they first came to greet us. I forgot all about them. "Wait . . . Why aren't we using those? It'd be so much quicker."

"Quicker and more dangerous." Beckway holds out one hand, letting sunlight flash across the nyxia implanted over each knuckle. "We traveled that way through Grimgarden because the risks were minimal. Most species there would have been easy enough to deal with. But out here?"

He gestures to the surrounding mountains. Light peeks in from the west. Each of the waiting giants has snow frosted over jutting shoulders. A pair of faded valleys carve paths to the north.

"This continent is far more dangerous," Beckway concludes. "And certain creatures are drawn by the use of nyxia.

Our carriers are especially attractive. The faster prey can move, the more appealing the hunt. So we've chosen to march slowly and deliberately. Does that make sense?"

It sure does. On my left, Katsu immediately pretends to walk in slow motion. Each stride is taken with exaggerated slowness until he's fallen well behind. "Is this better? Am I safe now?"

Beckway laughs. "You will be eaten last. Congratulations."

"It's interesting," I say after the laughter dies down. "Something being lured by nyxia."

"It is knowledge for which we paid dearly," he replies. "There are historical accounts of entire traveling parties vanishing. Certain primes began following the scent. They learned to recognize our use of nyxia, and knew following those trails would lead to a good meal."

"One more thing Babel never told us," Noor complains.

"One more thing they didn't know," Beckway corrects. "There is a great deal Babel could never understand about our people. Their time here has been short. Just thirty years. For all their talents, Babel has not paid the necessary price for such knowledge. They never discovered that nyxia came from the moon Magness. They never learned that our people avoid the substance when it first lands on the surface, because it emits a mind-controlling poison until it chemically settles. How could Babel ever know such things? They are outsiders. They always will be."

We march in silence after that. The passing hours prove Parvin right. We are starting a very gradual descent. The path winds downward until we reach an overlook. And the sight waiting below forces a deeper silence. The scene is beautiful and bright and painted with blood.

There is the valley.

But there are also bodies. Hundreds of them stretched across rivers and over hillsides and through the ravines. I've only ever seen pictures of battles like this in history vids. It's a carnage I've never had to know. The sight presses permanently into my memory, even though none of it makes any sense. One section of the valley flickers black. My brain irrationally labels it as a soccer field. A flawless rectangle that veils one section of the battle. It's hard not to notice the high concentration of slain Imago skirting the edges.

Feoria organizes some of the units at the front, just in case of an attack. But it becomes all too clear that the valley— and the dead—have been abandoned. No one speaks. Our group descends in silence. The waiting images are oppressive. The way they haunt us through every gap in the trees. How our approach brings out the bloody details we could not see from above. Dirks flap from body to body.

At ground level, the smells hit. There's so much death.

Isadora is the first one to transform a piece of nyxia into a bandanna. She ties the thing over her face like a mask. We all follow suit. They look like mourning colors. Whispers echo back from the front lines. Feoria and the rest of the Remnant are clearly stunned. It's not hard to figure out why. From above, I was expecting to find a mix of Imago and Babel. Even if Babel won the fight, there would be a few casualties at least.

There aren't, because this battle was Imago versus Imago.

Our group picks their way toward the black field. At

ground level, I couldn't tell that it was three-dimensional. It looms before us now. Not a flat square, but a series of massive cubes. The whole thing looks like a grid. Slightly darker lines show where one section ends and the next begins. The cubes are at least twice our height. It doesn't take long to remember we've seen them before. Back on the Sixth Ring, there was a single cube. Emmett and I watched it together.

"Grav fighters," I mutter.

Beckway is the closest Imago. He looks around at a field full of his own people, all slain. After taking a deep breath, he confirms my guess. "The gravity cubes are also used in warfare. A general will rig the grid in a section of the battlefield. His fighters would know the full layout. Some cubes have extra gravity. Others have less. It's supposed to give them the advantage."

He pauses. It's clear that advantage was not enough. The dark grid initially obscured our vision, but at this distance, everything becomes clear. Even more bodies line the interior of the grid. The ones inside cubes with less gravity float up into the air like puppets. It's impossible to breathe.

Beckway points to the nearest corpse. "See the tattoos?"

Around one wrist, planets are in orbit. I know the tattoo far too well. Jerricho had one. So did the three assassins who tried to attack us at Foundry. I speak the title aloud.

"Slings."

Beckway frowns. "I never imagined there were so many."

Jerricho—and every other sling—thought it was their destiny to launch into the stars. Jerricho even kidnapped Emmett in the hopes that he knew how to return to Earth. Speaker described them like they were a terrorist organization, operating outside the boundaries of Sevenset. Feoria created a plan to help her people survive. She called the slings selfish for trying to carve a path back to Earth at the expense of everyone else. A better word would be *desperate.*

Looking around the plain, it's easy to spot the tattoos. On wrist after wrist, scattered around like obvious clues. Beckway's eyes roam the scene. His voice is all but broken.

"The slings waited for them in this valley," he says. "Only a few people knew the exact coordinates of the bases. But there was a whole council who knew the general route. Someone tipped them off. I'd guess they came here, set up their trap, and waited. They were smart enough to let the group get fully into the valley. No retreating at that point."

He points west. A series of massive tracks cut across the ground, turning up mud.

"One group came down from the western hills there. Another from the east. The Second Ring would have formed up ranks. They had the numbers to turn them back easily, but . . ."

"Slings were marching with them," I note. "A lot of them."

He nods back. "You can see the wounds along the outer line. Most of them come from behind. The general panicked. Summoned a grav field, but it wasn't much of an advantage because half his soldiers were traitors. They knew the layout as well as the loyal Imago did. Likely there are more ahead. A wise general would have pushed his troops deeper into the valley, but the slings were ready for that too. I would imagine they had their own grav fields ahead."

Beckway starts walking again. The other members of the

Remnant are moving forward too, looks of devastation on their faces. I realize this is the whole reason we're heading to Launch Bay 2. This carnage is the only reason we have a chance to survive. We're here because the evacuees from the Second Ring marched right into a trap. And thousands died.

It is an outcome Feoria believed impossible. I haven't forgotten her words. She thought her people would march toward the end of their world and not become less than they had always been. Every way we look on the bloody plain, there's more proof that she was wrong. At other stations, maybe there's order and honor and sacrifice unfolding. But not here.

We pick our way through the valley. Someone asks if we'll bury the dead. Beckway quietly replies that the moons will do that before long. After that, no one in our group speaks. We realize it isn't our place. And even if it was, what could we possibly say to comfort them?

Over the next hill, we find more of the nyxian grav fields as Beckway predicted. Smaller skirmishes, but all of them just as bloody and doomed as the main one. I keep expecting survivors. Someone to call out for help. No one does. Maybe they kept marching? But Jacquelyn's sensors showed no movement at the base. Best guess: they killed the person who knew where the base was.

Beckway motions for us to follow him to one side. I walk that way—staggered by all the grief and loss—and he points out a third party. There's a small battalion of dead marines. So Babel was here, but clearly later in the game, and without much consequence. Our crew circles around. Beatty's bold enough to lean over one of the marines and examine the equipment. A snapped whisper from Parvin has him holding up both hands innocently.

"I was just looking," he says.

Beckway points out the obvious. "This isn't a full unit. We'll keep an eye out. Babel's groups usually travel heavier than this. I suspect the rest of their crew is out here somewhere."

The last light leaves the valley by the time we clear the killing fields. Feoria doesn't order us to a halt. Instead, we keep marching. How far will we have to go—I wonder—to not be haunted by these ghosts? Feoria doesn't offer any sweeping speeches. Instead, she mourns her people. She walks side by side with Ashling. The two queens link arms. They bow their heads.

And they march on.

It is the saddest thing I have ever seen.

CHAPTER 13

ARABELLA

Morning Rodriguez
11 days 20 hours 15 minutes

This brutal world is not done with us.

We march through the dark. Over hills. Away from the dead. At some ungodly hour, a golden glow cuts through the blanketing black. My eyes flick that way. An Imago scout stands just fifty meters ahead of our front lines, and he looks like an actor who has stumbled into the bright lights of a stage by accident. He straightens, clearly confused. The little globes of light dance around him in a circle.

"What on earth . . . ," I start to say.

No one else speaks. There is an almost song in the air. Beneath the ethereal strains, I can hear the slightest buzz. Our entire group comes to a halt. We stare as the hovering insects dance around the scout in an enticing rhythm. I'm close enough to see the scout's lips tug up into a smile. And then his eyes lose focus. He starts to laugh. And we all start laughing with him.

Except for Jacquelyn.

Vaguely, I notice her breaking through the ranks, sprinting in that direction. What is happening? Why is she shouting? I watch as she lifts a short-handed mace into the air. My eyes are drawn back to the scout. He is the only bright thing in this dark, dark night.

It's like a huge spotlight. Or a target.

I'm still smiling when a claw punches right through the scout's chest. The lights all flicker out, like dying fireflies, and the spell breaks as Jacquelyn raises her weapon, but she's too late. A shadow hovers over the shrieking guard. The creature's round head is as wide as a set of double doors. In the failing moonlight, I can just make out thousands of empty eye sockets.

Nightmare gives birth to nightmare. Pincer legs unfold from a slinking insect body. It pinches the guard's neck and stomach and thighs. There's a bone-chilling slurp as the creature pulls the guard into a lover's embrace. Folds of skin collapse around him like stage curtains, and the shrieks cut off sharply. The creature—a massive, toothed worm—shivers with pleasure.

I manage to pull my scouter down over one eye. It pings an identification: *arabella*.

Jacquelyn lets out a war cry as she swings her mace. The strike is solid. The creature's body flexes with the blow, though, and goes slinging to one side. The arabella shivers again, and its whole body unfurls like a rotten flower. Hundreds of squirming legs appear, and it dumps the guard's mangled corpse back to the ground.

Five seconds. It took five seconds for the thing to feed.

Jacquelyn swings again, but the creature back-dives and

vanishes. Her head whips around, and there's terror written there in the boldest letters. *"What are you waiting for? RUN!"*

And the entire Remnant lurches into motion. Our group was only a hundred or so deep, but the sudden threat and the surrounding darkness make it feel like thousands pushing and shoving their way to safety. The person in front of me stumbles. I catch a flailing elbow and get them standing upright again before realizing it's Isadora. "Come on," I grunt. "Stay with me."

All around us, the Imago are shouting orders.

Feoria's voice thunders above the rest. "Watch your footing! The burrows! Make noise!"

The warnings sound ridiculous until Isadora shoulders me to the right. We stumble together and just barely miss the gaping mouth of a tunnel. It's carved with precision. Just wide enough for the arabella to crawl back through. "Underground!" I shout uselessly. "It's underground!"

There's too much chaos to check for stragglers. I just have to hope all that training instinct we learned in space is kicking to life now. I thought Isadora might slow me down, but she keeps the pace, vaulting with me over hills and around random formations of stone.

Our progress stops abruptly. Another glowing ring to our left. I *know* we should run. I *know* we need to keep moving, but that almost music curls back into the air. All I can do is stand there and wait for what happens next. Isadora frees herself somehow. She pulls at my shoulder and lands a brutal slap across one cheek. The pain shocks my system.

"What the hell?" I snap.

"Don't let it lure you in," she hisses back. "Keep moving."

And just like that the music fades. On our right, lights flicker around another target. The person stands there the same way I did. Hypnotized by the song and the light. It takes about two seconds to figure out *who* they're circling: Beatty. One of the Genesis 13 survivors.

Isadora shoves me in that direction. "Save him!"

My body wakes up before my mind does. Arms pumping, chest heaving, eyes narrowed. An arabella spirals out of the nearest tunnel and towers over its next meal. It takes less than a breath to cross the distance, to leave my feet, and to wrap both arms around Beatty's shoulders. We hit the ground hard as jaws snap shut on the empty air above us. The creature shrieks before falling angrily back into its tunnel. Around us, the entire plain glows. Rings of light in every direction.

"Keep moving!" Feoria shouts from somewhere ahead. "Be *loud*!"

Beatty stammers his thanks as Isadora helps both of us to our feet. A second later, we're all hurtling onward. Beatty is almost hyperventilating. Noise thunders to life around us. Not screams like before, but shouts. The Imago bellow and curse. It takes a second to realize what they're doing.

"Drowning out the noise," I gasp. "They're drowning out the noise."

Our group veers left as a new set of dangling lights appears. We're close enough to see that they're floating insects, about the size of a fist. I add my own roar to the surrounding noise.

"To me!" Jacquelyn calls. "To the stones! To me! To the stones!"

Isadora's grip on my hand tightens as we leap over shattered stone rises and come stumbling down a final hill. Beatty's just ahead of us. Several units of Imago soldiers wait in the distance. They've chosen to stand along a shoulder of raised stone. Of course. The hunting ground ends where it meets the stone. No way to bore through something that thick. Their ranks open long enough for us to come barreling safely through. The second we reach a safe spot, all three of us whip around. We blink through the shadows. The plain has gone silent. No one else is coming.

"Where are they?" I shout. "Parvin? Where's the rest of the crew?"

A second passes. Then Parvin calls back. "Morning. We're over here."

We shove through the ranks and find Genesis waiting. My heart skips a few beats. Are they all here? I make a panicked count. Seven, eight, nine. Nine of us. Relief floods through me as I realize Parvin's making the same count as me. "Thank God," she says. "Everyone's here."

Beatty shoulders forward. "Where's Gio? Where's Vic?"

No one answers. We all look back across the plain. A few more Imago stumble free of the deadly field. Beatty paces from side to side. For a heartbreaking second, I think he's about to go back for them, but then Gio limps out of the shadows. There's a nasty wound running down his right hip. Words shake unsteadily from his gaping mouth.

"It took her. I need your help. It took her. We have to go back."

The Imago avert their eyes. It's not hard to figure out the truth. Arabellas do not give back their prey. Up and down the ranks, unit leaders start gathering soldiers. I can hear Jacquelyn's and Feoria's voices echoing louder than the rest. It's not hard to see the gaping holes in our forming ranks. We lost soldiers tonight. More death and heartbreak. When will all of this come to an end?

Gio's chest heaves. "Come on," he begs. "Someone *help* me."

He turns, ready to march back by himself, but Beatty grabs him by a shoulder. The two of them struggle until Katsu steps forward. Together, they drag Gio carefully out of harm's way.

"Let me go!" he shouts. "Get the hell off me, man!"

And underneath it all, Beatty whispers: "She's gone. Gio. She's gone."

It takes a second to realize the rest of the Genesis crew is waiting on my command. This isn't a situation for Parvin. It's not about logic or arguments or any of that. They need to hear that the strongest person in the group is still with them, still ready to walk fearless through the night. I take strength from the trust in their eyes.

"Get your stuff," I order. "Let's get the hell out of this place."

PART II

COLLISION

CHAPTER 14

BROODLORD

Emmett Atwater

11 days 19 hours 12 minutes

Having Bilal back is like breathing in a new kind of air. He's tired and hungry—both of our recovered prisoners are—but he still smiles like this world has only ever loved him. Back aboard the *Colossus*, I sit at the edge of his bunk. I can tell he's fighting sleep just to stay up and talk with me.

"I have prayed for this," he says. "Every day in captivity."

He has a handful of bruises. He looks thin too, but at least he's alive.

"Did they hurt you?" I ask.

"I was treated well enough."

I nod at him. "It's hard to imagine someone being mad at you."

He smiles. "Up in space, the guards would ask me to make tea for them. We discussed politics and our favorite sports. Down here, though? The marines were cut from a different cloth. I think I might have suffered more if not for Roathy. He did his best to take the guard's attention away from me. I didn't want him to do it, but you know how stubborn he can be."

Stubborn is one word for it. Roathy's sleeping a few bunks above. It's hard to square the idea of him sacrificing himself for Bilal with the Roathy that I encountered in space.

"You would make tea for the guards."

He smiles again. "I have a gift that shouldn't go to waste. Once it was said I made the best tea in Palestine. Now there is a rumor that it's the best tea in the galaxy."

"When all this is over, I'll take a cup."

He asks about the others. I walk him through what happened after we landed. I try to steer clear of the deaths, but it's like ripping off a bandage, better to do it all at once. He takes the news about Jaime as hard as anyone. I walk him through the escape from Sevenset and the Imago's plan of attack, but after a while he's struggling to keep his eyes open.

"It's good to have you back," I say. "Never felt right without you."

"Brother," he replies sleepily. "It feels like home."

As he sleeps, I watch him and wonder if this is how Pops and Moms always felt. Like I was something precious, something to protect. My mind still can't grasp the impossibility of it. The day that Anton told me Bilal was dead, I closed that door in my heart. And I needed to close it. I didn't have any energy left to put into grief. I had to focus on surviving. Survive Babel. Survive the Imago. All of it. I closed the door, because what good was leaving it open?

Bilal's return is a bright and hopeful light. There's still

darkness. Out in the world and inside of me, but Bilal's return is too bright for them to keep their claws in me for long.

Azima's in the bunk above him. I try not to see the specks of someone else's dried blood on the elbow of her suit. Small traces of dark deeds. On the top bunk, Roathy turns in sleep until he's facing me. He's been quiet since we found him. I'm still not sure how he feels. Does he still hate me? He opens his eyes, blinks, and nods my way.

Then he asks the only question he cares about. "Isadora?"

"Safe." I take a deep breath before saying, "She's pregnant, you know."

He nods. "She told me. That's why we were so desperate. She didn't want to do this alone."

Those memories replay in my head. I was in the hallway when they argued back and forth in one of the comfort pods. And then they cornered me down in the Rabbit Room, ready to put me out of the competition for good. He was desperate in our final fight too. It's amazing to think of all the reasons we had to kill each other, and to think of all that's gone down since.

"If I could go back, I'd let you go instead."

He frowns. "No, you wouldn't."

"Trust me, I would. I wish I had never boarded *Genesis 11* in the first place."

He considers that. The two of us have always had this in common. We dig down under the surface of things and try to figure out what's really there. He must see I'm telling the truth.

"What about the others?"

"Jaime's dead," I answer. "Defoe killed him. Omar's gone too."

Roathy shakes his head. "Babel."

"Babel," I agree. A glance back shows Speaker hunched over the ship's dashboard. He's guiding us quietly through the shadowed depths. "Their plan was to eliminate the Imago."

"The who?"

Of course. He doesn't know. He doesn't know that their real name is the Imago or that the moons are going to collide. He and Bilal have been in the dark for so long.

"Maybe I should start from the beginning. . . ."

It takes a few minutes, but Roathy's a patient audience. From the start, he and Isadora had been imagining their new life here. He's as shocked as we were about the coming apocalypse. He asks a few questions about our rendezvous at Launch Bay 2. I can tell he's relieved about Isadora, but there's still a lot of terrain between the two of them. The people we love are somewhere else, crossing some other ocean. We'll have no idea how safe they are until we meet them in the middle. Babel hovers over it all like a dark cloud.

"Do you believe me now?" I ask. "About who the real bad guys are?"

His glare is stripped of hatred. "I believe you."

The sonar pulses behind us. I turn in time to see Speaker straighten. His eyes are alert. I nod once to Roathy. There's an understanding. Our past is still there, but it feels like we're taking the first step in the right direction. Looking away, I cross the cluttered room. Greenlaw's off to one side, sleeping on her gurney, her knife wound neatly bandaged now. I take my place at Speaker's shoulder. The screen looks empty.

"What was it?" I ask.

He's frowning. "I am not sure. It vanished right after the alert came in."

Together, we watch the empty screen. The next scan shows a mass spreading over the northern half of the radar. It spans the entire quadrant, a dark bulk with sprawling limbs. I can't help but picture a huge octopus. "Look. Right there. That's what made the noise?"

"No," he answers. "The ping came from behind. I recognize *that* shape."

As we watch, a second mass bleeds out above the first. Both forms defy any natural shape. And I'm amazed they take up that much of the radar. They must be huge.

"What are they?"

"Broodlords. One of our more peculiar primes. The two larger masses you see? Those are the mates. Both of them are bigger than buildings. Inside each one are hundreds of broodlings. An entire litter of hunters. The broodlords send them out to bring back food."

"Great," I say. "You're heading right toward them. Shouldn't we change directions?"

Speaker shakes his head. "They're much deeper than we are. And we're not really large enough to be worth the time it would take to chase us and feed. I'll show you."

His fingers run through a sequence on the control panel. Several of the data screens shudder to black before images replace them. We're getting a live feed. The underbelly of our ship glows softly. Each camera transmits fifty meters of swirling ocean, and then a veil of ominous dark waits beyond. Speaker taps another configuration, and the central camera twitches with thermal imaging. We see body heat outlined below. The creatures are a massive ball of red and orange light.

"Those are broodlords?"

"Mating broodlords," Speaker corrects. "With stomachs full of broodlings."

It's straight out of a horror movie. "You're sure we're safe?"

"At this depth, we'll be fine."

He looks ready to say more, when consecutive pings sound. Less than a second passes and they ping again. Two marks are coming up behind us, and they're coming on fast.

"Incoming, Speak."

He cycles through a quick sequence. On the screen, I can see our defensive shields on the back half of the ship increase. Clearly, something is on our trail. "Broodlings?" I ask.

"It's Babel," he replies, dumbfounded. "Those are Babel ships. It must be a random patrol that stumbled right on top of us. There was no one alive to track us from the coast."

The noise of the approaching enemies echoes.

"So what do we do? Is there a gun station or something?"

Speaker looks over. I almost don't recognize the emotion, because I've never seen it painted across his features. He's terrified. "The *Colossus* was built to survive. It is not a fighting boat. There is an avatar defense system, but if they use long-range weapons . . ."

Every beep comes more frequently now. I've seen enough

submarine movies to know what happens next. The big dot will give birth to a smaller dot. Missiles launch. We die.

"Come on, Speak," I say desperately. "Give me something to do."

He answers calmly, "I am thinking."

Behind us, the others are waking up. Azima drowsily asks what's happening. Roathy climbs down the ladder and shakes Bilal's shoulder. Greenlaw is sitting up—in spite of her wound—eyes completely alert. Speaker's still staring helplessly when she speaks.

"Dive," she orders. "We have to dive."

Babel's ships are gaining on us. My shoulders start to flinch inward, bracing for an impact that might come at any moment. Speaker hesitates for exactly one second before obeying Greenlaw's command. The *Colossus* isn't quick, but before long, we're clawing down into deeper and darker waters. My eyes flick back to the radar.

"What about the broodlords?" I ask.

The screen shows we're heading right for them. I'm not sure how deep we have to go to get their attention, but it's still not a theory I'm eager to test.

"The broodlords are our only hope," Greenlaw answers. "We have to get their attention."

I'm thinking about how insane that sounds, when Speaker confirms her decision.

"Brilliant," he says. "That is brilliant. If we get close enough, they'll fire broodlings."

"Am I missing something?" My eyes dart back and forth. "How does that solve anything?"

"It reduces the fight to our greatest strengths," Greenlaw

says. "Foundational tactics. Always highlight your strengths on the field of battle. We can't win a race to shore. Our weaponry isn't sophisticated enough to turn and face them directly. The *Colossus* has two strengths. The protective avatar system attached to the exterior and the defensive shields. We just have to hope Babel follows."

My head is still spinning when Speaker breathes a sigh of relief.

"They're matching our descent." He looks triumphantly back. "Now we fight to survive."

Everyone goes quiet as we pass directly over the floating masses of color. On the live screens, I can just barely make out limbs spiraling and unfolding. At the creature's core, a burst of bright red. It blooms wildly as something fires out. Three slashes of color hurdle through the sea.

And they're heading straight for us.

"Broodlings," Speaker confirms. "It's working."

Greenlaw rises unsteadily to her feet. "I'll suit up."

"No," Speaker replies. "Not with that wound. It is a good plan, but we have to execute it now. I need someone with full mobility in the avatar. Prepare Emmett instead."

That earns me the biggest side-eye I've ever seen, but Greenlaw eventually nods. A loud *thud* hits the exterior of our ship. A second is followed by a third. Broodlings making first contact. On one camera, I catch sight of tentacles and eyes and teeth. There's fluttering movement as each one suctions to the hull. They're about half the size of an average human, and ugly as hell.

"Stay focused," Greenlaw orders. "With me."

She crosses the room and stands before a panel of encased glass. The ship lurches as I stumble her way. A glance back shows the others are terrified. No one wants to die, but especially not in the dark of an alien ocean. We have to survive this. We made promises.

"Everyone strap in!" Speaker shouts. "Greenlaw, it's the standard military code."

She punches a sequence in and the borders of the encased glass start to glow. There's an audible click as the door slides open. A suit hangs inside. Greenlaw unhooks the thing and hands it over. I'm amazed how light it is. The material is delicately thin and covered in half-faded blue circles. A cord uncoils from the padded stomach section and connects back to the *Colossus*.

It's my turn to side-eye Greenlaw. "The hell is this thing?"

"Get in the suit," she orders. "I'll explain as you go."

Panicked, I fumble with the leggings. My eyes keep flicking back to the screens. Our exterior cameras flash tentacles and teeth. More and more of the creatures join the hunt as we finally pass over the mating broodlords below. The Babel ships are closing in, but I can see the genius of Greenlaw's plan now. If our ship is covered in broodlings, so are theirs.

I'm shaking so badly that Bilal has to come over and calm me down. He sits me against one wall and helps me slide off my boots. With his help, I manage to get both legs inside the thin-layered suit. When I've got both arms in, Greenlaw seals the front. A hood flaps against my neck. I pull it overhead. The material hisses and suctions until only my eyes, nose, and mouth are exposed. It feels like some kind of futuristic swimsuit.

"What do I do now?"

Greenlaw turns to the control keypad. "I'm going to activate you. You have one job. Defend the ship. Remove as
many broodlings as you can. Understand?"

As she punches the sequence, I find myself staring back
in confusion.

"Wait? I have to go outside?"

A deafening pulse answers. All the blue dots on my suit
hum to life in perfect sequence. The glow fills our cockpit
with ghostly light. Power vibrates—enough to chatter my
teeth—and something *forceful* snatches my body from the
room.

I am in the dark and endless ocean. A scream tears from
my lungs. There are noises all around, but my own screams
conquer everything. I turn and turn, but there's only darkness.

"Emmett." It's Bilal. Somehow I can hear his voice. "My
friend. Be calm. Listen."

His words are the only reason I keep it together. Dark
objects glide and move and swirl. I turn and turn, but can't
find Bilal in the darkness. How the hell did I get out here?

"B-Bilal?"

His voice comes back even clearer. It's like he's speaking
right into my head.

"Emmett," he says. "You're controlling the avatar attached to the exterior of the ship. Greenlaw is explaining it
to us. Your mind is connected to the device. You're hooked
into the ship's protective avatar. Do you understand?"

"Bring me back. I don't want to be out here."

Bilal answers calmly. "You are mentally controlling our
defense system, Emmett. And we need defense right now,

yeah? Take a deep breath. Calm down. Your physical body is in here with us. I can see you right now. You are safe. Fathom?"

I manage to nod. It's not real. Or it is real, but I'm not *really* out here.

"Fathom."

"All right. It's time to start punching things," Bilal says. "If I recall, you're quite good at that."

Slowly, I turn. The movement grates. It is not a normal turn of a neck. Everything about this body feels slow and foreign. I glance down, and it helps to see that this isn't *my* body. It's a mechanical one. The avatar is made of metal gears. I have arms like sharp blades. It takes my brain a second to accept the disorienting truth: I am controlling something that's wired to the ship.

Movement stirs in my peripheral. I look up to find one of the broodlings sucking at the bold emblems etched on the hull of our ship. It's a struggle to make my hand move, to force the limb to obey, but finally a metal claw extends. I'm trying to grab the thing by a tentacle, but metal slices through skin and bone like paper machete. Oily blood spews, and the creature flashes a toothy hiss.

"Emmett." It's Bilal's voice again. "We need you to do some damage. You can slide around the exterior of the ship. Your avatar's back is sealed to it. Just push left or right, up or down, yeah? When you punch, the avatar punches. When you kick, it kicks."

Nodding, I slap a backhand across the path of an incoming broodling. Blood blooms out. Other creatures start to notice. The nearest lunge hungrily forward, but I am more dangerous than they are. I hack sloppily through their ranks, and even though the movements are heavy, each blow leaves behind a new carcass.

I'm finding my rhythm as the swarm turns its attention from the ship to me. It takes focus, but I can sense what Bilal meant. If I shove with my legs, I can glide around the ship's exterior. It's like I'm attached to tracks. A new wave of broodlings dart forward and I shove left. My foot plants as I bring a mechanized left hook around. The blow cuts through four of them.

Pushing off again, I find new targets. I'm the hunter now.

The ocean swallows each shriek as I find my rhythm. For a while, I think that I'm winning. But there's no break in their ranks. The broodlings never stop flowing forward.

"Too many," I whisper. "There are too many."

"We're almost to the coastline," Bilal replies. "Emmett. There were two ships following us. One faded from the radar. But the other is fighting their way through. They're right behind us."

I swing my bladed arms in a clearing arc. The broodlings scatter before trying to snap their way back at me. "What do you want me to do?"

"Can you circle to the back of the ship?" he asks. "Move to your right."

Another swing clears a path. I plant my left foot and shove myself in the opposite direction. My vision skews as broodlings scatter in every direction. Momentum carries me to the back of the ship. I can tell I'm in the right place because even if the *Colossus* is moving slowly, torrents of water are streaming past as the ship's propellers work in the opposite direction.

"Now what?"

"The remaining ship is trailing us," Bilal explains. "They are almost directly behind. On the count of three—" I catch a snap of static as another voice argues; then Bilal's back. "Four? I guess on the count of four. Greenlaw's going to undock you from the ship. We want you to jump."

All around me, the broodlings are still swarming. I swat back at them, but my mind is focused on what Bilal's asking me to do. "Jump? And do what?"

There's the briefest hesitation. "Act like a missile," Bilal whispers. "On the count of four."

I can tell how much it pains him. Bilal was not meant for war. I do my best to clear a space in the water around me. The broodlings are still working at the edges of our ship, but Greenlaw's right, our defensive shields are holding. I squint into the distant dark as Bilal begins the count.

Muscles steady. Feet planted. Eyes focused. Fear tries to nestle into my heart, but I beat it back. There's no time for fear. There's no room for hesitation. We have to survive.

". . . three, four!"

There's a thundering metallic *click* as I launch myself away from the *Colossus*. A few broodlings pursue, but as I tuck my arms in tight, I become a living and breathing bullet. One second passes. Two seconds. Three . . . And then there's the bright flash of a ship. I get a perfect glimpse into their cockpit. Five marines in battle mode. All their expressions are predatory.

They are hunters.

Or at least they used to be.

I arrow both arms forward. The sharp blades strike the window dead center, and the whole damn thing shatters. An ocean vacuum swallows their screams, and all that light *explodes*.

My heart rate spikes, but my throat is too dry to shout. I wake up to Bilal ripping the hood off of my head. Faces stare down at me. Everything is blindingly bright.

"It's okay," Bilal whispers. "You're okay, Emmett."

Except I can't *breathe*. My whole body spasms. I can feel chills running up and down my arms. For a second, my mind jumps back to the ocean. I'm surrounded by debris, body parts, swirling tentacles. I'm drifting off into the cold nothing. Another violent tremor shakes my body.

"Damn it, Speaker!" Azima shouts. "He's going into shock."

"It's just transference delay. Give him time."

"We don't have time."

A warm hand. I can feel the calluses. I force myself to focus on the feeling. The warmth of that hand in mine. My mind tries to trick itself again. I get a distorted glimpse of the ocean before blinking back to the interior of the ship. Bilal's hand tightens around mine. Azima is at his shoulder, staring intently. I know them. I recognize them. But I still can't *breathe*.

"They're about to breach!" Speaker shouts. "Everyone hold on to something."

Bodies press tight around me. "It's going to be okay," Bilal promises me.

Speaker's voice echoes. "In four . . . in three . . . in two . . . in one."

A sonic boom ends everything. Time rotates and claws, and I can only feel the pressure of Bilal's shoulder against mine. Some kind of electric charge snuffs the lights. The only reason I know I'm not dead is Bilal's steady breathing. He's so damn calm.

"What was that?" Azima asks.

"I blew the ship's electrical system," Speaker answers. "It creates a blast radius. Killed every broodling within fifteen meters of the ship. The two broodlords are still down below, but we're out of their range now."

Azima asks the obvious follow-up. "How long until the systems come back on?"

"They don't. Our unit is done. There is a backup generator. It will give us enough energy to reach the shoreline. Emmett took care of Babel's ships. We should be in the clear."

"Right," Azima replies. "Everyone okay?"

There's a shifting of hips and shoulders. The entire group calls out all clears as we stumble to our feet in the dark. Emergency lights flicker to life at the front of the ship. I can see Speaker leaning over the control panel and mashing a red button over and over. The rest of us crowd around as he continues to work. "Could have used a little more information on the whole suit thing," I say.

Speaker grins back. "I thought you did very well."

The overheads finally flicker on. I expected to feel exhausted, but instead there's an onrush of adrenaline. I feel like I could run through a wall. "My heart is about to beat out of my chest."

Greenlaw explains, "You will feel that for the next hour or so. It's a post-separation kick. Every first-time user experiences it. Your body is trying to reclaim your mind by reminding the brain just how alive it is. Make sure you don't overexert yourself."

I nod back to her. There's enough light now to see the others' faces. Azima's got a cut on one cheek, but looks fine otherwise. Roathy somehow looks bored, but Bilal shoots me the same look he used to give me aboard the *Genesis 11* at the end of a long day. I can't help laughing.

"See what you've been missing out on?"

He smiles. "My lifelong dream of being attacked by sea creatures, finally realized."

There's a groan as the ship starts to edge slowly toward the shore. A single camera shows the sputtering view of our approach. The rest of our exterior feeds are too damaged. We all stand there—listening and watching—as the ship gets close enough to scrape the bottom. Lights shudder as Speaker buries us in sand. He leaves the controls, and Azima helps him spin the hatch wheel.

Bilal wraps an arm around my shoulder. "Friend. Let's go home, yeah?"

A dark coastline waits for us. There's about ten meters of water between us and freedom. Speaker leaps down. Greenlaw struggles enough that Bilal detaches from my side to relieve her of some of the extra equipment. Roathy and Azima follow with splashes of their own.

"Emmett," Speaker calls. "Toss down the last few bags."

It takes a second to dig behind the cargo harness for them. When I'm sure the landing area is clear, I toss both down. It's a surprise to hear Bilal and Roathy laughing together in the dark. I never heard them trade jokes aboard *Genesis 11,* but they were in captivity for a while. It's not hard to imagine a bond forming in all that time with only each other to depend on.

I'm setting up for my leap, when the ship lurches. I barely keep my footing, but a second jerk sends me stumbling back into the cockpit. Desperate, my hands reach out and snag the cargo netting fronting the luggage bay. And then the ship starts to tilt for real. The movement draws the ship—and me—away from the shoreline. Gravity's teeth dig in, and I know I have two seconds tops.

Shouts echo from outside. "Emmett! Get out! Emmett!"

A quick shove off the wall, two gravity-defying strides, and I leap. It is not my most athletic moment. The raised lip of the doorway catches my right foot. It sends me spinning out awkwardly through the hatch. I see a blur of shadows before the sand and the water both wreck me. Up into my nose and all through my suit. Hands pull me gasping out of the water. We crawl to shore, half choking and spitting. When we're finally clear, we all turn back and look.

In the water, the *Colossus* spins in the grasp of something out of nightmares. Tentacles the size of full-grown oaks twist around it. A head looms beyond, double the size of our ship, with thousands of eyes glaring out from the folds of blackened skin. We all watch the head sink down beneath the waves. The tentacles follow, and the *Colossus* is dragged into the deep.

It takes a while, but Bilal's the first to break the silence.

"Wow. We really blew the roof off the doors."

We all laugh like fools. We all need to laugh. It's the only way to keep from counting all the ways we could have just died.

"That's not the phrase, Bilal. Not even close."

"No?" Bilal smiles. "I thought I read that somewhere. . . ."

We all laugh again. Speaker's the first to shoulder some cargo and lead us on. We move into new territory. Right now, Launch Bay 2 is just a distant speck on the map. We have more marching ahead. I find myself praying that Morning is marching too.

"Meet you in the middle," I whisper.

Above us, the moons promise the same.

CHAPTER 15

HONOR

Emmett Atwater

08 days 08 hours 53 minutes

Speaker's evasive maneuver landed us well south of our target drop zone. It shouldn't make or break anything. Our lead on the Remnant is gone, but at least we're still alive. We move as quickly as we can through the unfriendly terrain. The sun rises and sets, rises and sets.

The third day of our march offers as breathtaking a view as any I've ever seen. The sunlight slips through gaps in the forest and makes patterns on the path ahead. Leaves tremble from branches to kiss the ground. The sky to the north is finally clear. We get our first glimpse of this continent's namesake—the Ironside Mountains. I've only seen places this pretty in calendars I couldn't afford to buy.

It's all beautiful, but it's hard not to see each new stretch of forest as an obstacle. It stands between us and the safety of the launch bay. I'm thinking about all that we still have to accomplish to survive—starting to feel the weight of it all—

but Bilal's constant smile keeps the bad mood at a distance. His presence is as bright as a second sun.

"Such colors," he's saying. "Speaker, do your people ever visit these mountains?"

Speaker smiles. "One does not visit those mountains and return alive."

Bilal marvels at that. "In our world, people climb the mountains for sport. There are even lifts to take them up to the top so they can ski back down to the bottom."

"Truly?" Greenlaw asks, fascinated. "And the arabellas don't devour them?"

"There are no arabellas in their world," Speaker answers. "No centuries. No everhounds. No broodlords or vayans. It is a different world with different rules, Greenlaw. You will learn that."

She frowns at us. "So what is the most dangerous creature in your world?"

Bilal and I exchange a glance. We answer at the same time: "Humans."

Our march grows quieter after that. Some of it is exhaustion, but every now and again Speaker has us come to a stop. We all wait and watch as some new creature trots across the empty plains. Most of them blend into the backdrop easily. Speaker insists that the creatures that don't bother with camouflage are the ones we should really worry about.

The next obstacle comes halfway to Launch Bay 2. Speaker pauses our progress again. He stares for a longer time than usual before summoning us forward. It doesn't take long to figure out what caught his attention. In the rocky valley to our right, there's a Babel ship. The front end of it is cratered into the ground so that it sits at a slight angle, almost ready to topple over. The funky landing forced the exit ramp open, but only about halfway.

We wait for fifteen minutes. Nothing moves.

"Do you recognize it?" Speaker asks.

The ship has Babel written all over it. All those standard trademarks in the design, but Azima and I haven't seen any ships since landing on the planet. It's definitely bigger than the original escape pods. Roathy and Bilal nod knowingly, though.

"We came down in something like that," Roathy says. "They launched a bunch of them on the day of the attack."

Greenlaw kneels and carefully removes her rifle in response. We all watch as she checks the ammunition. "Approach with caution," she says. "I will cover you from here."

She sets up at the base of the nearest tree. The view gives her a good look at the whole valley. The rest of us take out our close-combat weapons and prepare for the approach. It's not too far away, but the second we step out into the open, everything feels like it's happening in slow motion. I keep Bilal tight to one side as we walk, mentally preparing for whatever comes.

About one hundred meters away, we see the claw marks. All around the half-opened hatch. Bad news for the Babel marines. Good news for us. The scores in the metal are massive. It's like Godzilla was trying to force his way inside. My stomach tightens as Speaker reaches the ruined entrance.

"No footprints," he notes. "Coming or going."

He manipulates his nyxia into a sturdy rod. It takes him a second to wedge the thing in at the right angle. A few

cranks and the ramp starts to lower. There's a little hiss of
air as the whole door releases. Speaker stumbles back, and
we all raise our weapons as lights flicker on inside.

"It never activated," Roathy says in disbelief. "Look at
them."

I'm the only person in our group who's seen this sight before. Down in the basement of Foundry. Again in the Myriad
Station. Frozen soldiers line the interior of the ship. All in their
own cryogenic chambers. I'm guessing they were supposed to
wake up when they landed. Whatever the group's marching
orders, it clearly didn't go as planned: they're all still asleep.
Our crew enters cautiously. It's hard not to notice the specifics
of each face. A sharper nose, a scatter of freckles, a hooking
scar. All of them have stories and families and friends.

All of them came here ready to kill the Imago and steal
their planet too.

"The control console broke," Speaker notes. "I do not know
much about their technology—that was always the province
of Jacquelyn and Erone—but broken is broken, I suspect?"

He's right. Either the pressure of the descent or the
momentum of the crash snapped the panel clean in two.
There's a mess of exposed wires and switchboards scattered
at the base. Speaker considers the frozen soldiers one more
time before turning back to us.

"We should keep moving," he says. "I can leave behind
a detonator."

Azima's eyes widen. Roathy raises a curious eyebrow.
Bilal looks horrified. There's a shrinking part of me that
knows I should argue for the sleeping marines. It scrapes at
everything I know of honor. No one deserves to dream their

way to an explosive death they never saw coming. But that part of me has been quiet for weeks now. That part doesn't get as many votes as it used to get. Bilal watches me as the seconds pass. His horror doubles when I shrug back at him.

"Look, man, he's right," I say. "What if they wake up and follow us?"

He shakes his head. "Emmett. You are better than this."

"We are at war," Speaker answers. "Do you think these soldiers would hesitate for even a moment if the situation were reversed? It was their intention to bomb every ring in Sevenset. They did not ask our people's permission before attempting to destroy them."

"And that is the difference between us and them," Bilal flings back. I realize this is a bolder version of my friend. Once he would have bumbled his way through an explanation. He was always this kind, but it used to go hand in hand with a shy awkwardness. My friend has changed. "Act as they would act, do as they would do, and you are no better. I will not let you fall that far, Emmett."

And in truly typical Bilal fashion, he plunks down in the abandoned captain's chair. He crosses both of his arms and looks at Speaker. "If you blow the ship, you'll have to do it with me inside."

It's the first time I've ever seen Speaker speechless. I note that he already has one of the Imago-style grenades ready for the task at hand. He takes the temperature of the room, though, and realizes we're all going to side with Bilal. He fastens the device back to his utility belt.

"I believe this is a tactical error," he says. "But I admire you for it all the same."

He leads us back down the ramp.

Bilal answers, "We'll move faster without this burden on our shoulders."

I spy a smile on Speaker's face. Even he isn't immune to Bilal's charms. Azima pats Bilal on the shoulder as we press back into the open field. Roathy just shakes his head, like he's been putting up with this kind of thing ever since the two of them landed in prison together. It's impossible to be mad at the kid for longer than a few seconds, though.

"Damn, Bilal." I wrap an arm around him. "Didn't realize how much I missed you, man."

As he grins back, a bullet hisses overhead.

Our whole group ducks instinctively. Nyxian shields bloom out. Bilal stumbles into no-man's-land, and I barely manage to pull him back to safety as another shot sounds. It takes a second to figure out that Greenlaw is the one firing, and another two seconds to find her target.

About ten meters to the left of the ship's gaping entrance, right behind us, a Babel marine collapses to the ground. His gun falls from an outstretched hand. I wonder if he was aiming it at us. I wonder how many seconds we had until he opened fire. We watch as he takes his last breath. Greenlaw's shots struck true.

Azima raises her spear, eyes on the entrance. "Are they all waking up?"

"No," Roathy replies. "He was awake. The captain's chair. I thought that was odd. I was trying to figure out why it was there. Babel doesn't do anything just for looks. This must have been the guy in charge of the ship. He couldn't wake the rest of them up."

Speaker looks to Bilal. "Do you still want to leave them alive?"

My friend nods. "Isn't one man dead more than enough?"

"Your choice." Speaker signals for Greenlaw to join us. After a second, she stands and starts packing up her weapon. "Come. There is still a long way to go."

And just like that, our march continues. Bilal's quiet for a while, but eventually Greenlaw coaxes him into conversation. They trade questions about human and Imago hobbies for a while.

I'm half listening to their chatter when I catch the faintest rumble in the distance. Bilal doesn't notice. Azima strides at the front of the group, unaware. But Roathy glances up like a startled rabbit. He immediately catches my eye. We both look in Speaker's direction.

The Imago doesn't say a word. He keeps marching, eyes fixed on what is ahead of us. The rumble leaves as quickly as it came. My eyes flick to Speaker's utility belt. One of the devices is gone.

Roathy and I lock eyes. There's a silent agreement there. We will not say anything to Bilal. Clearly, Roathy sees Bilal the way that I do now. Someone worthy of his protection.

Beneath that first agreement, there's a second one: it's easier to march forward without having to look over one shoulder. Roathy and I have always been cut from the same cloth. The two of us understand Speaker's decision, messed up as it might be. He's right.

This is war.

I fix my eyes on the approaching hills and keep marching.

CHAPTER 16

LAUNCH BAY 2

——————

Emmett Atwater

07 days 17 hours 42 minutes

For the first time on Magnia, we see something with our own eyes *before* we see it on a readout. Launch Bay 2 does not come up on any scans. According to Speaker, it won't register on any Babel satellites either. Jacquelyn's teams built the bases into the natural terrain. They also designed everything with as much stealth technology as they could come up with. It shows.

Launch Bay 2 nestles flawlessly into a fractured ravine. Two rows of waiting ships run the length of the opening, with just enough space for all the flanking catwalks that connect the structure. Not a single ship peeks out above the natural cliffs. The visible tops are painted to match the surrounding terrain too. Even if Babel combed the area with satellites, they'd never see these. Our crew pauses along a looming cliff to admire the scene.

This is our way home.

And then light pulses. All of us drop to the ground as the entire base hums to life. Blue light scales the sides of the standing ships. It hums in the pitted circles beneath them too.

"Someone is here," Speaker hisses. "Weapons out."

The entire ravine is starting to glow. My mind leaps to the obvious guess: slings. If they've already reached the base, we're screwed.

"Hey," a voice calls from behind. It's a voice I'd know anywhere. "You ever gonna show up *before* me to anything? Punctuality is a virtue, you know."

Morning strides up the slight rise with the world's biggest grin on her face. Feoria and Jacquelyn are there too, looking a little more subdued. I barely manage to get my arms out in time for the bone-crushing hug Morning delivers.

She whispers into my chest, "Meet you in the middle."

"We made it," I whisper back, and I almost can't believe the words. "We're going home."

She unhooks herself from me long enough to see we brought back a few rescues. Her face lights up at the sight of Bilal. She knows who he was to me, and how hard the thought of his death really hit. I can see the understanding and the weight of all of that in her expression as she rushes forward to give him a hug. "Bilal! I thought you were dead!"

He hugs her back and smiles. "In this, I am happy to disappoint."

She smiles before glancing Roathy's way. "And look: another dead man walks among us."

He gives his wicked grin. "Isadora?"

"Is a real piece of work," Morning throws back. "But she's down below. She's fine. The baby's fine too. Come on. We can all head down together."

It's like letting out a breath I've been holding for weeks. She's safe. We're safe. The Imago are busy preparing the base, following Jacquelyn's guidelines. Morning's voice is quiet as she recaps their journey. I can't help grinding my teeth together as she describes the carnage of an abandoned battlefield and the creatures that hunted them the same night. Activity around Launch Bay 2 is too chaotic to make a proper count, but I haven't forgotten that only sixty people will launch into space. Our crew is thirteen deep. Sixteen if the Imago are counting the Genesis 13 prisoners.

A roar of celebration greets us in the loading bay. The recovery of Bilal and Roathy acts like a new sun. It's the start of a brighter future that we can all rally around. We're not just going home. We're going to go home *together*. There's more to do. Necessary tasks and difficult fights. But for the first time in weeks, anything feels possible.

Off in a corner, Roathy and Isadora reunite. Ida watches the scene with a half smile on her face. I'm so used to seeing the two of them as a threat that it's hard to really grasp this side of them. Roathy is down on one knee. Isadora has his head pressed to her stomach so he can listen for kicks or heartbeats or both. After all we've been through, it's strange to celebrate them. But there's something *right* about it too. It's almost like we've reversed Babel's curse on us.

Back in our group, Katsu has lifted Bilal into the air and is spinning him around. Azima grins wildly, and Jazzy's clucking like a mother hen, warning them to be more careful. Morning nudges my shoulder, and I feel like my face is going to break from smiling so much.

"Let's go home."

"Not before you take me on that date," she says with a grin.

I nod through the glass. The lights of the nearest ship flicker. I want to keep smiling and laughing, but the hard conversations need to happen too. "What are the numbers?"

That wipes the grin off her face. I hate myself for taking these brief joys from her, but neither of us has ever danced around the truth. She has me follow her off to one side.

"We lost half of the Remnant," she says. "There are twenty-seven of them left. Each one gets a seat. Bilal and Roathy will be added to our count automatically. So that's forty seats accounted for and only twenty seats left for the rest."

"Better numbers than we originally planned on."

Morning sighs. "You're right. I should be thankful, but it doesn't make things much easier. Thirty-eight other Imago survived the march. Only two of the three Genesis 13 survivors made it."

My heart sinks. "Who'd we lose?"

"Victoria. She—" Morning shakes her head. "So there are forty other survivors, but only twenty seats. Feoria decided to give everyone a chance. She's running it like a lottery."

"Damn."

"Right? And it's not exactly something we can argue. Beatty and Gio are lucky they're even being included. I really like Gio. He gets what our group is all about. Beatty's an ass, but still, he signed up to come here for the same reasons we did. I don't want to leave them behind."

My eyes flick back across the room. The two of them are sitting in their own corner playing a game of cards. Every now and again they side-eye our little reunion. Every day I find myself living more and more in the gray. Nothing is easy. Nothing is black-and-white. I feel for the two of them. They lost their whole family when they landed. All the pipe dreams about going home richer than kings have vanished. And they took from us too. Omar and Jaime are *dead*.

Nothing is easy.

"It sounds like that's the best we can do."

Morning nods. "I'm starting to hate the word *best*. On the ship, *best* meant I was on top of a scoreboard. Down here, *best* is nothing but bare-bones victories and silver linings. It sucks. Okay. I'm going to go talk with Jackie about Bilal and Roathy. I want to make sure they're counted right."

A thought hits me. "Wait. Don't tell Bilal."

She frowns. "Tell him what?"

"Anything. Just tell him he's launching up into space. Don't mention the lottery and all of that." I'm still thinking about the frozen marines he tried so desperately to spare. "If he knows we're going to strand people down here, he'll never go."

She offers a tight nod. "Got it. Be back in a little."

I turn back to our crew. Everyone's laughing it up, except for Alex. I spy him standing off to one side, eyes fixed on the waiting ships. I cut across the room and join him. It's quite a view.

"Ready?" I ask.

He tries to smile, but the look doesn't reach his eyes. "Anton's up there."

"I'm sure he's fine."

Alex nods. "I'd know if something happened. I'm not sure how to explain it, but I know he's alive. But it's like in all the stories, you know? Bad stuff always happens at the very last second."

"Those are stories. This is Anton we're talking about. Hell, I wouldn't be surprised if he was running the whole ship already. Wouldn't be surprised at all."

Alex smirks. "That's exactly what has me worried. Anton doesn't do subtle."

The entrance opens again. Jacquelyn and Morning enter. There's a flush of red coloring Morning's neck. I know that look by now. She was getting heated about something. All our conversations die away as Jacquelyn waves us forward.

At the center of the room, she accesses a waiting console.

"Gather around. I want to run you through a quick tutorial."

We circle up as the holographic images hum to life. A scaled version of the spaceships outside appears in the air, reduced down to about the size of a football.

"Every single one of these ships operates the same way. They are incredibly limited in function, which was kind of the point. Here's a glance at the cockpit."

She brings up a new image. Inside the ship, there are two seats facing each other. *Simple* is definitely the right word. There's a single console between the two seats and touchscreens facing each astronaut. Slit windows provide diagonal glimpses outside the ship, but there aren't many other bells and whistles that I can see.

"Launch is controlled by the station," she explains. "All you do is lock in and hold on tight. Once you're beyond the atmosphere, the ship's internal systems do the work. We've explained before that every ship is going to automatically attract to the largest deposits of nyxia they can find. That means Babel's ships. There is a way to override the ship's controls and fly manually, but we strongly discourage that. You are not trained pilots. Our tech is smarter than you. Let it work.

"The one thing you *do* control is the air lock mechanism. Once your ship finds the right target, it will seek that target out. Every ship is designed to latch and suction. Initial punctures will seal automatically. You have to activate the boring drill mechanism, though. It will carve a doorway into the metal and function as an air lock. We're giving you control of that function because we don't want the ship to automatically carve a path into enemy territory. If you suspect Babel troops are waiting outside the door, you can try and wait them out. That decision has its own risks."

We're all focused and listening. It's no surprise when Parvin asks the first question.

"So when we dock, what then? What is your plan once everyone is on board?"

Jacquelyn sighs. "We have very little information about the ships. One of our own was intentionally captured by Babel before you came." Her eyes flick briefly my way. "Our last report was not promising. I'm not sure we can count on Erone as a rallying point. What of your man?"

"Anton is up there," Morning answers. "But we haven't heard anything."

Jacquelyn nods. "So it goes. We have little information to go on. I think our general goal is to attach the escape pods, infiltrate Babel ships that we suspect will mostly be empty, and commandeer every section. Once we've neutralized the station, we'll discuss our options for returning to Earth."

"When do we launch?" Parvin asks.

"Now."

A current of surprise runs back through our ranks.

"I thought you were coordinating a specific date with the other launch stations," Parvin says. "Wasn't that the whole point? Launch all at once so Babel doesn't have time to react?"

"Our estimates of the time of the collision are just that— estimates. It would be best to launch as soon as possible." Jacquelyn hesitates. "And our scans show that Launch Bay 3 is active. All the ships have launched."

"So Babel knows?" Parvin asks. "Fantastic."

"Our people are desperate. Feoria chose to believe the best of them. The battlefield we saw to the north . . ." She shakes her head sadly. "I hope you understand how heart-breaking it is. We expected some rebellion, but thousands have died. Thousands will die. The people of the Fourth Ring gave in to the same desperation. Can you blame them? They're scared. We all are."

Parvin nods. "So we launch now?"

"In the next few hours," Jacquelyn confirms. "Morning has promised to arrange seating preferences. Once I have that list, I'll assign each pair to a specific ship. Beatty and Gio, I need you two to come with me, please."

There's an ominous silence as the Genesis 13 survivors separate from our group. I watch them both go, and all I can do is hope that they're chosen. I'm not sure what they deserve, but no one should die this far from home, on a planet they never really knew. Morning glances my way, and there's even more heartbreak in the look she gives me. It's like no matter what we do, no matter how hard we try, someone always loses. It makes it that much harder to celebrate the victories.

And this *is* a victory.

We're going home.

As our crew crowds the windows and admires the ships that will take us into space, Morning and I stand back like proud parents, too busy counting the costs to see how bright a day it is.

CHAPTER 17

LAUNCH SEQUENCE

Emmett Atwater

07 days 14 hours 57 minutes

An hour later and our whole crew waits in pairs.

Noor and Parvin will launch together. Azima tracked down Beckway and convinced him to launch with her. That one raises a few eyebrows. Alex snags a spot with Katsu, claiming if things go wrong, at least he'll die laughing. As the others discuss the launch, Morning pretends to adjust her makeup in the reflective glass. When Holly asks what she's doing, she just says she's getting ready for a hot date. I roll my eyes, but can't help throwing her a grin that would make Pops proud.

Roathy and Isadora stand together. I realize their ship will be the only one that launches *three* people into the sky. Their reunion left Ida as the odd one out until Holly swooped in and threw an arm around the girl's shoulder. The final pairing is Bilal and Jazzy.

My stomach tosses a little at the idea of leaving his side. I know it's a necessity, but I've only had him back for a few days now. Losing him again would wreck me. Bilal looks unconcerned. It takes him and Jazzy about thirty seconds to catch up, all smiles. I realize I've given fear too much power. I want to carve out the space it's claimed in my heart, replace it with hope.

Jacquelyn returns. Speaker and Feoria follow in her wake. I'm a little surprised to see the two of them holding hands. "Launch stations are active. Final checks are complete. We have specialized exosuits for everyone. Take a second to get dressed before going out to your stations."

Everyone slips over to the far wall. The suits hang there. Generic sizes that stretch or shrink depending on what we need. I take advantage of the distraction and cross over to Speaker.

"Thanks, Speak. For everything. You were brilliant from jump."

He smiles. "From jump?"

"From the beginning. Thank you for being so welcoming to us."

"It was my duty," he says. "But it was also my honor. Before we part ways, I wanted to apologize. I have felt guilty over the past few weeks. I do not feel as guilty now that we have successfully arrived, but it is still weighing on my conscience. I would free myself of the burden. Your name? It was not chosen by Parvin. I might have influenced the results."

I stare at him. "What? There's no way, man. I put my name in the hat myself. It never left Parvin's hand. You couldn't have influenced it. There wasn't time."

He raises an eyebrow. "No? You wrote with a nyxian writing utensil, didn't you?"

I nod back, remembering now. "We all did."

"Our people banned such writing implements. We quickly discovered that people could forge documents. Change what was written with a focused thought. You see, when you write with a nyxian tool, the ink is made of nyxia too. It becomes its own, separate piece of the substance. It was not difficult for me to manipulate the names to look like your slip.

"I hope you will forgive me. It was not intended to punish you through separation. After parting ways with Feoria, I know how it must have felt for you to be without Morning. No, I chose you because you are the person from Earth in whom I have the most trust. It made my decision all too easy, and for that I apologize."

"And I thought you chose me because you liked my jokes or something." I smile at him. "Thanks for trusting me, Speak. I'm just glad it worked out."

No point being mad now, I realize. After all, we made it here in one piece. Instead, my mind wanders back to the first thing he said. Not about rigging my name into the hat, but about parting ways. It takes a long second for me to accept the truth. "You're not coming with us."

He shakes his head. "I removed my name from the lottery."

"Why? We could use you up there."

Feoria leans over. "He removed his name after finding out I had removed mine."

That news sinks in.

"He's a good man," I reply quietly. "You are a good queen."

"Everyone's so nice when they find out you're about to die," Feoria says with a smile. "I know that you are still angry with me. I know we invited you into all of this and that you will always hold some of it against me. Please promise that you will reserve your anger for *me*. The Imago that will launch across the universe with you are our very best. They deserve to go to your world and make a new beginning. Treat them the way you treat each other. With respect. Like family."

I offer her a nod. "Deal."

Speaker smiles. "I still find you all marvelous. After all we knew of Babel, I cannot fathom that people like you exist, Emmett. And Bilal? Your other friends? Where did you learn to live this way? When did it go wrong for the others we have met from your world?"

"We're not all good," I reply. "And they're not all bad."

He lifts an eyebrow. "I suppose that is the simplest truth of all."

We clasp arms, and I nod one more time before joining the rest of our crew. I'm fully suited up by the time I notice Morning having one more whispered conversation with Jacquelyn. Both parties look equally frustrated and helpless. I cross over as Jacquelyn detaches from her.

She calls a final order to the entire room. "Let's get to stations. Follow the markings on the catwalks. Make sure your suits are sealed. Don't forget your numbers."

I nod at Morning. "What's up?"

"Lottery is done," she says. "Gio's name got chosen. Beatty's didn't."

I let out a breath. "Damn."

"I tried to negotiate with Jacquelyn. She told me I'm more than welcome to replace one of our people with Beatty. She also pointed out that Gio is taking a spot that could have gone to one of the Imago. It's freaking gutting me, but our hands are tied. The Imago are running the show."

All I can do is nod. It feels wrong to leave Beatty behind, but the last thing I want is for Bilal to get wind of it and sacrifice himself. Better to let it all play out. "We should get moving."

Morning nods once and raises her voice. "Genesis. Bring it in."

The group gathers without hesitation. The laughter cuts out. Morning steps naturally into the role she's always held: our captain. "All right. I'm just gonna be honest. I have no clue what happens next. All I know is we got this far. We fought this hard. Let's take some ships and get back home. Number one priority once your ship locks on to the Tower Space Station is *survival*. We'll rally together and set up defenses. If the plan works, it's the Imago who will do most of the heavy lifting. Fathom?"

There are nods all around. I hadn't thought about it much, but what we're about to do should be terrifying. We're launching up into space in alien ships and praying they're smart enough to attach us to an orbiting space station, instead of just floating off into the void forever. And the only reason it *isn't* terrifying is that we've done all this before. We launched into space. We came down like conquerors from the stars. We've been fighting and grinding and shouldering our way through the flames since day one.

We're made of iron now.

Unbreakable.

In pairs, we start toward the entrance. Outside it's noisy. The engines of each ship have kicked to life and are throwing dust over the catwalks, up the faces of the nearest cliffs. I barely have time to process everything. It feels so good to finally set a few burdens down. Morning takes my hand and leads me out. We trace the markings and find our ship in the farthest corner of the ravine. It takes a few minutes to get there, but it's time well spent.

We walk together, thinking about all that's happened, all that's still to come.

"Finally," Morning says. "We *finally* get to go on our date."

"I've been thinking about it all *week*," I say with a smile. "You know, in between taking over Babel bases, recovering long-lost prisoners, and fighting off sea creatures."

"Right," Morning replies. "It's been the only thing on my mind too. As long as you don't count the field of glowing, truck-sized worms we had to escape. Other than that, yeah, this is all I've thought about."

I shrug back at her. "Gonna have some great stories to tell at parties."

She grins. "There is that."

Ahead, the ravine narrows. Instead of running two ships wide, now we're at the end of the line, where lone ships wait to be boarded. Jazzy and Ida are crossing the second-to-last catwalk, poking their heads into the gaping doorways of their assigned craft. At the very end of the ravine, the last ship is waiting just for us. Morning races up the catwalk ahead of me, because of course she always has to be first.

I grin my way into the cockpit after her. Jacquelyn's blueprints were spot-on. There are two seats, the central console, and a handful of levers. Otherwise, the place is bare-bones. Morning shoves her knapsack into the corner compartment and starts strapping in. The heat from the engines keeps gusting, relentless. The whole launch station is building and pulsing.

It's hard to fathom that we're really doing this, really launching back into space.

"How do I close the door?" I ask, looking around for a handle.

"It won't close," Morning replies. "Not until we're both strapped in. The station controls it anyways. I think whoever's manning the central console has to give the all clear."

I take my seat across from her, but my knapsack jams uncomfortably against my back. I groan a little and start working the straps of it around one shoulder. Morning smirks.

"You know, you're kind of far away for a proper date," she says. "It's almost like mi abuelita is here or something. Making sure we don't sit too close in the back row of the movies."

I grin at her. "No telling what we'd get up to then."

"No telling."

The look on her face about ends me. All I can do is shake my head. "Come on, now. If I'm going to be buckled in over here and you're going to be buckled in over there, you can't be giving me looks like that. . . ."

I watch the playful look vanish. I can't help thinking I'm a little rusty at flirting or something, but the playfulness leaves so quickly and so fully that I know something else is wrong. A shiver runs the length of my spine. I see fear flash in her eyes at the exact moment metal presses to my temple. The contact is paired with a hissed warning. "Do not move a muscle."

My jaw clenches disobediently. I only talked to him once or twice, but that was enough to know that Beatty's the one with the British accent. I stare at Morning in disbelief. Beatty has the barrel of his gun pressed to my head like a promise.

"Cut that out." This warning is for Morning. I saw it too. Her hands started reaching for her hatchets. They're stuck, though, wedged at the back of her hips against the chair. "Do you really want to risk it? At this range, I won't miss. You're quick, but you're strapped in, yeah? Hands up, please."

Morning's chest is heaving. She lifts her hands into the air. I start to do the same, but Beatty snaps at me. "Not you. Leave your hands at your side."

"Beatty," Morning warns. "This is a mistake."

"I think not." His voice trembles. With fear? Desperation? "You were all going to leave me. So I just stay down here and die? Suffocate or whatever happens when a world ends? Not a *chance*."

Outside, there's the slightest uptick in engines. I can tell we're closing in on the launch. I'm half praying there are cameras or something, some way the Imago can see what Beatty's doing. But I remember that Jacquelyn's only way of monitoring the bases was through movement sensors. My stomach is doing backflips.

"I want you to stand up," Beatty orders. "Slowly."

The fury is building in Morning. I can see all that dark rage threatening to break through, but she sees what I see: there's no direction for it. I could try and duck. I could shoulder into him. Maybe she gets a hatchet out in time? I doubt it. More likely Beatty puts a bullet in my head and all of this would be for nothing. I realize my hands aren't shaking. When did I stop being afraid to die?

"Now," Beatty snaps. "Slowly. Keep your hands down."

I start to rise. Morning's emotions break. "I saved you, Beatty! You can't do this!"

"Look. It's nothing personal. You think I wanted the ship with the two of you on board? Not a chance. I just picked the ship at the end of the line. You heard the launch announcements. It's happening soon. Too late to change. Bad luck. I swear, though, if you move again, I'll shoot him. Please don't make me do that."

It's awkward because I'm a little taller than he is, but he manages to keep the gun pressed to my temple as the opposite hand grabs a handful of the suit fabric at my shoulder. He pulls me through the entrance and stands me just outside the doors. My eyes flick back down the catwalks, but we're the final ship, down here at the end of the row. Jazzy and Ida are already safely tucked away. Their door has closed. No one is coming.

Beatty gestures. "Down on your knees."

My jaw tightens as I obey. He positions me just outside the ship and circles, letting the barrel of the gun drag around the back of my head. He rotates until he's standing just inside the escape pod. "Move closer."

It's insult on top of injury. I struggle forward on my knees. Both hands are tight fists. I do my best to breathe in and breathe out. I'm waiting for just the right moment, begging him to make just one mistake. Beatty sits down and—without looking—starts to work the seat straps overhead. He gets one shoulder through before copying Morning, fastening it down between his legs. The effect is instantaneous. A glow fills the room. In that bright light, I catch one final glimpse of the monster who's taking my spot and sentencing me to death.

I look into his face and wonder if I would have done the same.

"Nothing personal, Emmett."

A loud ping is followed by a hiss. Beatty pulls his gun back as the doors slide shut. He aims it at Morning. She starts to scream, but the doors mute the sound. I'm left with a razor-thin view inside the cockpit. Beatty keeps the gun extended. Morning stares out, mouth twisted in a scream.

All around me, the base begins to *thunder*. The noise picks up, and Jacquelyn's voice fills the whole area, echoing out louder than the voice of God.

"All hands off the catwalks. Launching in one minute. I repeat: clear the catwalks."

Inside the ship, Morning is crying. I can see her begging for Beatty to open the door. All I can do is stumble away. There aren't handles on the exterior of the craft. No way to drag him back out, and too much risk even if there were. What happens when I break inside? He shoots Morning?

I look back down the walkway. Ships are firing. The heat intensifies. The run back to the main command bay would take longer than a minute. "Damn."

Glancing back, I see a narrow exit ramp. Our ship really is the last one. That's how Beatty kept out of sight too. There's a rift in the ravine. The ramp cuts down before giving way to sand and desert. I take one look back inside the cockpit. Morning locks eyes with me.

"I'm coming for you!" I shout. "I'm coming!"

And then I duck out of sight. The thunderous roar of the engines consumes everything, burns away every thought. I sprint down the ramp. My feet almost slip up as the texture changes, but then I'm shoving through the narrow ravine, out into the open. The sky's so damn bright and blue and such a lie. I don't stop running.

The air feels like it's made of fire. Distantly, I hear Jacquelyn's final commands. She's in a ship somewhere. My friends are all about to launch. I'm going to be left behind. I keep pumping my arms and my legs because running is instinct. Nothing else makes sense.

Explosions. The sound pulls my attention back to the base. I stumble to the ground and watch as our one escape route—my one escape route—takes to the sky.

The first few ships pulse into the air. Jacquelyn has them sequenced, I realize. There's a pattern to the launches so that none of them go side by side into the air. Five take flight. Eight. Fifteen of them. I'm staring, jaw open, as my friends leave me behind.

And then there's another *hiss* in the distance.

It's not the same sound, not the same ships. My eyes dart to the western sky just in time to see three Babel jets come soaring through the blue. They move into formation, and their target is all too clear. I'm close enough to see trails of smoke as missiles spiral out from the tips of wings. The missiles split—from one to five—in less than a breath. There's a flash of sparks as they chase their targets through the blue. My eyes rake back to the launch station. More ships are launching.

Their flight paths drag right across the incoming missiles. In all the chaos and mayhem, I find the ship that I should be on. It's the closest one, the easiest to locate. The first streaking missiles hit just above Beatty and Morning's ship. Explosions spread through the sky.

Death arrives faster than the snap of two fingers.

Morning's ship fights through. They barely miss another explosion. I watch as her ship claws its way through the clouds. A second set of missiles detonates just below. I watch until she clears the danger zone. All three Babel pilots soar past the base.

The Imago answer. Gun towers.

A brilliant flash of blue. The projectile moves faster than my eye can follow. The three birds spiral in an attempt to escape, but the nearest one isn't fast enough. The Imago strike hits its left wing and sends it into a deadly spin. It clips the central jet, and both of them go down, smoke and fire pouring into the air above them. Only one of the pilots manages to bail.

The third jet slips through the clouds and out of sight.

Overhead, our escape pods are doing their job. Several climb higher, out of sight. I'm staring up when a massive scream of metal sounds to my left. One of the pods has crashed down into a hulking tree. The whole thing goes up in flames. Both passengers are clearly dead.

My body wakes back up. I realize I'm in the landing zone. Other crashes are scattering around the canyon cliffs. Some look worse than others. Direct hits are all too clear. Those ships are just burning pits of twisted metal. But some of the pods look damaged by secondhand explosions. I take a second to look up, make sure nothing's coming down overhead, and then I scan the field for the most intact-looking ship. I make a line for it.

Halfway there, I hear the *hiss* again. The final jet is returning. I frown up, because most of the pods are clear by now, but then his target becomes obvious.

"Get out of the base! Everyone out!"

No one hears the warning. I can see Imago up on the cliffs, down near the base's exit points. None of them see the missiles coming. The base's gun tower answers, but not before a series of missiles spiral free of each wing. Direct hits. Explosions rake the sides of the base and all I can think is that Feoria and Speaker were still inside. "Speak!"

A second blue streak shreds the final jet. It goes down, but all the fire spreading over the scene takes away any taste of victory. I pick my way through the battlefield. My eyes flick up to the sky once or twice—searching for Babel ships—but nothing comes. The hull of the nearest intact pod is scorching. Waves of heat lash out, so I skirt around it for a minute, trying to see who's inside.

It takes the survivors just as long to figure out the escape sequence. The doors open and I get a glimpse of curly blond hair. "Jazzy!" I shout. "Over here! You all right?"

And then it hits me who Jazzy was with.

"Bilal is knocked out," she calls back. "Blow to the head.

He's still breathing, though. Come around to the side and I can pull you up!"

It takes a few seconds to find a part of the ship that doesn't feel like it's on fire. The closer to the nose the better. Jazzy reaches down, sets her feet, and lifts. I use a few footholds to help bear the weight, and we both stumble on the imbalanced surface. The entrance hangs open.

"I'll lift him up," I say. "Let's get him to the ground together."

Carefully, I climb down inside the cockpit. A nasty-looking gash cuts across Bilal's cheek, but Jazzy is right, at least he's still breathing. I take a second to clear the straps and then lift. He's lighter than he used to be. All that time in captivity thinned him. I get him over one shoulder before turning. The footing's awkward. Eventually, though, I find the highest point inside the ship and anchor myself. Jazzy reaches down. Together, we get Bilal's bulk above the lip of the entrance.

"Got him?" I ask.

She nods. "Got him."

It takes another second to pull myself up out of the cockpit. Jazzy scales down the side nimbly and turns to help lower Bilal. Once we're all down, we carry him well clear of the other fallen ships. I've seen one too many movies with delayed explosions and random fireworks. Not risking that with him. A few other ships have coughed up survivors.

But most don't. Looking around, I see about a dozen have been shot down. Maybe more. Only three of them show signs of life. My attention flicks back to the base. It's lost in flames too, but about eight survivors limp out onto the open plain.

Relief thunders through me at the sight of Speaker and Feoria fronting the group.

"Hey," Jazzy calls. "Where's Morning?"

I glance up. "She launched."

Jazzy scrunches her nose. "I don't get it. She launched without you?"

"Beatty." A name worth choking on. "He wasn't going to launch. He lost the lottery. We were going to leave him behind. I'm not sure where he got one, but he had a gun. He came around the side of the base. Our ship was the one farthest from headquarters."

Jazzy just stares. "You've got to be kidding me."

I shake my head and look skyward. The ships are gone now. How far up are they? How much longer will it take them to find their way to the right targets? I picture Morning staring seven layers of hell in Beatty's direction. "I almost feel bad for him."

"For Beatty?"

I nod again. "She's going to kill him. Slowly."

Jazzy starts to smile, but there's too much smoke in the air, too many casualties on the ground. "We were so close," she says sadly. "So close to going home."

There's not much I can say to that. I glance up again, and my stomach tightens. There aren't any more Babel ships, but my eyes find the half-faded moons. Even in daylight, the next step looks obvious. Both moons stretch like eggs. Jacquelyn said they're getting too close to each other. Something about tides and gravity and all of that. Now there's less than a finger separating them.

"How long did we have?" I ask.

"A week," Jazzy replies. "At least that's what Jacquelyn said."

I shake my head. "Does that look like a week to you?"

She doesn't answer. We both look helplessly around the burning landscape, and the truth hammers in our hearts like a dark, nail-sharp promise: we're going to die down here.

CHAPTER 18

CROSS FIRE

Emmett Atwater

07 days 12 hours 33 minutes

I still remember my favorite painting. We went on a field trip in fifth grade. I spent most of that day making fun of things with PJ. All those white dudes in their wack outfits. It was like walking around a historical zoo full of rare birds stuffed into bizarre costumes.

But there was this one painting of Mount Vesuvius that stopped me dead in my tracks. In the painting, the volcano has just exploded. There's fire carving rivers down the side of the mountain. Smoke chokes out most of the stars. The distant town sits abandoned. A single bridge is clogged with all the folks who used to live there. It is pure chaos.

Sometimes you forget that those things happened to *real* people. I always thought about it as a painting, but some mother clutched her child tight as she fled across that bridge. Actual people scrambled into boats out of desperation. Some of them never made it out alive.

History remembers the darkest moments. No one wants

to be in one of those paintings, but we're standing in one now. Our group of survivors gathers along the nearest cliff. Feoria stands at the edge like a windblown queen. She waves her hand to clear the smoke, but it just keeps curling up in unnatural shapes. The escape pods below are still burning.

Speaker asks, "How many made it through?"

"Seventeen ships," Feoria answers. "Only seventeen."

Everyone looks up. Another painting hangs in the sky. Both moons are on the verge of collision. It won't be long before our secret is out. Babel's smart enough to put the pieces together. Both moons look distorted and swollen. A brightness hangs between them like permanent lightning. We get to watch the end of the world happen in slow motion. Do we have days? Hours?

"We should start moving," Speaker says. "We have a long way ahead."

His words are nothing but wind. We're all too bruised, too broken to do anything but stare at the first signs of apocalypse. No one moves. Even Feoria says nothing as she considers the black pit that used to be Launch Bay 2. Most of the surviving Imago are unfamiliar, but I do recognize one. Greenlaw stands at the edge of our camp. Her ship was shot down too. The chosen queen, the future of their kind. Burns run up an exposed shoulder. She looks like she's had the entire world ripped out of her grasp. Her nyxian gloves clench into useless fists.

Only two other Genesis survivors didn't reach space: Jazzy and Bilal.

After Bilal regained consciousness, we had to explain

what happened. For the first time, he looks hopeless. I have to admire Jazzy, though. While I sat there staring up at the moons, she took one deep breath and plunged back into the chaos. She helped free a few Imago who were stuck behind jammed doors. It almost makes me smile. I remember her telling stories about all the pageants she lost. What are the winners doing now? I doubt they could hold a candle to her.

My mind jumps back to Morning. Her desperate shouts muted by bone-thick glass. I think about her sitting inside our escape pod across from Beatty. That asshole. He's pointing a gun at her, but I guarantee she's figured out eighteen different ways to kill him. The thought of her lights a fire in my chest. I've let my anthem get too quiet.

Now it rises. It claws free: *Today is not the day that I die.*

"What's the next move?" I ask. "Where do we go now?"

"How 'bout the other launch stations?" Jazzy throws out hopefully.

But Speaker shakes his head. "The other stations are activating. All of them will launch within the next few hours. Seeing the moons will only quicken that process. If we head there, we'll find empty bases waiting for us."

I realize that leaves one option. "Babel. They're our last way out."

Speaker frowns. "Apologies, Emmett, but our goals have shifted. Babel will react to our ships launching into space. We believe that our window for escape has closed."

"So we give up?" I ask. "Just like that?"

Feoria turns, and it's like trying to stare directly at the sun. That fiery spirit burns back brighter than ever, and she answers my question with iron in her voice. "We do not give up. We will do what we always intended to do. We will *strike*. Babel will burn."

And just like that, her sleeping soldiers awaken. There are about a dozen Imago soldiers left. All of them rise. Every look promises blood. I exchange a glance with Jazzy and Bilal. Clearly we're not on the same page. None of this is about revenge. It's about home. We've had our hearts set on Earth for too long to give up now.

It takes a second to remember that Morning and Parvin aren't here. No one's going to argue for us. It's my turn to step up. "Speak. I thought we had a pact. We're supposed to go home."

He gestures to the sky. "Have we not honored our pact? The ships have launched. Your brothers and sisters made it to space. We promised we would do everything in our power. Have we not done that and more? It is out of our hands now. So is the fate of our own species."

My mind races through the possibilities. There has to be a better alternative than just setting it all on fire. I have to fight for some kind of compromise, but you can't compromise if you don't have a better plan. "Okay. Babel burns. I get it. Where will we go?"

Feoria taps her scouter. "The nearest Babel stronghold. Back to Grimgarden to cause trouble. If we can strike quickly, it might give our people a better chance in space."

An idea echoes and thunders and pulses. Of course. Babel's bases.

"Foundry," I say out loud. "That's perfect."

"Myriad," Feoria corrects. "It's closer, and Jacquelyn believed that Babel was using it as their main port. We avoided sailing south for that reason. We will travel to Myriad. We will kill *anyone* we find there. We will march to the next place and the next. Until the moons come for us."

The surviving Imago answer with a war cry. Their shouts echo over the cliffs. They're finally getting a chance to draw blood and destroy the unwelcome invader. I know they deserve this. It's been two decades of sheathed blades and putting on a peaceful show. But we have our fight waiting.

"Let us go to Foundry." I hate that it sounds like begging. Feoria glares back at me, but I won't back down, not this late in the game. "It's our last chance. Kit Gander is at Foundry. He's just a kid. He's one of us. If we can get there, I know how to launch back up into space. Anton did it the same way. He used the supply silos. It's dangerous, but it might be our last chance."

Dark stares greet the idea. I'm trying to think of what else I can possibly say, when Greenlaw steps forward. Her face is determined. "I want to go with them."

Speaker looks offended. "Your *queen* has given an order."

"My allegiance is to the next generation," Greenlaw cuts back. "Feoria and Ashling gave me their seal. I promised to lead our people, and I cannot fulfill that promise if I'm stuck here on a dying planet." She pauses meaningfully before turning to me. "You can get us into space?"

"Definitely," I answer, before realizing it's not that simple. "If we make it there. And if Kit is still at the base. There's a lot that could go wrong, but I don't see any better options."

She nods once. "My presence only strengthens that chance. I'm coming. Who will join us?"

I'm surprised by how the numbers split. It's the opposite of what I expected. Of the eleven soldiers, only two step forward to join Greenlaw. Sometimes it's hard to tell with the Imago, but I'd guess they're the youngest two. The rest grew up serving Feoria. Her name is the one they would have screamed as they ran into battle. Like Speaker, they've chosen to stay and die with their queen.

Greenlaw turns to Feoria. "With your permission . . ."

Feoria actually laughs. "Queens do not ask for permission, and you are most certainly a queen. Take them with you. Let's set coordinates for the nearest harbor town. When we arrive, our group will head for Myriad, but the rest of you must go your own way. It is time for you to rise."

She offers one final smile before stumbling. I stare in confusion. The movement is so unlike her. She's always been so steady. Speaker figures it out before the rest of us.

"Feoria!" he screams.

Greenlaw's command follows. "Everyone down!"

We hit the deck as Speaker lunges forward. He reaches for Feoria's hand, but a second bullet punches through her chest, just beneath the right shoulder. I can hear the concussive shot that echoes in the distance. There's a sniper. Nyxia blooms out, but too late. The next shots are deflected away, but the damage is already done.

Speaker is there. He leans down and applies pressure. I can hear him begging Feoria not to die. I force my eyes past him. Along the opposite canyon, the first line of Babel troops emerges. There are too many of them to count. It's a full squadron. The crew picks their way through the flame-gnarled ships and keeps weapons pointed in our direction.

Another set of marines fans out to the left, hoping to close the circle around us. Feoria's body goes frighteningly still.

Greenlaw takes charge. "We need to get out of here now."

Queen or not, no one listens. Instead, the group watches Speaker. He quietly closes the eyes of the woman he loved most in this world. He brushes her outstretched hand with his, and then reaches for the mace strapped to his back. He whispers one final word, something meant only for his dead queen. Maybe it's a promise that he'll join her soon.

And then he rises.

He takes his place at the edge of the cliffs.

"Greenlaw. Take them to the Old Volgata harbor. Pick the boat with the best engine. Go to Foundry. Move quickly. My queen's final words are not to be taken lightly. She says you are to be a great queen. Rise to her final challenge."

He draws nyxia into the air. It spirals into the form of a massive sphere. We've seen them before. The carriers the Imago have always used to travel. He looks back at the other soldiers and takes their measure. "For our queen. Ride with me."

As he climbs inside, a roar answers. The Imago manipulate matching vehicles, and I can barely blink before they thunder over the cliffs. I stumble to the edge and watch as Babel opens fire. Bullets ping off the hurdling spheres. Some lodge into the side of the ravine, spouting dust.

"There are too many of them," I mutter. "Babel has hundreds of soldiers."

"And all of them will die," Greenlaw replies. "We need to leave. Now."

I watch long enough to see the lead carrier spiral open.

Speaker rises like a demigod. His mace catches the first marine's jaw and spins him to the ground. The nearest soldiers aim and fire, but his carrier expands into a shield on that side, catching the bullets. Speaker pivots and marches straight through his own nyxian wall. I watch the substance drape around him like armor.

Another swing, another death.

"Emmett!" Jazzy calls. "We have to go!"

Bilal has to pull me away. My final glimpse of Speaker is bloodstained. He shouts Feoria's name at the top of his lungs. The dead surround him, but his eyes search for the next target and the next and the next. I'm pulled away from that final image.

And we're sprinting through the forest.

Overhead, the moons march toward their own war.

CHAPTER 19

THE PRODIGAL

Longwei Yu
07 days 12 hours 13 minutes

We disembark in an empty hangar of the Tower Space Station.

Before launching, Defoe altered our ship's identification codes. All he had to do was hold his watch up to the console. It took the ship about thirty seconds to make the necessary changes. For all the Tower's brilliant tech, we might as well have been ghosts launching into space.

It clearly worked. No one greets us in the hangar. Anton isn't here to have us arrested. No guards wait at strategic choke points. Our group arrives undetected.

Defoe's three chosen marines sweep the room and perform the standard protocol. He chose to keep the crew light. I walk beside him, and two techies trail us. Defoe spent the entire flight digging into me for every scrap of information I could give him. Questions about the Imago mostly. He made all the logical leaps except for one. He guesses that the launch stations were designed to take over the Tower. From there, he assumed the Imago intended to return to Earth. He hasn't figured out the moons. He thinks this is an act of greed, not one of desperation.

Instead of pressing into the depths of the station, Defoe guides us to a room in the far corner of the hangar. An empty command bay. It's not big enough to be the central hub, but after taking a long look through the window and into the room, Defoe smirks back at us.

"This way." He holds his watch up to the door scan. The circuits fire with new codes, and the door gasps open, green-lit. "They've shut down the primary systems. Clever of them. But they've forgotten that in this world I am one of the gods. Let's set up in here."

Our obedient techies unspool the device Defoe used down on Magnia. It takes some time to feed the wires into the right veins and nerves. He lies down on the floor, gets as comfortable as he can, and nods once to them. "Activate the link."

In answer, the techies fire up the device. I watch it all with drowning eyes. I'm still not sure what I should do. A nyxian sword hangs on my back. But what does killing Defoe in this moment accomplish? Will it be the deciding factor? I don't have enough pieces of the puzzle to decide.

So I wait and I watch.

Last time they used the device, Defoe was out cold for about thirty minutes. Somehow the technology allowed him to worm his way into space. I don't understand. How is he connected? More important, what is he connected to? As I watch, his hands tremble. A few seconds later and both of his eyes flutter halfway open. It's clear that he is not with us in the normal way.

"I'm in the command bay," he says. "He was sleeping. Anton left him. Time to explore."

The techies make slight adjustments. One asks, "What do you want us to do?"

Defoe's eyes snap briefly back into focus. "No one comes in or out of the hangar. Not even our people. Let's stay hidden for as long as we can. This connection is *much* stronger. I would prefer to exhaust this option before we make our move. Only give me the necessary updates. I need to focus. He's trying to fight back."

But the idea of a fight only widens Defoe's smile. I do my best to trace back through his words. He said something about the command bay. Someone was sleeping? The final sentence gives the biggest clue of all, though. *He's trying to fight back.* All the pieces link up. I guessed Defoe was tapping into the nyxia aboard the ship in some way. I thought they had rigged some kind of overarching system that only he could access. It would have been a clever fail-safe.

The truth is worse. Defoe's tapping into *someone.* An actual person. *Anton left him.* I take a deep breath as Defoe's eyes fog over again. His fingers twitch. His legs tremble. He's not just seeing through the person's eyes. He's controlling them. Walking them around like a puppet. But who?

"What the hell?"

The techie's voice pulls me away from my thoughts. Defoe gives a slight twitch, but it's clear his mind is centered *elsewhere.* I follow the techie's stare and look back into the hangar. It's not hard to find the source of his alarm. The hangar walls are still shut tight, but a pair of . . .

. . . drills? It sounds impossible. A pair of drills are boring through the metal. We all stare at their progress. The three marines move like magnets toward the spot, guns raised and ready. I stare from behind the protective glass as the hole widens. The drills retract slowly. Hooks slip through the gaps, attaching to the interior walls and flexing tight. A second passes before the newly made door collapses inward.

I stare in awe as a girl floats forward. Gravity snares her. She lands neatly. Her skin is dark, and her hair is dyed a bright blond color. I've never seen her before. I blink as others follow her through the carefully made gap. There are ten of them. All teenagers. All of them wearing the same nyxian masks we did. My mind pieces together another clue. Defoe mentioned *Genesis 14.* This must be the fourth crew they launched into space. But if Babel brought them here, why are they drilling to get back inside the station?

Uncertain, Defoe's marines spread out. The new Genesis crew keeps a tight formation, backs pressed to the hangar bay's exterior wall. The leading girl raises both hands innocently. She heaves the biggest sigh of relief I've ever seen. I can't quite hear her words—everything is muted by the glass—but I watch as she unleashes a choking sob and rushes to hug the nearest marine.

He lowers his weapon. What a mistake.

The knife at the girl's hip becomes the knife in the girl's hand becomes the knife in the marine's neck. The scene unfolds like a dying flower. His partners react, lift-

ing their weapons, but the bullets lodge into spawning nyxian shields. I watch their crew move in flawless harmony.
Ducking around one another, lifting summoned weapons,
circling their prey.

The two marines realize they're trapped.

Backpedaling.

Dead.

As blood splashes to the floor, I reach out and pull one of
the techies flat to the ground. My whispered command snakes
through the air. "Stay down. Out of sight. No one moves."

Silence reigns. Defoe's lips continue to move and mutter.
Each second weighs an hour. There's a slight gap between
the door and the wall. It's open just enough to hear the echo
of movement. Their group is debating something. For the
thousandth time, I wrestle with the correct action. Do I be-
tray Defoe now? This crew is a question mark. Where are
their loyalties?

They just killed Babel marines. Does that mean they're
on our side?

I realize I could never convince them to trust me.

So I wait in the room. Eventually, the hangar grows quiet.

"I'm going to look," I whisper.

Both techies are sweating and panicked. Before they can
protest, I push carefully up from the ground. My eyes rise
above the bottom rim of the glass window. I spy the three
corpses, but the rest of the hangar is empty. My heart hammers in my chest. I'm debating what to do next when Defoe
lets out a satisfied laugh. He whispers the last thing I want
to hear.

"Hello, Anton."

CHAPTER 20

EYES

Anton Stepanov

07 days 12 hours 14 minutes

I stand at the rear of our makeshift command center. Aguilar picked this place as a containment strategy. The room boasts a less complex system than the main command center. It allows her to monitor her team more closely. Fewer chances of betrayal. I like the place because there's a hidden back door in one corner that leads to all my favorite places.

It's hard to stop thinking that way.

Back doors. Tunnels. Hiding.

It takes effort to return my attention to the task at hand. Every console glows with blue light. Hands dance over schematics and layouts. Quick swipes silence the growing number of alarms. Our crew has been on high alert ever since the first alarm announced objects leaving the planet's atmosphere. Patrols roam the corridors. Vandemeer is sending reports from our detainment area. It didn't take Aguilar's team long to determine the incoming ships weren't from

Babel. That news had my heart beating with a new kind of hope.

The Imago are coming. Maybe my friends are with them.

"Twenty-three breaches," one of the techies announces. "Most of them are along the hull of the *Genesis 12*. There's only one outlier in the mix. A breach near the auxiliary hangar."

My eyes narrow. "That could be the Genesis 14 crew."

Aguilar shakes her head. "There's no way to know. We don't have eyes on any of it after shutting down the main security system. We can bring it back online, but we risk giving anyone loyal to Babel a foothold if it's up and running."

"Let's focus on the main breaches," I say. "Is anyone aboard the *Genesis 12*?"

"One of our techies was performing maintenance there. Her name is Lilja Gudmundsson," the nearest techie says. "The no-grav areas are patchy at best. We can't get any contact. But we have an open line with the person that was posted on guard rotation aboard the *Genesis 12*."

It takes her a second to scan down the list before she selects the right name. A photo appears on her console, and she transfers it to the main screen for the rest of us to see. A pale face with dark raven eyes. "Dr. Karpinski," Aguilar announces. "Let's get him on the comm."

It takes a few seconds for the link to work. A hesitant voice echoes back to us.

"He-hello?"

"This is Commander Aguilar. Are you at your post aboard the *Genesis 12*?"

"I'm here."

Dr. Karpinski's file is up on the screen. The more I read, the less confident I feel. He was one of the caretakers aboard the *Genesis 11*. His two wards were Roathy and Isadora. I can't help noticing the demerit listed in the bottom right corner of his file. It describes the doctor's actions during their flight as "reckless" and "treasonous." It goes on to say he "intentionally endangered the life of Emmett Atwater, a valued asset . . ."

All I can do is shake my head. Not the most promising option.

"Dr. Karpinski, our systems are showing breach points in the *Genesis 12*. We believe a number of Imago ships have made contact. Based on information provided by Erone and Anton, we believe that the Imago are launching into space and intend to join us in the fight against Babel."

There's a long pause. "Did you say breach points? They're actually up here?"

"Yes. They've breached the ship." Aguilar glances at me. "You are under no obligation to approach, but we could *really* use some eyes on what's happening while we organize a more official welcoming committee. We also don't want the Imago to damage the ship in any way. If you're willing to help, we can walk you through it."

There's too much fear in Karpinski's voice. No way in hell he actually goes.

Aguilar mutes her headset and glances at me. "Erone?"

I've been trying to contact him. There's a good chance he's still passed out in the original command center. I shake my head. "No response. I'll go find him if this doesn't work."

Tension fills the room as we wait. Karpinski's voice finally breaks back through.

"Just tell me what to do."

Aguilar shoots me a surprised look before walking him through the process. It's a nice twist of Babel's tech. She has Karpinski go into the settings of his scouter and invert the screen. She feeds into his individual line, and in less than a few minutes, we're seeing what Karpinski sees. Aguilar converts it the main screen, and we watch the frightened doctor perform his first act of bravery: he reaches down and swipes his card.

The entrance gasps open. An empty hallway waits. There's a slight blue glow coming off his headset. It makes the edges of our camera angle look thick with fog. Aguilar guides him down the right hallways. I activate my own headset and brief him on the situation. He still looks like Babel. The Imago will see him as the enemy. Unless he tells them we're with Erone.

I stare at the POV screen and find myself hoping for a familiar face. I want him to round a corner and run into Morning or Parvin or Alex. Hell, I'd even take Katsu at this point. I just want some proof that they're still alive. The room takes a collective breath when Karpinski rounds another corner. In the distance, the Imago are waiting.

It's a far larger group than I expected. Fifty of them? Maybe more? They wait in a proper defensive formation. Each gap in their front lines is accented by a flickering nyxian shield. My eyes are drawn beyond the group too.

About twenty drill tips have punched through the side

of the ship. Each one expanded out wide enough to allow a person through. Nyxia blankets the gaping holes neatly.

"Air locks," I realize. "That's clever."

No one replies. Everyone is too busy staring. Karpinski looks frozen too. He stands by the entrance, and I have no doubt that it's the most terrifying thing he's ever seen in his life. Babel showed them the same videos they showed us. In his mind, the Imago are brutal warriors. Erone hasn't done much to soften that reputation either. And while the waiting Imago don't all look like soldiers, all of them are definitely armed.

"Translator active?" Aguilar asks.

Karpinski takes a deep breath. "Active. Engaging now."

And the doctor starts bravely forward. He's smart enough to lift both hands innocently into the air. An Imago soldier slips around their summoned barrier. He wears a simple off-white jumpsuit. There's a single black sash crossing his chest. He matches Karpinski step for step, his head tilting slightly as he studies our lowly emissary.

Karpinski begins. "I come in peace."

I can't help rolling my eyes. Aguilar shoots me a God-help-us-all look.

"We're not with Babel," he continues. "Our commander is one of your own. Do you know Erone? He's an Imago like you. We're following his orders."

"Erone?" The leader's voice is smoother than silk. "The Tinker?"

Our POV camera shakes as Karpinski nods. "I think so. Is that what you call him?"

"It's what we *called* him," the leader corrects. "Erone was kidnapped. Every ring saw the footage. We have not forgotten that betrayal. The queens believed he was dead."

Karpinski shakes his head. "He's alive. He's in control of the ship. He sent us to greet—"

But a look from the Imago leader buries the rest of his sentence. Even watching it through the safety of a screen, I can't help flinching. Hatred breathes through the expression.

"Alive? Perhaps. In control of the ship? I doubt that. But the idea that Erone would send you to greet us? Clearly you know nothing of Imago custom. None of our kind would ever send a stranger in the place of a friend. You have lost my faith."

Aguilar senses the encounter slipping through our fingers. She hisses a command through the headset. "Tell them Erone is watching the prisoners. Leaving risks our control of the ship."

And her mistake seals Karpinski's fate. The bright blue at the edge of his vision flashes as his headset receives the inbound message. Before Karpinski can even process the words, an unmistakable sequence begins. The Imago leader's eyes widen in suspicion. He plants his back foot. The black sash running across his chest *smokes* into the air. It forms back into the shape of an ax.

"Wait!" Karpinski shouts. "Erone. He's with—"

The POV camera offers front-row seats to the murder. Aguilar flips a switch in time to mute Karpinski's screams, but the screen shows more than enough. Our newly converted techies watch as their fears come true. The Imago prove as brutal as their employers always promised they were. I can feel our footholds vanishing as Karpinski slumps to the floor, camera shaking.

The nearest techie looks back and asks the question on everyone's mind.

"I thought you said they were on our side?"

I know it's too late for empty promises.

"Seal *Genesis 12*. I'll find Erone and take him down. He'll set all of this straight."

"You heard him. Seal the ship," Aguilar orders. And then she leans toward me and lowers her voice to less than a whisper. "We are about to *lose* this ship. Find Erone. Take him down there. We'll activate your POV camera. I need you to show them this was all a misunderstanding. If you don't do that and do it *soon,* we're going to have a mutiny on our hands."

I nod back to her. "I've got this."

I cross the room, mind racing. Fear runs through every vein. I'm already counting all the ways this could possibly go wrong. I can't help wondering if leaving Aguilar behind is a mistake. What if she decides none of this is worth the risk? If she decides to load the rest of the survivors onto a ship and leave, there's nothing I can do to stop her.

I turn a corner and run right into Erone. The blow knocks the wind out of me. Erone stumbles before righting himself against the nearest wall. When he sees it's me, his eyes light up.

"Hello, Anton."

That strangeness is back in his voice. His eyes roam around the hallway like he's seeing the ship for the first time. I'm not sure what's wrong with him, but right now it doesn't matter. He's our best chance at keeping the Imago from slaughtering the rest of the crew.

"Imago have boarded the ship," I say. "You were right. They launched. But they still think we're with Babel. They killed the first person we sent down to speak with them. You and I need to go down there together, Erone. We have to show them you're still alive."

Erone takes longer than normal to process that. I eye the purpling bruise on his forehead. Our last conversation didn't make any sense. He fell at the end of it and hit the floor hard. Perhaps he has a concussion? After watching what happened to Karpinski, we'll have a hard time convincing a doctor to actually treat him.

"Take me to the command center instead."

I frown. "We really don't have time for that, Erone. Your people just killed one of our guys. If the Imago don't see that you're alive and working with us, we're going to have big problems."

Erone nods. "We can use the communication system. Let me speak to them."

I'm about to push back when I see the way he's looking at me. A familiar danger lurks. I haven't forgotten Katherine Ford or David Requin. How quickly both of them fell when Erone decided their end had come. I take a deep breath and nod. "Back this way. Let's give it a shot."

"This way will be more efficient," he promises.

I scan back into the control room. Aguilar raises an appraising eyebrow before noting Erone trailing me. The whole room flinches a little at his arrival. They all just got a live look at what he's capable of doing. Most of them avoid eye contact, just in case.

"Can you pipe Erone through to the *Genesis 12*?" I ask. "He thinks broadcasting his voice will be enough. It's worth a shot, right?"

Aguilar looks annoyed, but nods anyway. "We can definitely try it. Sierra, will you get those systems back online?"

Erone takes his place on the command deck. I stand beside him, and my eyes are drawn back to the main screen. We're still watching everything unfold from Karpinski's perspective. The only difference is that the angle is looking out from the ground. I try to ignore the puddled blood on the right side of the screen. Imago scouts are testing the boundaries of the room. Most of them are still huddled in defensive positions. Erone considers the scene for a few seconds before glancing back at Aguilar.

"So you are in charge?" he asks. "Of all this?"

Aguilar frowns at him. ". . . I've been handling the technical side of things, yeah."

And something powerful fractures the air around us. I'm shoved to one side. My shoulder bangs into the nearest console, and the techie at that station jumps back in surprise. I whip my head around in time to witness the impossible. A black sword has pierced Aguilar's stomach. Erone has her shoulder in a vise grip. The last thing she does is look at me.

There's disbelief and confusion and fear there.

In an elegant motion, Erone slides his sword free. A deadly arc brings it swinging back around at my neck. I gasp when the blade stops just short.

"I am in command now," he says. "Anton's game is at an end."

Disbelief dominates the room. Aguilar is dead. I am a hostage. Erone has rebelled again. I know we represented hope to them. These were the Babel employees who dared to dream we might take them home when their employers would not. That hope just died.

"Where are the Imago?" Erone asks.

The techies aren't foolish enough to play games.

One answers, "All of them are aboard the *Genesis 12.*"

Erone watches the screen for a few seconds. Was this his plan the entire time? Overthrow Requin. Play nice until his people arrived. Anger burns to life inside me. There's nothing I can do about it with a sword at my neck, but the betrayal digs down beneath my skin.

I actually *helped* him.

"How many are there?" he asks.

"Over fifty of them."

Erone nods decisively. "Seal the ship."

A few techies look up in confusion. "We've already sealed the ship."

"Unlatch the *Genesis 12.* Send them into space."

Now everyone looks back. The command doesn't make any sense. These are his own people. Somehow, I manage to find my voice again. "I don't get it. They're Imago."

Erone's blade slips across my throat. My eyes widen, but it's not a killing blow, just a warning. He brings the hilt of the sword slamming into the nearest console. Glass shatters, and the seated techie has to leap out of the way.

"I said *unlatch* them."

This time the techies don't hesitate. I hear one of them mumble the name of the other techie that we couldn't get in contact with—Lilja. She'll be just as lost as the Imago.

I watch helplessly as a series of codes unlock the mechanisms that moor the *Genesis 12* to our station. Erone oversees the strangest betrayal I've ever witnessed. None of this makes any sense. When the sequence completes, a blue grid of schematics flashes into midair. We all watch as an outline of the *Genesis 12* flashes red. The whole ship floats quietly away from the main structure. All the surviving Imago begin their unwanted journey into space. It's not hard to imagine what happens next. Without pilots or an understanding of the navigation system, they're all going to die. Erone nods to himself.

"Now," he says. "I want a full report of *every* ship leaving the atmosphere."

It takes a few seconds for the techies to respond. When he's convinced they're working busily at the task, his attention turns back to me. Erone's eyes lock with mine, and for the first time, I see a flicker of something *else*. It's just the ghost of an image, there and gone, but I swear that for a single breath I'm not looking at Erone at all.

He smiles. It's both strange and familiar at the same time.

"Anton. It is time to discuss your punishment. You have been *very* busy."

CHAPTER 21

SHOWDOWN

Morning Rodriguez
07 days 12 hours 07 minutes

I hate how tight the straps of my seat are. I hate how the pressure shifts and the ship rattles and all the other signs that we've exited Magnia's atmosphere. I hate the determined glare on Beatty's face. He's not supposed to be here. It wasn't supposed to happen this way.

"Nothing personal," he says. "I did what I had to do."

I hate his British accent and the way he shrugs, like this is somehow *my* fault or *Emmett's* fault. And that name burns a path from my head to my heart. Emmett. He's gone. We *left* him. Even from the safety of the escape pod, Beatty and I both heard the arrival of Babel's ships. We felt the shaking explosions in the air as we cut through the first layer of clouds. How many Babel marines attacked the base? Is Emmett . . .

No. I will not think it. I will not speak it, because it can't be *true.* Emmett would survive. Emmett would fight.

I know he's doing everything he can right now to get back up into space.

Hopelessness still claws at my chest. What chance does he have now? We pinned our survival on the launch station. We let ourselves celebrate a safe arrival there because we knew there wasn't another option. That was our only way home. And it worked.

I glance through the slanted windows. We've been rising steadily for a few minutes now. There's a slight haze of blue in every direction. I know we're out of Babel's range. It should take a few more minutes for us to clear the atmosphere.

This is when Emmett would make a comment. Something meaningful, about how small we really are. Or maybe something funny. A joke about the weather up here.

My heart crawls up into my throat.

He's not here. Beatty is.

I lock eyes with him and grind my teeth. He's pointing the gun in my direction. He's not extending it anymore, because his arm was getting tired, and that might be enough distance for me to work with. Usually, it'd be as easy as breathing. The manipulation I need to do isn't even that hard. I need to draw the nyxia out of my knapsack and up into a shield. Beatty's first shot would deflect off it. I'd seal the barrier and free myself. The plan ends with me floating this asshole out into space.

But there are too many variables. A whole list of things that could go wrong, and at the top of that list? Distance. Beatty is so close. I know I'm faster than him, but fast won't matter at this range. He doesn't have to be quick. A bullet will hit long before my nyxia can answer. I need a piece of it in hand for this to work.

So I wait.

I grind my teeth and settle my breathing and burn with hatred.

But I wait.

There is a question that Beatty is going to ask me. All I have to do is wait for him to ask it. I mentally focus on the way my body will move. I'm going to use an old magician's trick. Make them look in one direction while you work in another. I just need the right moment to come.

Another few minutes and our escape pod starts to lose momentum. Beatty's eyes stay trained on me. He has to keep a vigilant watch. He doesn't get to enjoy the view. Emmett's not here, but I know he'd want me to look. So I glance out the window and see Magnia sprawling below. The slashing darks of oceans. The curling green continents marked by looming mountains and slithering rivers. Emmett would say that we're going to be the last ones to see it this way.

Space starts to affect the ship. The nose of our craft rotates gently, floating and turning. The Imago were smart enough to seal the interiors, though. So while the ship groans with obvious movement, we stay upright the whole time. No loss of gravity either. Beatty's eyes flick briefly around the room. He's starting to get nervous. Good.

Out the windows, I can just make out the lights of other ships. The bright blue of their burning engines. There aren't nearly as many as there should be. The ones that did make it into space start to move. I watch long enough to see them *activate*. Little bursts of light that guide them in the right direction. It's like Jacquelyn planned. Each of them is seeking out nyxia. It will have them heading straight for the Tower Space Station.

Beatty asks the question I've been waiting for him to ask. "Shouldn't we be moving?"

I keep my face as neutral as I can. Beatty's eyes glance out the window, and I slide my right hand just slightly to the side. Just a fraction. It slides clear of my leg and hovers in the air to the right of my chair. My knapsack is on that side.

I take a second to bring up a mental image of the contents. Most of the nyxia is stuffed in there at random. Larger chunks too, which won't work for what I need. But I remember there's one piece that's dangling like a keychain. I attached it to my knapsack after Omar died. It was a way to remember him. A little black pyramid that's small enough to fit in my palm.

Eyes pinned on Beatty, I mentally reach for it. I'm just trying to establish the connection first. There's the slightest whisper in the air as my grasping thought touches the edge of the pyramid. Beatty stares back at me, so I raise a distracting eyebrow and answer his question.

"You have to activate the console, asshole."

My mind closes around the image of the object. Our bond kicks to life. I take a steadying breath and wait for Beatty to ask the question that will inevitably follow the first. I know that I'm only going to have one chance at this.

He eyes me. "Well, do you know how to activate it?"

I make the most annoyed face that I can. It's actually hard to summon annoyance when what I really feel is hopeless, pounding rage. But I do my best and then I use the distraction to do *several* things at once. My left hand reaches out, finger pointing, in the direction of the central console. That's the hand I want Beatty to see, and sure enough, his eyes follow its progress.

At the same time, I open my right hand. My knuckles face Beatty. My palm faces the bag behind me in the corner. It takes all my focus to speak at the same time that I summon the more important thought. *Fly into my hand. Fly into my hand. Fly into my hand.*

"You just press and hold that button down." The words almost sound like they're being spoken by someone else. "If you press it down for three seconds, the ship will activate."

Beatty shifts uncomfortably, and the noise of his suit bunching is the only reason he doesn't hear the whispering *thwack* of nyxia striking my palm with force. I close that hand into a fist. The point of the pyramid digs into my palm. My face remains neutral.

Beatty gestures with his gun. "You press it," he says. "Slowly."

I make sure to show off my empty left hand as I reach down for the button. He stares at me as the seconds tick off. The ship shudders before following after the others.

Beatty relaxes as I lean back in my seat. He doesn't know it, but he just died. I'm close enough to see the obvious relief on his face. He thinks he *won.* He escaped the end of the world. He doesn't realize I'm his apocalypse now.

Beatty's story ends here.

I imagine he's keeping me alive with a purpose in mind. Maybe he thinks we'll attach to the Tower and he'll hold me at gunpoint as we board the ship. Was his plan to rejoin the others? Or did he want to join up with Babel again? Doesn't matter now. He'll never make it inside the Tower.

The passing minutes stretch. Each one feels like an eternity. Scraps from science class come floating back to the front of my brain. The International Space Station took an hour and a half to orbit Earth. It's not hard to imagine the Tower pulling about the same rate. Are we chasing after it? Or are we circling in the opposite direction on a collision course?

In answer, the console stirs with blue light. We get a displayed image of our ship and a distant object that can only be the Tower. It flashes angles and distances. I can feel the ship tugging itself into the right position and working to buffer the inevitable impact. I take a deep breath as the console shows us closing the gap. Grinding mechanical noises sound within the ship's walls.

I already have the manipulation in my head. I stare across at Beatty. He looks pale in the ghostly light of space. His forehead is so thick with sweat that the hair at the front of his scalp is a shade darker. It runs down his temples too. We're both counting down the seconds. But we both have very different ideas about what happens next.

Equipment extends from our ship. Some kind of claw or suction. The walls tremble as the escape pod kisses against the side of the Tower Space Station. My eyes are fixed on Beatty. The final piece of his failed puzzle is about to click into place. Gears grind. Our ship flashes with blue light again, and I can hear the sound of a drill. The escape pod bores into the side of the Tower.

I keep watching Beatty.

There's a *click*. The drill stops. The job is finished.

Beatty's curiosity betrays him. He flicks a glance that way, and I summon my nyxia. It stretches across and forms a flawless shield. Beatty looks back a second too late. His eyes widen. His finger itches over the trigger. He fires twice. The sound is deafening, but my shield absorbs both blows easily. The material trembles before flexing straight. The bullets drop uselessly to the floor.

My summoning cuts the room in two. Beatty reaches out, but he's too weak, too unfocused. It's like shoving away a child's hand. I am stronger than he could ever dream. My translucent curtain adjusts with less than a thought. I carefully cut Beatty off from the control panel. I tighten the opposite side too so that he has no access to the hatch.

He fires one more shot, and I can't help smiling.

Maybe it's cruel, but I take my time now. Beatty fumbles at his own twisted straps as I carefully unclip myself. I stand up and crack my neck. I don't even look at him as I gather my belongings. I shift my belts so both hatchets hang up front, tight and ready. I add a few wristbands and rings. All the right tools for what waits for us in the Tower.

Finally, I turn back to face my enemy.

Beatty's free of his own straps. He's set the gun aside and has both hands pressed to the wall I've summoned. I can see him gritting his teeth as he tries to take control of it. The console flashes repeatedly. It's waiting for permission. We're sealed to the ship. All I have to do is leave.

So I look Beatty in the eye.

"Please," he begs. "Please don't do this. What was I supposed to do?"

I ignore him. I walk over to the door and put my ear against it. There's movement on the other side, but no explosions or gunfire or anything. We've leeched onto the ship without Babel noticing. Or maybe they just don't have the defenses in place to react? I turn back.

"Emmett would let you live. He's got a good heart like that." I walk forward. "It's a shame you just tried to kill him. It's a shame you left him behind, instead of me. It might have saved your life. I'm not like him. Nowhere close. You hurt someone I love. That doesn't work for me."

I pause at the edge of my nyxian shield. Tears streak down Beatty's face. His eyes flick toward the entrance, and it's like he's hoping Gio will come bursting through the door to save him. He looks back at me and begs again, "Please, Morning. I'm sorry, okay? I didn't . . ."

I reach through the barrier. The nyxia pulses. It feeds on all the anger I have humming in my chest. It wraps around my hand like an armored glove. I catch Beatty by the throat. I stand there, eyes locked on him, and start to squeeze.

His face contorts. I'm close enough to see the veins widen. His eyes start to go bloodshot. His pale face whitens to the color of snow. In the back of my mind, though, Emmett's voice echoes. He wouldn't do this.

I pull my shaking hand back through the barrier. Emmett would show mercy. I'm about to tell Beatty that when I realize he's still choking. I removed my hand, but the nyxian glove is still there, its grip still firm. My eyes widen. I reach for the nyxia . . .

. . . and it rejects me. There's a sickening twist as the gloved hand snaps Beatty's neck. He falls like a rag doll to the floor. I stagger back, chest heaving. I'm flooded by the same darkness I felt when I killed Jerricho. I can almost hear the nyxia arguing. Beatty *deserved* this, didn't he? But I'm hyperventilating.

It takes a minute to actually draw in even breaths. Cautiously, I reach for the nyxia again. All the resistance is gone. It feels the way that it always feels. I wait until my breathing is steady, focus on the substance, and force it back into the shape of a little pyramid. It shivers into the smaller form, and I feel instant relief. Sitting in the palm of my hand, the substance feels like something I can control again. I keep my mind sharp and steady, though, just in case.

It still takes me a few minutes to stand up. I feel the scars of this moment already forming, but I don't have time for scars or tears or any of it. I remind myself of the one thing that matters now. "Emmett," I say. "I have to save Emmett."

I wipe away the tears. When my breathing steadies, I slam a palm down into the release button. There's a gasp as the hatch gives way. Blinding light dives into the cockpit. I slide both hatchets free from their straps. Beatty's ghost haunts me as I step into the quiet of the hallway.

Guilt tries to claw into me. I fight past it. Everything changed when Beatty boarded our ship. It's not just about surviving Babel now. I have to help Emmett. I have to save him.

So I grit my teeth and walk into the light.

CHAPTER 22

IMPACT

Emmett Atwater

07 days 11 hours 31 minutes

Our escape is not cautious. Greenlaw loads us into individual nyxian carriers and has us vaulting toward the coast in minutes. The trip takes less than an hour. The village harbor—Old Volgata—is barely worthy of the name. Four buildings circle a pair of half-rotten docks. A handful of boats toss at sea. Greenlaw eyes them for a few seconds before picking the one she must think is the fastest and sturdiest. It's a tip of the hat to her that I don't think twice before boarding.

As the others prep the boat, I summon a nyxian shield. It hovers between us and the shoreline. I'm not taking any more risks. It's starting to feel like Babel could come around the corner at any moment. I can still hear Feoria's final, gasping breaths. I can still see the way fury pulsed like a living thing in Speaker's chest. I watch the shoreline and find myself hoping he killed them all.

Of course, Bilal takes a second to introduce everyone.

The other two Imago are brothers. Diallo is the younger of the two, slender as a knife. He buzzes with so many questions that even Bilal struggles to keep up. His older sibling—Craft—is the exact opposite. He takes his post at one of the front defensive stations and doesn't say a word. Unlike Diallo, he's old enough to count the score. We're losing, and it might be too late to catch up.

As our boat hums out into the blue, I find myself praying. For this to work. For us to make it. Can't the world give us two hours without someone trying to bury us in too-soon graves? Thinking about all the steps it will take to get home has me overwhelmed. We have to reach Grimgarden. And then march to Foundry. And then find Kit. And then . . .

. . . I take a deep breath and remember one of the lessons Pops drilled into me. Our favorite quarterback for the Lions—Quincy Rising—explained it in a postgame interview. Pops always had me watch the clip when things with Moms got too stressful. Rising's team had clawed back from being down twenty-four points to win. In the interview, the reporter asks him how he did it.

Rising just smiles. "One play at a time, baby. Not worried about the next set of downs. Not worried about how many touchdown passes I have to toss. I'm just taking *that* snap. I'm throwing *that* pass. I'm on *that* play. One at a time. It's the only way I know how to play."

Watched it so many times that I can close my eyes and see the smile on his face, hear the sound of his voice. I take another deep breath and focus on our first step: cross the ocean.

Bilal and Diallo talk through the first hour. Jazzy rides

at the front of the ship, eyes pinned to the radar. Craft and Greenlaw brood quietly. Night is coming. Darkness grinds away at the horizon. Our boat is gliding silently over the waves when red light sears the sky.

We all look up as the moons collide.

The growing dark makes each moon look brighter. Magness breaks first. The familiar red scars triple in size as the moon's core suffers the blow. Fire rages out of every crevice. On the moon's swollen side, it bursts free in a bright column. But it's the point of collision that draws our attention. The explosion there grows like an open wound. Glacius—always more reserved and proper—shows off a quieter destruction. A delicate feather of red light frames her blooming edge.

The end is here.

Jacquelyn's prediction was off by only a few days. Now a new countdown begins. This time it is a race with Babel to get off-planet and escape the inevitable apocalypse. A shiver runs down my spine. I feel like the second hand is already ticking. "So much for the element of surprise," I say. "Babel definitely knows now."

Jazzy nods over at me. Bilal frowns, though. He opens his mouth to speak, and all I can do is stare. His mouth moves, but the words don't make sense. "What, Bilal?"

When he speaks again, it's the same unrecognizable sound. It takes me about two seconds to figure out that his graceful Arabic is cutting through the air. Bilal frowns and gestures to his throat. Greenlaw tests her own voice, and my jaw drops. Her words pour out in a polished and rolling tongue. It's not a language I've ever heard before. Craft answers in the same dialect.

Jazzy's eyes go wide. "What the *heck* is happening?"

"The translation . . ." I start to connect the obvious dots. We spent all that time aboard the ship with translation devices. Long enough that the nyxia actually rewired something in all of us. We could speak to each other *without* the devices. It's been an unexpected advantage until now. I take a second to dig back through my knapsack. It takes a few seconds to find the nyxian translation mask I abandoned months ago. I press it to my jaw, and the whole thing suctions.

"Can you understand me?" I ask hopefully. "Bilal?"

But as my words hiss through the device, the translation feature clearly isn't working. Bilal looks back blankly at us. He seems to recognize his name, but the rest is lost. Greenlaw and Craft exchange a glance before gesturing up to the moons overhead. She speaks in short, rhythmic bursts. Diallo chimes in excitedly. Craft's reply is something I'd recognize regardless of language. It's short and crisp and has to be a cuss word.

My eyes trail back up to the moons.

"It's Magness."

"Magness?" Jazzy asks.

I find myself nodding. "One of the Imago soldiers told me about it. Nyxia is created on Magness. The moon's core produces it. Then it rains down during certain seasons."

"And it just exploded," Jazzy catches on. "The core exploded."

Bilal tries to say something, but the rest of us can only stare helplessly back. The Imago are having their own debate. "Nyxia is like that," I say. "Remember when Jaime stabbed me? Nyxia made the wound. So they couldn't use nyxia to fix it. It was like the pieces remembered or something. Like all of it was kind of connected."

"So the moon explodes," Jazzy says. "And now the other nyxia is reacting?"

"That's my best guess."

Greenlaw waves to get our attention. She waits until all of us are focused on her. Using both hands, she walks through a few signals. She points in the direction we're sailing. She signals something that has to represent marching or walking, and then the final gesture is a clear-cut launch into the sky signal. At the end of it, she uses a signal I remember.

Her fist double-clenches: *Keep going?*

She repeats the signal again, and I realize she's waiting for an answer. I nod over in Jazzy's direction. "She wants to know if we should keep going. Can we still launch?"

Jazzy nods once. "It's our last chance."

I lock eyes with Greenlaw and double-clench my own fist. Jazzy mimics the signal. We all glance in Bilal's direction. He looks a little lost, but he's smart enough to just agree with whatever I'm doing. He raises a fist and double-clenches it.

Greenlaw glances up one more time at the growing destruction before taking her captain's chair. We might be a little lost in translation, but there's nothing confusing about the burst of energy she shoves into the nyxia. My body shakes, and my teeth start to chatter.

Her message is clear.

It's time to get the hell out of here.

PART III

AFTERMATH

CHAPTER 23

SIGNAL INTERRUPTED

Longwei Yu

It is time to act. For the last five minutes, I've pretended to watch the empty hangar. The techies have continued monitoring Defoe. I don't have to look back to know that he's slipped more fully out of his own body. He's controlling Erone.

And Erone has Anton.

Anton. It is time to discuss your punishment. Those words send a shiver down my spine. I am trying to be wise. I have tried to wait for the perfect moment. I wanted a wider perspective and the assurance that when I struck it would be a crucial blow. Maybe I've waited too long.

The Prodigal device is powerful. Defoe now controls the ship remotely. He's taking over without any risk to himself. And it will not be long before he kills Anton.

I study the reflection in the glass. Both techies hover off to one side. They are looking down at the device and listening intently to Defoe's continued muttering. The deeper he

slips into Erone's conscience, the less intelligible those mutters sound.

I swallow my fears. It is time to take action.

My brain reaches for the most believable lie. I realize
the newly arrived Genesis crew made my job a lot easier
when they dispatched the three marines. It makes my task
simple and clear. I have to remove the two techies. I have to
destroy the device. Finally, I have to convince Defoe that I
had nothing to do with either outcome. I consider the position of my two targets: how are they seated and which way
are they facing and where are they looking.

A deep and steadying breath. I remind myself this is war.
These are our enemies.

I turn around slowly. My hand glides up to my shoulder and settles on the grip of my sword. One of the techies
glances up. The other remains focused on their task. It
makes my choice easy.

"Did you hear that?" I whisper.

I tilt my head slightly. It shows the techie what he is supposed to do. He mimics the motion, arching his neck and
looking out into the hangar, widening my target area. My
sword comes slashing down. It is what I was trained to do.
The blade sings across his skin. His eyes bulge in surprise.

But no blood comes. No damage is done.

We're still staring at each other, and I realize what's
happened about a split second before he does. I drop the
sword and summon a pair of nyxian bracelets from my
wrist. There's no time for detail or elegance. They form like
weighted rocks in my hand, and I drive the first one into

the techie's temple. He crashes into the wall on our left. The other techie follows his instincts and dives for my sword. I realize he didn't see the result of my first swing.

As I move forward, blunt object in hand, the techie shoves the sword up into my stomach. His eyes widen when it slips straight through my body, and yet I keep walking. He says something, and I'm shocked to hear it in another language. Words I somehow can't translate.

I bring the crude stone swinging down a second time. He falls. Both of them lie motionless on the ground. My chest is heaving, and I struggle to steady my breathing. The truth trembles through me. I was this close to killing another person. It was to save my friends, but now that I've thought about it, I can't stop my hands from shaking. I turn my attention to Defoe.

He didn't wake. Good.

I realize Anton doesn't have much time. He could die at any moment, and it would be my failure to act. But I also have to remain with Defoe. I have to avoid his suspicion. I set about the task carefully. It takes effort. I have never had to move a body before. I awkwardly ferry both of them to the closet at the back of the room. It's a tight fit, but I wedge the door closed and seal it.

As I return to Defoe's side, my eyes find the sword. It is the sword Defoe returned to me down on Magnia. I should have known that he only trusted me so far. He gave me the same kind of weapon we used in the pit. Something that can fend off a blade, but that can't take a life. I was surprised by our proximity, by how often I was in a position to kill him.

The truth makes far more sense.

I could not have killed Defoe, because he gave me a blunted blade.

Time to turn the tables. It takes concentration, but I set one of my crude chunks of nyxia down next to the sword he gifted me. Focus, thought, transformation. A duplicate appears, but with a slight adjustment. I lift the sword and slide the blade against the back of one finger.

Blood rises in answer.

I nod to myself. Now I am a weapon when Defoe suspects I am not. I hide the fake sword in one corner. Defoe is still whispering commands. I'm surprised again by the sound of a clearly foreign tongue. Why can't I understand him? No time for those questions now.

I take the other blunt stone in hand and position myself over the device.

"For Anton," I whisper.

My fist slams down. The plastic dents inward. I bring the stone down again, harder this time, and the whole thing breaks. I can feel the air fracture as Defoe's connection with Erone severs. I slip quickly to the right, out of Defoe's vision, and brace myself for the plan's final touch.

With a tight grip on the object, I bring it slamming against my bottom lip. The blow is awkward, but it still staggers me. Dizzied, I let myself collapse to the ground. It's not a knockout blow, not even close, but I lie on the ground and pretend to be unconscious.

I resist the urge to watch Defoe. Instead, I listen. He heaves a massive breath. It takes him a few seconds to sit up. It takes him a few seconds to process everything. I'm not sure if it's the transfer delay, or if he's just trying to piece together the puzzle of what happened.

He doesn't speak immediately. He's too smart for that. Instead, he cases the room. I hear him glide off to one side. I can imagine his eyes darting over every detail, resting in suspicion on my unconscious form. The absence of the techies. All of it. I hear him slip over to the entrance. He pushes the door quietly aside and pads lightly out of the room.

Everything is quiet. Will he leave me behind?

Footsteps as he returns. I hear him lean over the device. It scrapes against the tiled floor as he picks it up. He whispers to himself. I catch the anger in his tone, but the words still don't translate. A brief silence follows. I struggle to stay calm, because I know that he is watching me. He is weighing all his options. He's trying to understand how we survived when the marines outside did not. I have my story loaded and ready. The moment arrives.

"Longwei?" He moves closer. "Longwei . . ."

He shakes my shoulder, and my eyes snap open. I blink up at him.

"Mr. Defoe. What happened? Did the . . ." I look around the room and pretend to search for the techies. "There were ten of them. . . . They must have doubled back. . . ."

Defoe watches me. I flinch a little under the weight of his stare, but when he responds again—and again it's in an unfamiliar language—I realize the issue. He can't understand me. I catch a word or two of what he says—leftovers from my time in school—but most of it is unintelligible. I shake my head when he finishes and know this is *perfect* timing. I can't mess up my explanation if he can't even understand it. I point to my lips and then tap the side of my head.

"I can't understand you."

Defoe frowns again. The barrier creates more chaos. More things are breaking. It has his mind chasing all the wrong rabbits. He gestures out through the observation window. He points at the marines emphatically. I can see him concentrating. I am so accustomed to the polished sound of his voice, always delivered in flawless Mandarin, that the struggling words barely sound like him.

"Who? Who? Name?"

He struggles to ask the question. I shake my head.

"Kids. Like us. I've never seen them. They're strangers."

My answer clearly frustrates him. I can't tell if it's because he doesn't like the answer or because he can't understand what I'm saying. He gives up speaking and crosses the room. He leans close enough to inspect my bloodied lip. Something about the sight of it satisfies his suspicion.

After a second, he gives one more command. I'm not surprised that he knows the translation for it either. It is the one thing he expects from everyone he meets.

"Come. Follow me."

Silently I obey. My heart hammers as he steps over the device and leaves it behind. It worked. I put an end to one branch of his power. A connection has been severed. More important, he marches with his back to me. He thinks I do not have a weapon that can harm him.

The element of surprise is on my side.

But as Defoe leads me past the dead marines, I can see he has not lost confidence. I thought that I had ruined something important to him, but every single door slides open at his approach. We make our way through the labyrinth hallways, and I wonder if I've acted too late.

Clearly, Defoe has what he needs.

He controls the station now.

CHAPTER 24

ESCAPE

Anton Stepanov

All I can do is stand there and grind my teeth.

Nothing makes sense. Erone takes over the ship, but his first move is to float his own people off into space. Did he recognize them? Are they enemies of his? Or has he gone insane?

His next order makes even less sense. It does show how closely he's been listening to us, though. He has the techies fire up the main system of the ship. It's a decision that will hand power back to Babel when they arrive. I know better than to speak. Right now, my only goal is to keep my head on my shoulders. So I stand motionless and wait for the right moment.

There's a reason Aguilar chose this command center. She liked it for the reduced complexity. It allowed her to control the basic systems of the ship and eliminated concerns over untrustworthy recruits getting too much access.

My reasons for liking the choice were entirely different. I

recognized this room from my own explorations. I liked this choice because there's a back door, a back door that I'm very careful not to look at because I don't want Erone to know that it's there. It waits about fifteen paces away. There are exactly three computer consoles between the exit and me.

It's the same kind of door Babel installed all over the ship. Service entrances to reach the parts of the ship that are less pretty, but no less vital. I've used them enough to know that it takes about three seconds to open one. I have to pop the hatch, twist the handle, and shimmy through.

Three seconds. There's no way I have that much time.

"Oh, smile, Anton. This is where the game *really* gets fun."

My eyes lock on Erone. He sounds like an entirely new person. Did I really do such a poor job of reading him from the beginning? When I don't smile back, he turns to the main screen.

"We're seeing more breaches," someone reports.

The techies are doing what I would do. Answering questions. Providing new information. I don't blame them at all. They're fighting for their lives too. Erone considers the news.

When he speaks, though, the words slam into one another. There's a rhythm to the sound, but no meaning at all. A few of the techies are brave enough to look back. Erone repeats the command, and there's no denying it this time. The words aren't translating. He's speaking in the Imago tongue.

A techie throws a question back, and it's like being dunked in cold water. All I've heard for weeks is the nyxian-filtered Russian. Now stubborn English cuts through the air.

I can barely translate the sentence. "Babel ships. On the way. Advice?"

Erone eyes the man. His mouth opens, ready to issue another order . . .

. . . and he unexpectedly staggers.

I watch him drop to a knee. His off hand lifts briefly to his temple, and it's like someone just landed a punch there. His sword lowers, and the tip of it scrapes across the blue-lit floor. It's the moment I've been waiting for. I launch into motion, snaking between consoles and sprinting to the back corner. Erone shouts something.

Pop the latch, twist the handle, pull the door.

I risk a single glance back and see Erone's face twisted by surprise and confusion. He raises his sword and points it at me, but he's too far away. I ignore his final shout as I shove into the waiting darkness. It's a tight tunnel, the ceilings lowered, but I know the way by heart.

Lights flicker overhead, and Erone's screams chase me into the tunnel. I don't stop moving. I slam around every turn and keep my arms pumping. I trace back through my memories of the schematics and remember an air lock two floors down. I veer right and find one of the ventilation shafts. Deeper and deeper into the rabbit hole I go.

At the bottom of the shaft, I put my back against a wall and listen. I want to know if he's chasing me—or if he sent anyone else after me. Five minutes pass. And then ten. I have always been patient. The dark does not scare me. No one is coming.

I take another fifteen minutes to breathe and think. What should I do next? Erone won't have eyes on me until

I appear back in the normal corridors. The real question is where do I go? Who can I trust? How quickly will Erone gain complete control? My best option is Vandemeer.

Down to the prison warden.

I'm about to start moving when the tunnel ahead of me *explodes.*

A concussive blast thunders my way and presses my back to the tunnel wall. Fire races briefly inside before flickering back out. I cover my face and listen as voices echo through the opening. Shouts are followed by the sound of heavily armored boots. Marching soldiers. The battles are beginning. I try to remember where I am on the ship. Are there more Imago boarding? Maybe our loyal soldiers are marching on the command center? I'm thinking back through the blueprints when a voice tears its way through my thoughts. I'm almost startled by their clarity. The words reach my ears in blessed Russian. The voice is familiar, the command clear.

Morning shouts, "Shoulder to shoulder! Hold the line!"

CHAPTER 25

GRIMGARDEN

────────────

Emmett Atwater

The collision in the sky is already affecting the planet.

We skirt the coastline of Grimgarden and see a fire raging through one of the forests. The result of falling debris. The coastline shows signs too. The whole ocean has receded and left an extra hundred or so meters of the shore exposed. Every time I look up, it feels like there's more debris crashing through Magnia's atmosphere. We're running out of time down here.

We eventually make land east of Foundry. The retreating tides haven't fully impacted the inland waterways. We cross the same sections that Jerricho used to escape from Myriad after she kidnapped me. I shiver a little thinking about that night. This moment is far worse. That night my life was on the line, but now the entire planet is staring down an apocalypse. I take a deep breath and try to focus on the one hope I have left. We don't plan to be here when the end comes.

Greenlaw guides our ship to the westernmost banks to

disembark. It's just before sunrise. Mist curls through the waiting forest like a living thing. I keep looking up, but our vision of the moons is cut off by the trees and the fog. No one wastes time tying up the boat.

We're either going to launch into space or die down here.

"Foundry has some anti-Imago weaponry," I remind them, and then remember they can't understand anything I'm saying. Greenlaw glances back at me, an eyebrow raised. I try to signal with my hands. "Never mind. I'll try and explain it closer to the base. . . ."

Bilal laughs and throws an arm around my shoulder. "Emmett! I can understand you. It's working again. Can you hear me now?"

Greenlaw smiles. "The whole forest can hear you. Keep it down."

I can't help smiling as I lower my voice to a whisper. "I thought that break was going to be permanent. That would have made all of this *really* difficult. Especially in space. All those Imago running around the Tower. A lot could go wrong if the language breaks down."

Jazzy nods. "Ever seen anything like that happen before, Greenlaw?"

She shakes her head. "Never."

"Because you're too young," Craft says. "Same with Diallo. There hasn't been an echo like that for decades. The scientists believe it starts in the moon's core. Any seismic event on Magness creates an echo, a ripple. Nyxia always reacts to it. Usually it's a temporary breakdown, like the language gap we just went through. Sometimes it reverses the manipulation process. Or lashes out at random. The only echo I lived through resulted in stolen memories. The nyxia works that way normally. It takes a thought and shapes it. But the echo from the moon caused it to dig deeper. There was an uncle whose name I suddenly forgot. My parents had to reintroduce us."

"Why does it always have to do such creepy stuff?" Jazzy asks.

Bilal shrugs. "I have a few memories from childhood I wouldn't mind it stealing."

"Same here," I say. "Let's hope it picks the right ones."

Craft doesn't smile. "Let's hope that the first echo was the only one."

His warning brings focus back to the group. In whispered voices, we discuss our plan. Greenlaw explains that we have to get through this stretch of forest first. Once we're on the plains, we can use the nyxian carriers to move more quickly toward Foundry. I remind them of the anti-defense system and explain that we'll have to get Kit to disable it.

Overhead, we're joined by clippers. The swinging pack of winged monkeys moves thirty or forty deep. Diallo hoots up at them until Greenlaw tells him to be quiet. Bilal walks so close to my side that I almost trip over his feet. It takes a second to realize he's freaked out.

"They're safe," I tell him. "We saw them our first night. Not like the broodlords."

He eyes them suspiciously. "If you say so, friend."

Craft actually reaches into his bag and produces a little silver hoop. Several of the clippers come swinging down at the sight of it. He tosses the disc into the air, and the nearest clipper snags it deftly. When Craft catches us watching, he shrugs. "It's good luck."

I smile and think about Morning offering up her lucky coin that first night. I'm not sure how much luck we got out of it. Thinking about all that's gone down slowly peels the smile off my face. Morning is gone. She and the rest of the Genesis team are up in space. It was hard enough figuring out how to survive taking over the Tower. I hope she's smart enough to focus on the rest of the crew and not on me. There's nothing she can really do for me now anyway.

It takes our group less than thirty minutes to reach the edge of the forest. Bilal eyes the clippers again before asking a question that has his cheeks blooming bright red.

"Is it safe to use the bathroom?"

Jazzy makes a face. "As long as you don't mind them watching."

"Number one or number two?" I ask with a smile.

Bilal's face burns even brighter. Jazzy smacks my arm. "Don't be gross."

I laugh a little as Bilal slips behind the nearest veil of trees for privacy. A few clippers decide to follow him, and Jazzy actually laughs with me when they swing down for a closer look. Greenlaw stands at the forest's edge, eyes fixed on the waiting plains. She has the look of a proper general. Getting back into space isn't just about us, I remember. We're fighting for them too. The Imago wanted a new start in a new world. They deserve to have the right leader at the helm.

Footsteps announce Bilal's return.

"Clearly you weren't shy about . . ."

But the joke trails off as he comes into sight. Bilal's jaw is tight. His eyes wide. He breathes heavily through both nostrils. There's a man walking behind him in Babel fatigues. A gun is held to the back of his head. Jazzy retreats to my side as snapped branches and footsteps sound all around our group. Craft draws Diallo carefully behind him. Greenlaw tightens our formation, but we all know we've made a huge mistake. Babel got the drop on us.

I make a quick count. There are at least eight of them that we can see.

"Hands in the air." The marine holding Bilal hostage has a dark beard that's slashed with white. Old and sturdy. He keeps one gloved hand on my friend's shoulder. Something dark sings to life inside me. No one threatens Bilal. "Take it easy. No need for someone to get hurt."

My mind races. A fight is too risky. I'd like our odds if that was all this was, but they have Bilal at gunpoint. Make the wrong move and he dies. My claws are still hanging along my utility belt. It'd be easy enough to snap them on and lunge for the guy at this distance. But that won't work.

A glance back shows Greenlaw's nyxian gloves on the edge of form. She's ready to transform them into something far more dangerous. The soldiers tighten their circle, and I'm running through the details so quickly that I almost skip the familiar face on my right.

He buzzed his head, but I recognize the high cheekbones and narrow face. It isn't Kit, but it does look a hell of a lot like him. "Mr. Gander?"

His expression briefly unlocks. He looks even more like Kit when he's not determined to kill us. His eyes flick over to the marine holding Bilal hostage. I realize the man must be their captain. The guy gives a subtle nod, and Gander engages with us. "Who are you?"

"We're friends with Kit. We were with one of the Genesis crews that came through Foundry. I talked with Kit all the time. We both like the *Illuminauts*."

He might be hard-core military, but he's a dad too. The detail brings a brief smile to his face. Too bad the captain cuts off our momentum. "We heard the Genesis teams went rogue," he says.

I throw him a confused look, trying to buy myself an extra second to think. I'm racing through all the options and decide to play the card that they're most likely to believe: naïve kid.

"Went rogue? Is that what they told you? All we did was what Babel told us to do, man. We went into Sevenset, and Babel bombed the place. We've spent the last few weeks as hostages. Is that seriously what they call going rogue?"

The captain shifts his disbelieving look to the Imago with us. "And who are they?"

"They helped us escape," I lie. "They didn't like what the Imago were doing to us."

Above, the clippers continue to hoot and swing and shriek. Some of the marines glance up nervously as the captain considers my story. "The higher-ups said we could accept surrenders."

"If that's what you want to call it," I say quickly. "We'll surrender if that's what it takes. I'm just trying to go home, man."

"We accept your surrender." The captain pauses meaningfully. "Not theirs."

I'm trying to figure out a way to argue for the Imago to come with us, when a clipper swings in from overhead. My eyes go wide as it reaches for the shiniest toy in the clearing: the captain's gun. He looks up just in time to catch a shoulder to the chin. I hold my breath as he stumbles back and as the clipper's hand closes around the weapon and as the captain's finger slams down the trigger. Bilal flinches as the shot explodes above his left ear, barrel pointed skyward.

And chaos echoes.

As the captain stumbles back, wrestling for his gun, I sprint forward. One smooth motion clicks both claws over my wrists. The marines raise their weapons, but I hear the whispering bloom of nyxian shields in the air behind me. I don't have time for anything but saving Bilal. The captain wins his battle against the clipper just in time to see me coming.

Too late. My lowered shoulder crushes his exposed ribs. The tackle takes us both rolling through the brush. I control my weight on the second roll and pin him against the dirt. He might be a lifelong soldier, but I've got the drop on him and it's not even close. He slaps a hand out, reaching for his fallen gun, as I bring my right claw slamming down just below his shoulder. All three blades cut clean. He screams as the force of the blow shatters his collarbone.

I try to spin away to the right, but my blades catch. The impact recoils back through my body, and I stumble awkwardly. The captain takes advantage. He brings his right hand around, and I barely throw my off hand up in time. He's strong. The blow staggers me, but my claws are still stuck. My wrist twists painfully as the captain reaches for the knife at his belt. My eyes widen as I realize he's about to gut me and I can't do a damn thing.

Until Jazzy blurs in from the right. She drives a short sword down through the protective material covering his heart. It can't turn away a blow like that. Jazzy grits her teeth and thrusts down until the captain stops moving. I have to put a hand on his chest and pull to get my claws out.

"Thanks."

Her eyes are wide. It's her first kill.

"Come on. There are more of them."

We duck back into the clearing and almost run over Bilal. He's back on his feet and staring at the carnage. Of the seven remaining marines, only one more is still standing. Greenlaw and Diallo have him cornered. Craft is down, but a glance shows it's a shallow wound. Nothing that will kill him. Greenlaw sweeps beneath a blow and catches the final marine across the jaw. Diallo hamstrings him, and I know it's seconds from being over. My chest is heaving.

I take a step forward and freeze. Movement on my left. I look up and find Kit's dad about twelve paces away, gun raised. I realize he's standing in the exact same spot he was in before the fight. He never moved. I lift both hands carefully into the air and turn so he has to look me in the eye. We both hear the dying groan of Greenlaw's opponent. He's alone.

"We're friends with Kit," I remind him. "We just want to go home."

He shakes his head. "Go home?"

"Haven't you seen the moons?" I ask. "This world is coming to an end. If Babel hasn't told you that much, you really think they care about you? Or Kit? We're his last chance."

Genuine fear flickers onto his face. A few seconds pass and he finally takes the true measure of the situation. He sees I'm not arguing for my life; I'm arguing for his. Diallo bends over his brother to tend the open wound, but Greenlaw marches our way, gloves stained by Babel blood. It's an easy choice. Kit's dad makes a show of tossing his gun aside.

"I can take you back to the base," he says. "But the launch station is empty. We only had one ship here. A few marine units loaded into it a few hours ago and launched into space. Command said it was routine. We saw the moons, but when command didn't order an evacuation . . ."

He trails off. Of course. Babel abandoned him.

"Welcome to the damn club, man. Let's get to Foundry. We need to know *everything*. How many marines are there? What kind of orders have you been getting? All of it."

He frowns. "Okay. But you didn't hear me. There aren't any ships."

"But I'd guess there are supply freighters?"

"Of course, but they don't have seats. No regulated atmosphere. You can't launch in those."

"I know the manipulation to make it work. That's where we're going. It's our last shot."

He doesn't look confident, but he has to realize he has no other options. Greenlaw's been waiting patiently during the whole interaction. "I'm confused," she says. "Are we sparing this one?"

Gander's eyes widen in fear, but I come quickly to his defense. "This is Kit's dad. Our contact at the station. Kit's the one who can disable the defense system and let us inside. Pretty sure bringing his dad back in one piece is a good start. He comes with us."

Greenlaw inspects him from a distance. "Looks like Babel to me."

"Which one are you?" I ask him. "A marine or a dad?"

He doesn't hesitate. "A dad."

"All right. Let's go save your son."

Greenlaw nods her approval. Craft is back on his feet, wound already wrapped courtesy of Bilal. Diallo helps him into a freshly summoned nyxian carrier. Gander keeps his hands raised like a prisoner as we march after Greenlaw. Bilal and Jazzy take their places beside me.

Bilal lets out a sigh. "I am learning that life without you all was rather boring."

Jazzy can't quite bring herself to smile, not after what just happened, but she still entertains her own dream of home. "After all this, sign me up for the most boring life ever. I want to live on a farm and do crossword puzzles and sleep for a decade."

"Agreed," Bilal says. "Just give me a good cup of tea and the sunrise."

This is a game our group has always played. What would we do with all that money? What will we do when we finally get home? And I've always struggled with it, because what's the point? Both of them look over expectantly at me and I tell them the truth that's hammering through my head.

"We have to get there first."

One step at a time.

Next up: Foundry.

CHAPTER 26

FOUNDRY REVISITED

Emmett Atwater

We're on our way to Foundry, when we see the smoke. I panic a little—thinking that fire might have reached the base—when I realize we're still a solid hike away from the Babel-made buildings. And the smoke in the distance isn't the normal haze of gray. "Anyone else seeing this?"

Over one more rise and we finally get a view of the source. A hunk of the shattered moons has fallen from the sky. We're seeing mostly the entry point from this angle. Half the thing is sticking up from the ground, unburied by the fall. The nyxia looks the way it always does, that reflective black color, but there's green smoke rising around it like a backlit fog. I'm walking curiously forward, when Craft hooks me by an arm.

"It's a wonder you all survived this long," he says. "Did no one teach you about this?"

I stare back at him. "Nyxia comes from the moons. I know."

Craft scowls at that. "Your kind are too comfortable with knowing only half of what is necessary to know. Nyxia is not to be touched when it first falls. The velocity and the impact create an instability in the substance. See that green smoke? Get close enough and it will control you."

Greenlaw frowns. "I've never seen a fresh one before."

Craft shakes his head. "You've never lived through a rain."

All of us look up again, like another meteor might come down that very second. Craft has us moving well clear of the fallen shard. I glance back as we enter the next forest, and the green smoke is still shifting in the air, almost like it's alive.

It doesn't take long to reach the base after that. In the distance, Foundry rises from the cover of the surrounding forests. It feels like it's been years since we came here. Kit's dad shows his usefulness right away. After getting Greenlaw's approval, he accesses his headset and sends out a mayday. "Our unit commander is down. I'm pinging coordinates now. There are still three Imago here. Send back up now."

He shows me the location on his map. I nod my approval, and he pings it for the nearest Babel units to see. "What if Kit goes with them?" I ask.

"They'd never let him," he answers. "That was the only reason I agreed for him to come down here in the first place. He's not supposed to leave the base. It's the safest place for him."

It takes a few minutes of waiting, but we finally spy movement in one section of the base. Babel trucks come roaring out of the underground. Sunlight reflects off the chrome-black exteriors.

"We've got about thirty minutes," Gander says. "It's now or never."

"And the base is empty?" Greenlaw asks.

"It's not empty. Kit's definitely here. Maybe an off-duty soldier or two? But if they're off-duty, they should be down in one of the hives sleeping. This is as empty as it gets."

Greenlaw eyes the base again. "Time for your plan, Emmett. You're sure it's safe?"

I nod. "For me it is. Not for you. Come on, Mr. Gander."

After taking a deep breath, I start walking. Gander strides carefully at my side. I know it's a risk to let him get this close to the base's barriers—and to Kit—without the Imago hanging over him like the threat that they are. So as we walk, I remind him of the truth.

"If you're thinking about making a run for it, don't. That'd be a good way to get Kit killed. Hundreds of Imago have launched up by now. Babel's chosen who they'll send to retake the ships. By the time you get to another station, and board another ship, and launch up into space—the battle will already be decided. Babel wins and you're the traitor who abandoned his post. The Imago win and you might be launching up to a hostile space station. Your best shot is with us."

He lets out a held breath. "I know that."

"Mess this up and we launch without him."

Gander walks silently at my side after that. I can't tell when we actually trip the system, but it doesn't take long for Kit to stir from his crow's nest. A pair of turret guns unfold from hidden locations on our right and left. They don't open fire, but the system is active and the threat hangs over us. This will be like everything else that's happened since the beginning of this whole god-awful experiment. All it takes is one misstep for everything to go wrong.

Kit strides out to meet us, and judging by the look on his face, we're the most unlikely damn pairing he's ever seen in his entire life. My eyes flick briefly down to the glove on his right hand. I know that he controls the whole base with it. I haven't forgotten the night the slings came for us. Kit used the powers Babel gave him like he was in a video game.

"Dad? Emmett? What's going on? I heard your distress call. The location you pinged . . ."

"Is a decoy location," Gander answers. "We're leaving. Together."

But that answer just has Kit looking more confused. His gloved hand twitches a little as he weighs everything. Eventually, his eyes swing in my direction.

"I thought the Genesis teams rebelled. How'd you get here?"

"It's a long story," I reply. "We'll tell you the whole thing during the launch."

Kit doesn't budge, though. "I have orders, Emmett. I can't launch into space."

"Orders to die down here?" I point up to the moons. Daylight has made the scene look a little less devastating, but fire still burns at the core of the implosion. Both moons continue to drift. Clearly debris has already started hitting the surface. How long before the bigger chunks hit? How long before dust gathers and chokes out the atmosphere? "The moons collided, Kit. There's a battle in space right now. Anyone that stays down here is going to die."

Kit runs one hand back through his hair. I've seen him do it before whenever he gets nervous. His eyes flick over to his dad. "But orders are orders. Right, Dad?"

My stomach tightens. Kit's putting up unexpected resistance. He's always had a higher view of Babel than us, but I figured the second his dad came up with a new plan Kit would be on board.

"I know you've heard me say that," Gander replies. "Orders are orders. But I've taught you about trust too, Kit. We follow orders because we trust and respect the people giving them. Babel just lost that trust. They planned to leave you down here. That is unforgiveable."

It's the kind of thing my pops would say, but Kit barely blinks.

"Where's your weapon?" He finally notices the empty holsters and the barren utility belt. His dad doesn't have a speck of nyxia on him. We made sure of it.

"I surrendered my weapons."

"Of course." Kit pieces it all together. "You're a prisoner."

Again, Kit's hand trembles with movement. His dad is unarmed, but Kit has the full arsenal of Foundry at his disposal. A snap of his fingers could bring the rain. His eyes move beyond us.

"Emmett couldn't have captured you by himself," he says. "Who else is here?"

I exchange a glance with Kit's dad before signaling back to the forest. There's a distant rustle, and then Kit's eyes widen as our party emerges. Greenlaw strides forward with purpose. I'm guessing he remembers Jazzy, and it's not hard to figure out Bilal is one of ours. Diallo and Craft follow the others. Kit makes a disbelieving noise when he sees them.

"You brought Adamites here."

"They're with us," I say. "We're launching together, Kit."

He retreats a few steps, and I feel like we're losing our grasp on him.

"This is just like season three, episode eight," he mutters. "When that alien species kidnapped Captain Revere and brainwashed him. That's what they did to you. . . ."

"Brainwashed? Kit, that's a show. It's just a stupid show."

But I remember how attached Kit was to that series. He's expecting what he saw there to unfold here. It's replaced his reality. As the others close in our location, Kit raises his gloved hand. The familiar interface blinks into existence. I know there's only one way to fight that kind of logic.

"Not the best comparison," I say. "Revere was with the aliens for like two years, man. We ran into your dad about an hour ago. You really think we could brainwash him just like that?"

Kit hesitates. I can see the little symbol that must represent the turret system. His finger hovers in the air beside it as he waits for me to explain.

"I'm thinking it's more like in season two. You remember the Hangman Conspiracy?"

He's barely breathing, but he nods. "I loved that subplot."

I've got him now. "So the Hangman was with the Illuminauts. He was one of the good guys. But it turned out he was behind the underground slavery business happening on those two moons."

"Ku and Nareen."

"Right, Ku and Nareen. The Hangman did all this good stuff people could see, but it was so he could hide all the bad stuff people couldn't. Babel is the Hangman, Kit. The Imago are just like the natives of those two moons but if the natives had this badass plan to overthrow the Hangman."

Kit's nodding. "Which makes us . . ."

"The Illuminauts who figured out what was up and locked the Hangman away for good."

"Freaking cool." He reaches out and double-taps the turrets. I hold my breath—thinking he just activated them—but both turrets vanish back into their keeps. "So freaking cool. I get to be Lunar Jones. Come on! Let's get moving."

And just like that he turns on a heel and starts marching back into the base. Gander stares over at me, and I shrug. "It's a pretty good show. You should watch it sometime."

I throw the all clear back to the others, and we move through Babel's stronghold like welcome guests. If there are any off-duty soldiers, none of them show.

Kit's rattling off new strategies and ideas at such a fast clip that I decide to nod along for now. Anything to keep him from jumping back on board with Babel.

"We need to launch a supply shipment," I tell him. "Like you did when we were here."

"Cool, cool." Kit pulls up the interface as he walks. The whole process is as easy as point and click. We hear the slightest rumble in the distance. "What are we sending up?"

Mentally, I'm running back through the tricks that Morning taught me. If she hadn't taken the time to do that, we'd have no chance at any of this. It's the same trick that Anton used to launch back up into space. I find myself praying that the two of them both made it up. I hope our whole crew survived. Bilal and Jazzy stride beside me. Shoulder to shoulder.

"We're sending up ourselves," I say confidently. "We're launching into space."

CHAPTER 27

SURVIVAL MODE

Morning Rodriguez

I will save Emmett. I will save Emmett. I will save Emmett.

It's a new and dominating battle cry. It pulses so loud in my head that I'm struggling to stay focused. I know we have to get to the command center *alive* if I want to help him.

Our crew rallies in the hallway. I hear snatches of their conversations, but it's like everything has been muted. Apparently they experienced some kind of communication disruption as we carved our way through space. I listen as the others marvel over the language breakdown—and the sudden restoration—but my heart is racing.

I have to save Emmett.

No Babel troops greet us. Parvin starts to make a count, but it's pretty clear we're well short of the expected number. Only eleven Genesis members. Emmett's not with us, of course, but Jazzy and Bilal didn't make it either. My anger at Babel just burns brighter. When Azima realizes that I'm alone, she asks the obvious question. "What happened to Emmett?"

All I can do is shake my head. Beatty's name whispers through my lips like a curse. Our crew backtracks to the pod. Guilt tries to sneak back through the fences I've put up. I fight it back. No time for guilt. If the others are shocked by what they see in the pod, they do their best to hide it. Gio stands in front of the escape pod long after everyone else returns to the group. As he stands there—all alone—I realize he's the last surviving member of the *Genesis 13*. He turns back, and our eyes lock. I dare him with a look to say a damn thing about it to me. He's smarter than that. He's figured out what Beatty did to get inside that ship with me, so he stays quiet instead.

Jacquelyn and Beckway perform a count of their own. Including them, only twenty Imago soldiers are with us. About one-third of the original Remnant, and their acting queen—Greenlaw—didn't make it into space. There's a brief discussion, and I can feel nervous energy gathering inside me like a storm. I'm useless to Emmett in this random hallway.

We need to get moving.

I finally snap, "What are we waiting for?"

Jacquelyn raises an eyebrow. "For you to show us the way."

Of course. I glance back at our group and thank the stars for Parvin. She reaches into her knapsack and removes one of Babel's scouters. She must have snagged one before we left Sevenset. Girl has saved us more times than I can count, and she does it again now. After a few seconds, she accesses the least complicated map and starts leading us through the massive space station.

"We're on the second floor," she explains. "If we keep heading this way, there's a more central hub. It has about five tunnels connected to it. I believe the command center is one way. The docked ships are the opposite direction. About five hundred meters or so."

I know I should be leading, commanding, anything. But it's all I can do to stop myself from sprinting off through the halls and carving my way through Babel's soldiers to get to the command center. We press deeper into the center of the station. The lack of windows makes the whole place feel claustrophobic, more dangerous.

Our crew makes up the right flank of the advancing party. The hallway is wide enough to march seven across. I take my spot on the front line and walk side by side with our best fighters. Azima hefts that deadly spear. Holly marches between the two of us. She flexes her fingers inside the familiar nyxian boxing gloves. The sight of them breathes an image of Emmett back into my mind. I squeeze both hatchets tight. A whisper of fear runs through me at the idea of using the nyxia again. What if it reacts the way it did in the pod? What if it escapes my grasp? But then I remember I've been using these hatchets for more than a year now. They're mine, through and through. And I'm going to have to use them soon enough.

I'm coming for you, Emmett. Just hold on. Survive. Please.

"No welcoming party?" Katsu jokes. "It's almost like Babel didn't miss us."

No one laughs. We round another corner, and the hallway widens until we're clearly striding through the central hub Parvin mentioned. It's one massive honeycomb. We

exit our tunnel and find ourselves staring down four identical options. Parvin points to our right.

"The command center is that way," she says. "Genesis
ships are to the left."

Noor's voice echoes from our back ranks. "We're going to
the ships, correct?"

"The command center controls everything. We should
head there first," I answer quickly. I don't mention the fact
that it's also our best way to find out what's happening on-
planet. My best chance to save Emmett.

"We need to find Anton," Alex adds. "The command center is the best way to do that."

I watch Parvin swallow her first response. I can tell all
her logical engines are firing. She wants to knock down the
idea, but losing Omar has given her new perspective. She
understands why Alex wants to find Anton, even if it can't
be a priority for our group. That's why I haven't begged anyone to help me save Emmett. I have to make them think it's
the best thing for the group first.

"It'd be great to get eyes on everything," Parvin admits.
"But if we don't move toward the ships that are actually
designed to fly us home, Babel might cut us off. If we can
board one of them first, we guarantee we don't get stranded
out here in space."

The whole group spreads out as the discussion continues.
I can see the Imago getting restless. Even our own crew has
broken rank and started wandering around the hub.

We need to keep moving. "Why don't we—"

A sound cuts off my suggestion. We all hear the rattle. An
object bounces down the central tunnel and starts to roll.

Metal on metal. The thing rattles to a stop about five meters away from where Roathy roamed off to in his boredom. He looks back, almost in slow motion, and his eyes pulse wide. Isadora screams.

I realize he's going to die and there's nothing I can do to save him.

Alex shouts, "Grenade! Everyone get *down!*"

About half of us hit the deck. A figure blurs in from the right. It's moving so quickly that I barely recognize that it's Ida. She's been so quiet since Loche died. I can't actually remember the last time I saw her leave Isadora's side, but she does now. Those pale hands reach for him. She shoves Roathy headfirst to his left, safely out of the blast zone.

It leaves her exposed.

An explosion tears through the air. Our world temporarily mutes. Debris scatters. I squint through the smoke and see Ida motionless. My heart's pounding. "No, no, no . . ."

Roathy comes coughing back to us. Isadora's crying as our ranks open to let him through. I force my eyes back to what's coming. Someone threw that grenade. There's a gaping hole in one of the side tunnels. A brief fire has smoke clouding in front of us. We're all setting our feet when shadows press forward through the fog.

A group of Babel marines. I watch as they close in on us.

"Weapons!" Beckway orders. "Tighten up!"

His order wakes me up. "Shoulder to shoulder! With me, Genesis!"

They're close enough to see faces now. Babel's learned their lesson. None of the approaching ranks wields a gun. One too many helpless showdowns against the Imago to make that mistake again. The approaching crew is built for a melee. And they've divided into two clear units. The front line of marines sports a heaving, bulky armor. Behind them, I see a group of more mobile soldiers, all with long-reaching spears.

I set my eyes on the first target. I analyze him in less than a breath. His armor is bone-thick. Even the joints are sealed. No weakness I can see, but no weapons either. As he lowers his shoulder for a bull rush, I understand their plan. Break the lines and leave us weak. Expose easy targets for the second group. So I duck down and swing a hatchet at the marine's left knee.

The blow sweeps his legs out, and momentum sends him soaring overhead. I hear the Genesis member behind me cry out in surprise, but I'm already moving forward. The second soldier holds a raised spear, and I can tell he was expecting a distant target. I bring the fight far closer than he wants.

A huge first step and a fake jab with my left. He raises his spear instinctually, and my right hatchet buries into his hip. I bring the left around a second later. One down.

I spin away from a jab on my right and land my hatchet in the unsuspecting marine to my left. Their ranks react quickly. I backpedal, weapons raised, as spears dart in from all sides. Azima punishes one of the overeager offenders with a perfect strike of her own. That guard collapses.

But the bulky soldiers are doing damage. Our front lines are staggered, a crumbling half-moon. There's a shout as Holly goes down. I shove against the tide of bodies and find my next target. One of the bulkier marines is deep in our ranks, causing chaos. He's engaged with Alex and a staggering Roathy. He shouts insults as he fends off their blows with reinforced forearms. As he strikes again, I finally see the gap in his armor. Right at the back of the neck.

A lighter foot soldier has followed the guard into the opening, and looks ready to gut Alex. I shoulder him out of the way and bring my hatchet slamming down into the exposed area. He screams before collapsing.

Alex shouts a warning, but the attack leaves me vulnerable. I turn and catch an armored strike to the chest. The blow lifts me off my feet and slams me hard into the sidewall. Concussed, all I can do is stare up as the great chrome-colored suit approaches. My head's spinning as the marine steps into another reinforced punch. Grasping hands pull me away at the last second.

The marine crushes the wall where my head was. Gio's there. Pulling at my suit collar and dragging me away as Alex flails back into the armored marine. One of the Imago joins him. The two of them strike at the weaker joint areas until the marine buckles. Gio shoves me back to my feet.

"You okay?"

"Fine!" I shout back. "I'm fine!"

Except my head is still spinning. He rushes to fill the gap in our ranks. I struggle to keep my balance as I take in the whole scene. Holly's down, but still trying to strike at exposed legs. Katsu has a huge gash on his cheek and forearm. It doesn't stop him from swinging and swinging.

While our side of the room has caved in slightly, the Imago are pressing forward with brutal precision. Beckway and Azima fight together. They're surrounded by fallen marines.

Even with smoke hanging heavy in the air, I can tell Babel's ranks are failing. A fresh wave of vertigo almost drops me. Isadora is there, though. She gets an arm underneath and drags me back to safety. We skirt the fallen soldiers as Noor rushes forward to cover my retreat.

"Take it easy," Isadora says. "You've got a nasty cut. Let me take a look."

Her hands are shaking. I stare past her as the fight continues to unfold. The front lines are trading blows. I frown when one of the soldiers at the back of Babel's formation drops.

There's a shout. A second one falls.

I'm squinting through the smoke as the Babel soldiers spin in confusion. It's enough to put an end to the fight. The Imago break through on the left. Our crew hems them in on the right.

It takes another ten seconds for the final marine to fall.

I'm still watching when a figure strides through the smoke.

"About time you assholes showed up."

Anton grins at us as Alex runs forward. He lifts the Russian off his feet in a bone-crushing hug. Both exchange fierce whispers, followed by an even fiercer kiss. My heart breaks for Ida, but it beats with wild relief at the sight of Anton. We have lost so much. There is still so much to lose. But my friend is alive. When he and Alex finally separate, I shout over the noise.

"I thought you were supposed to take over the ship."

He flicks me off. "I *did* take over the ship. Lost control like an hour ago. No thanks to you!"

"Who's in control now?" Jacquelyn asks.

Anton's answer is drowned out by alarms. Three loud shrieks are followed by flashing red lights. Every eye goes wide as the entrances to the surrounding tunnels start to close. Glass seals extend down from the ceiling. The realization hits: we're going to be trapped.

"Get everyone on their feet!" I shout. "Let's *move!*"

Isadora helps me forward. I head straight for the tunnel that leads to the command center. It's all chaos. We're all moving and shoving and fighting to get beneath the closing entrance. We stumble over the dead marines, and in all of the panic, it takes me a second to realize that half our group went the wrong way.

Parvin led them toward the ships. Most of the Imago followed her too. Isadora forces me under the lowering partition. We all stare helplessly across the clearing. Parvin shouts something, but the descending glass mutes the noise. Ida, Noor, and Holly decided to follow her.

"Anton." I slam a fist into the glass. "How do we get these open?"

He shakes his head. "We don't. Erone reactivated the control system."

Jacquelyn's head whips up. "Erone? Did you say Erone?"

He nods back. After a few helpless seconds, Parvin waves to get our attention. When she's sure she has it, she holds up a signal. She raises both index fingers again and again. All I can do is nod. Her signal is clear. I throw my own index fingers back and nod firmly.

"*Genesis 11,*" I explain. "She wants to meet back on the *Genesis 11.*"

"We left her." The words come from Isadora. She's down on her knees by the far right edge of the glass barrier. She helped me get to safety, and we left Ida in the process. "It's not right."

"You want to honor her?" I ask quietly. "Survive. Live."

Anton nods at that. "We need to move before Erone closes off more sections of the ship."

"Can you get me to him?" Jacquelyn asks.

"No way in hell I'm going back there," Anton replies. "I don't know who you are, but I know what I saw. Erone just abandoned an entire ship full of Imago. He gave control of the ship to Babel. He killed our most loyal techie. I'm not going anywhere near him. We need to get to the ships and go."

"Tell me how to get there," Jacquelyn demands.

"Are you listening to a word I'm saying? I'm the one who freed Erone in the first place. He turned on me. What makes you think you can change his mind?"

"Because I'm his wife."

Anton's mouth snaps shut.

I step into the silence.

"Give her directions," I say. "Let's get moving."

A second alarm shrieks. More doors are starting to close.

We march down the tunnel.

I'm coming for you, Emmett.

CHAPTER 28

THE TOWER SPACE STATION

Emmett Atwater

Ten minutes. I used to watch the last ten minutes of class tick off in never-ending fashion. But this? This is the fastest and most frightening ten minutes of my life. Each one of us sits inside our own conjured nyxian environment. Person-sized translucent cubes stacked together and jammed into a corner of the supply freighter. The walls isolate the environment inside the nyxia. No sound in or out. No change in the temperature. It's the perfect way to hitch a ride into space.

Greenlaw took one look at my first demonstration of the manipulation and nodded.

"Stasis rooms. Of course."

Apparently, the Imago have used similar tech for centuries. It's a meditation practice for them. The three Imago had no problem learning the manipulation. It took the others a little longer. Kit's dad had an especially hard time. His struggles highlighted a strange and missing piece in Babel's preparation for taking over the planet. We were trained on how to use nyxia until our heads spun. We have an instinct for it that the marines lack. It might be a deciding factor in what's coming.

Our only view of the outside world is through a series of ventilation strips. Each one offers us a partial look at the rapidly shifting landscape. I watch a baby-blue sky tremble to midnight. I can tell the ship is taking a pounding. The windows rattle. I spy a few places where the metal dents inward. But none of us feel any of it. Instead, we focus on breathing steadily. Not wasting oxygen.

I keep staring through the tiny slit as a glimpse of space appears. That dark backdrop makes the destroyed moons all the brighter. Red light still burns and smolders at the center. Debris continues to scatter in every direction from the impact. A massive cloud of green-black smoke has formed at the edges. I've never seen anything like it.

I can't help thinking about what happens next. My mind drifts back to Speaker. Did he survive his attack on Babel's troops? What about all the other abandoned Imago? The longer I think about them, the harder it is to just breathe.

Movement snags my attention. Out the window, there's a herd of glowing blue dots. I squint out. It has to be one of the other rings. More Imago ships launching into space. I trace their progress, knowing they're designed to find Babel's Tower Space Station. The path has them heading straight for a gathering of thick debris. I squint and realize it's the same green-black cloud that Craft steered us away from down on the surface. That color curls through the pieces of shattered moon that are still drifting through space. I suck in a breath as the ships approach a looming wall of the stuff.

Half the ships skirt past. The other half dive straight into the gathered mist. The green-black curtain swallows them. I'm still staring—about fifteen seconds later—when they plunge through the other side. About twenty went in, but only fourteen came out.

And they don't come out unscathed. Green-black mist trails each of them.

"The hell?"

I glance around and remember I'm cut off from the others. Before I can get their attention, our ship lurches in a new direction. Our view of space shifts, and Gander signals us.

We're closing in on the ship. There's no announcement. No consoles flash to highlight our approach. Only the reaching shadow of the docking bay. Gander holds one hand out, palm flat, fingers stretching. The Imago signal to *wait.* He wanted to make sure no one deactivated their nyxia before we were back in a pressurized and safe environment. The seconds tick down in our soundless environments. The supply ship gives a final rattle. Gander double-clenches his fist.

My ears suffer a painful pop as I draw the nyxia back into a smaller form. Jazzy yawns wide like she's dealing with the same thing. Kit breaks the silence. "That was easy."

"Where are we?" I ask. "On the Tower Space Station or on one of the ships?"

Gander walks over to the window and glances out. It takes him a few seconds to get his bearings before he turns back to us. "I was hoping we'd go straight to the *Genesis 11.* Looks like that supply center is full. It rerouted us to the Tower. Their supply depot is up on the top floor."

"Not a good thing?" I guess.

"There's a lot of terrain between us and the ships that can take us home. The Tower is an *actual* tower of sorts. Kind of a large, cylindrical structure. It feeds back down and connects to what we used to call the underground. Babel keeps all the vital stuff in the lower levels. The command center is there. The living quarters. Even the Waterway you trained on."

"And the Genesis ships?"

"Attached on the back end of the basement," he answers. "There's a massive loading bay down there that connects to all the docks for the individual ships. We used to joke it was the only place on the ship big enough to host a full-length football game. Unfortunately it's as far from where we're standing as you could possibly be without floating out into space."

"Great. So what's our first move?" I ask.

He's thinking through the options when the back door to our ship glides open. Bright light cuts in from the loading bay, and we all whip around to face the intruders.

Make that *intruder*.

A single techie stands about five meters away. He has his hand jammed up against a black button, and he's facing the opposite way with headphones on tight overhead.

Craft glides forward with deadly ease. At the last second, the techie senses *something*. His neck stiffens and he starts to turn, but too late. A single blow sends him spinning to the ground. Craft moves forward to finish the job, but Bilal calls out, "He's down. Leave him."

Craft looks back and I can see the hunger in his eyes. He's making the necessary shift. Battles are waiting for us. Marines that will aim to kill. Bilal needs to understand that.

I'm a little surprised when Greenlaw nods. "Bind him. Bigger fights are waiting."

Craft frowns, but manipulates a smaller piece of nyxia and sets to work on the task. Gander strides across the central console in the room. We all watch him scan an identification card before looking through the summoned readouts. Kit stands at his side, chattering excitedly.

I pull Bilal and Jazzy aside while they work. "What do you two think? Straight to the ships?"

Jazzy nods. "The *Genesis 11* got us here. It can get us home."

Bilal sighs. "Home."

"Home," I agree. "We still have a long way to go, fathom? Bilal, we might need to fight."

He stares back at me. "I will do only what is necessary, Emmett. That man over there? He's no one to us. He's unloading crates and listening to music. I will not forget our true enemies."

"And if he patches our location back to Defoe, is he our enemy, then?"

"I am doing my best to not kill what is worth saving, even in myself."

I'm not really sure how to argue with that kind of logic. Bilal was always going to do this his way. I have to do what I do best too. I slide both hands inside my boxing claws and nod back.

"Fair enough."

The wait is brutal. It takes Gander almost fifteen minutes to gather all the necessary information. Kit comes back to us, buzzing excitedly.

"This is just like episode twenty-seven," he says. "It's so cool."

"We lucked out," Gander adds. "There's a freight elevator at the back of the room. It goes down all the way to the main floor. I'm not sure if you'll remember, but there's a circling corridor that feeds through the bottom half of the ship. That route will lead us around to the main loading bay that houses the attached Genesis ships. If we want to escape, that's our best plan."

"I want to find the Remnant," Greenlaw replies. "And I am sure that you want to find the other Genesis members. Do you think going to the ships is the best way to accomplish that?"

I shake my head. "No clue. If they're smart, they headed straight for the ships. Babel takes those and we don't have a way home. The station is just a hub, right? It can't return to Earth."

Gander confirms my guess. "It's designed to orbit and host. It's not going anywhere."

"So we walk down there?" Jazzy snaps her fingers. "Just like that?"

"The systems running in that console are Babel-designed," Gander replies. "I know for a fact that Babel launched a ton of marines into space. We have to assume they control the ship."

I feel my heart sinking a little. I was half hoping to get here and find Morning and company already in charge, or even Anton. It's not a great sign that Babel still has the reins. And if Babel still has the reins, our current company complicates things.

I glance over at Greenlaw and the two brothers. Every-one will notice the Imago.

"So we can't just walk down with them."

Kit leans into the conversation. "We can do a prisoner ruse! It's *perfect*. Here . . ." He manipulates a piece of nyxia into handcuffs and approaches Greenlaw. "I'll just put these on your wrists and—" Greenlaw offers Kit a knife-sharp glare. "Or you can put them on yourself."

"I will not be bound," she replies.

Craft steps forward aggressively. Tension briefly fills the air, but I find myself liking Kit's plan. It's the kind of thing that might be ridiculous enough to work.

"You won't really be bound," I say. "We'll use nyxia. You can manipulate it into anything you want in less than a second. It's just a decoy, Greenlaw. We pretend we're taking prisoners down to see Defoe. Any Babel marine that sees you three walking around without cuffs is going to call it in. We don't know how many marines are up here. This might be our best bet to get down to the ships without a fight."

Bilal chimes in. "I like this plan. Better this than cutting our way through Babel's soldiers."

Greenlaw eventually nods. "Fine, but we control the nyxia around our wrists. If there's even a hint of betrayal, I'll come for you first."

She points at Gander, and his face pales. "Of course. Yeah. Nothing to worry about."

It takes us about five minutes of arguing to figure out who should be doing what. All three of the Imago are ob-vious choices, but Gander suggests that I throw on some cuffs too.

"We'll tell anyone we meet that the higher-ups want to see you," he says. "They'll think it's weird if we're delivering a few random Imago. But a rebellious member of *Genesis 11*?"

I shift uncomfortably. It was one thing to argue for the plan when it was Greenlaw getting cuffed. I've spent most of my life doing everything I could to avoid the feel of iron around my wrists. But we're at the end now. Desperate measures are needed. I manipulate a pair of cuffs that match theirs and throw them around my wrists.

"Let's do it."

Our crew gathers in the back of the room. Kit sets a hand on Diallo's shoulder. Gander stands behind Craft, and Jazzy moves behind Greenlaw. Bilal will be my warden. We all watch Gander run his identification card and press the button. A nervous energy pulses through us.

"No way this goes wrong," I whisper.

There's a soft *ping.* The door opens. A blue light glows inside the massive elevator. Gander directs us to the right side of it, arranging us in believable order, before pressing the button for the lowest floor. The whole room lurches with movement. I can almost hear everyone's hearts racing.

Down one flight. Another.

And then the door pings again. The elevator heaves to a stop. We're about five floors away from our target and someone's about to join us. "Well, that's not good," Kit whispers.

The door glides up, and I hear Bilal gasp in my ear. We're staring at a full hangar bay. About seven smaller ships have docked. And there are literally *hundreds* of marines moving around the area, barking orders, organizing into squads. A stocky captain steps forward and cuts off our view. He eyes all of us before leading his soldiers inside. Bilal's grip digs into my shoulder. My jaw clenches as I make the count. Twelve Babel marines board with us.

It doesn't take long for them to realize who they're joining. The captain's face lights up at the sight of the three Imago with us. "No shit! Look at this! Adamites!"

The soldiers break rank briefly to get a look. Gander nods respectfully back to the captain. "Caught them in the shipping area." He reaches out and smacks my shoulder hard. "This tool was helping them board the Tower. The higher-ups want to see them right away."

The captain reaches out and punches the 3 button. I can see him turning Gander's words over until he frowns. "Aren't most of the higher-ups in the hangar?"

Gander doesn't hesitate. "Not *the* higher-ups."

"Straight to Defoe?" The captain looks impressed. "He must have something personal against them if he's breaking protocol just to bring them in."

My heart stops when the captain reaches out and pinches Greenlaw's jaw. He shifts so that his face is right in front of hers. "What'd you do, huh? Something awful?"

He laughs. The other marines join him. Craft is staring death at him. The guy has no idea that he just manhandled a queen. I try to steady my breathing as I wait for the other shoe to drop. It wouldn't take much for Greenlaw to cut him open from head to toe, but we're in tight quarters and completely outnumbered. Gut him, and the rest of us might not make it out alive.

Instead, she fixes her eyes on the doors. Their stop pings.

The captain laughs again and nods to Gander. "This is us. There were breaches on level three. Shouldn't have had time to spread down. But just in case we don't kill them all, keep an eye out, all right? You all have fun!"

Gander nods tightly. The rest of us stare as the doors slide open. The first pair of marines glide out, weapons raised, eyes scanning their surroundings. Our view doesn't offer much: a gray wall with the usual circuitry running underneath the glass. The soldiers move in pristine formation. The captain's the last one across. He turns back to say something, but a scream cuts him off. Gunfire erupts. My eyes widen when a soldier is thrown across the room.

Black forms slide with deadly grace through their ranks.

I almost mistake them for Imago, but this . . .

. . . this is something else entirely. The word that comes to mind is *corruption*. The creatures strike, and each blow fills the air with familiar green-black smoke. Marines scream. Their skin *erupts.* Their eyes go black. Arms sharper than blades burst through chests. I can see the make and shape of Imago underneath, but a liquid black covers their faces, their entire upper bodies.

It's the same mist I saw in space. The same fog that surrounded the fallen meteor shard. Craft said it was a mind-controlling poison, but this seems . . . beyond that. I'm still staring as one of the creatures lifts the disgusting captain off his feet. He screams as he's brought into a dark embrace. The green mist blooms out. Blood splashes to the floor.

Jazzy saves us.

She takes a deep breath and shoves through our frozen ranks. The doors weren't closing, because one of the marines backpedaled. His back foot straddles the gap. Jazzy lands a kick on his lower back. The marine sprawls into the chaos, and Jazzy jams one finger down on the Door Close button. The whole elevator shudders with movement.

Green-black smoke floods into the clearing. It starts to edge toward us. One of the creatures turns our way and lets loose a bone-chilling scream. But it lunges a second too late.

The elevator doors slam shut.

I almost collapse to my knees when it starts to move.

Kit's voice shakes. "Not my favorite episode so far."

"What the hell *was* that?" I ask.

For the first time, the three Imago look terrified. Craft shakes his head. "That was something more. I have seen what the substance can do on our planet. It was never so final. You could break someone free of its touch. But this . . ."

"If we make it back to your world," Greenlaw says quietly, "I suggest not bringing any of that with us. We'll have to move quickly. Leave it behind at all costs."

Their reaction triples my own fears. I realize I'm holding my breath, like I'm still worried the substance is in the air around us. No one else speaks as our descent continues.

CHAPTER 29
THE QUIETEST THING

Longwei Yu

I follow Defoe into the command center. He scans the room briefly, but it is clear that he expected the location to be empty. Our march through the corridors was unchallenged. Doors slid open with less than a wave from Defoe's hand. As in control as he appears, there is still a certain rush to his movements. Defoe has won some advantage and is eager to maintain it.

We move toward the main console in the room, but as our angled view of space changes, both of us briefly forget why we are here. The landscape windows offer us a view we cannot resist. Outside, the aftermath of a collision.

I realize we're both drawn forward by different reasons. I am looking at the fulfillment of what I already knew would happen. Defoe, however, sees the final piece to his unsolved puzzle. Both moons have shattered. The dark shards scatter in every direction. At the point of impact, there's still a little light from all the dying explosions. Backlit by those flames, the destruction looks all the more final. I note a strange green mist curling through the remnants of the collision.

Something about the sight shivers down my spine. My eyes trace a trail of debris that's making steady progress toward Magnia. Gravity will draw them slowly down.

The world will end.

Defoe speaks. "They were escaping. They *knew* about the moons."

I startle at the sound of his voice. His words are translating again. He turns my way, suspicious at my reaction. "I can understand you," I explain. "It's working."

Defoe frowns. I can see him trying to understand all the riddles, but he's smart enough to realize we don't have time for the smaller games. "Let's secure the ship."

I follow him. We are alone, and again I find myself wondering if now is the moment. Defoe turns his back on me and leans over the central console. He does not believe I can harm him. He thinks I'm still holding the blunted sword he gave me down on the planet. I take my place beside him and weigh my options. I can't kill him until I know what the situation is. . . .

"Breaches," Defoe muses. "The red marks are breaches."

A swipe of his hand brings the schematic hovering into the air. On the far left, there's the actual tower. Six separate levels all stacked on top of one another. One floor is full of blue-lit movement, but down on the third floor? All the lights are blinking red.

"Blue is our troops," Defoe explains. "They followed protocol perfectly. We've got at least three hundred marines on board now. But the only problem . . ."

He doesn't have to finish that sentence. I can see the problem. Red marks have appeared everywhere. Defoe spins the digital readouts, and it's like a body that's too infested and sick to save. There are breaches on the third floor, and matching marks appear on the *Genesis 13.* There are a handful on the *Genesis 14* too. I find our location on the blueprint—a small golden circle—and I can see we're nestled safely in one of the lower sections of the Tower Space Station.

But just two floors below us, more red dots are blooming.

"There are Adamites everywhere," Defoe concludes.

And are my friends with them? A new hope grows in my heart. Maybe they made it after all. Or maybe these are ships from the other rings? There's only one way of knowing.

"Can we bring up the cameras?" I ask, remembering security aboard the ship was tight. "We can get a better sense of the numbers we're facing that way."

Defoe shakes his head. "Opening up that system will give the techies one more way to slip past my lockdown. Besides, we know the numbers. The Imago launch station we destroyed had thirty ships. I inspected them myself. Each one was a two-seater. Sixty Imago per station. If every one of the rings had an escape route . . ."

He trails off. Maybe for the first time he realizes that there was no real victory that day. He is not the one who finally destroyed the city of Sevenset. He sees now that he can only claim what the Imago gave him freely. It actually brings a smile to his face.

"Clever bastards," he says. "They were *this* close to winning too."

I say the only thing I can think to say. "What do we do now?"

He scans the readouts again. "The station is lost. Time to amputate. Computer, highlight our best route to the Genesis Loading Bay. Create two routes. One from our current location, and another from the auxiliary bay on the fifth floor. Let's shut down the rest of the Tower. I want a full lockdown, not just the emergency grid. No access for anyone who isn't Babel. And extend complete control to my mobile device. We need to move."

The computer processes before responding, "Affirmative."

Defoe assesses the familiar data pad. I watch as it greenlights a safe path to the same docking bay we arrived in after our time aboard the *Genesis 11.* It's the same massive room where we first met the members of Genesis 12. Defoe's plan is clear. He used the word *amputation,* and it's just that. Instead of fighting off the Imago throughout the ship, he's severing a limb and reducing the battle to the one thing that matters: the ships that can go home. And of all the gathered ships, only one of them shows no sign of a breach.

"So we'll take the *Genesis 11?*"

Defoe nods once. "Ship statuses, please."

Statistics flash to life. *Genesis 12* returns no data. Something bad must have happened to it, but I'm not sure what. *Genesis 11* and *13* show positive numbers. Finally, I notice a red highlight circling the *Genesis 14.* "What does that mean?" I ask.

"It was never refueled."

At the corner of the screen, an urgent message. Defoe

reaches out and double-taps the square. It expands and shows a live feed of a glaring Babel general. "What are our orders, sir?"

"Evacuation protocol," Defoe answers. I can see the surprise on the general's face. "I've sectioned off the entire Tower. It won't hold the Adamites forever, but your path is clear and their path is not. I want all troops to head for the Genesis Loading Bay now. I'm uploading a list of updated breach points and containment areas for you. Proceed with caution. Ears open for changing commands."

The general hesitates. "We followed protocol upon arrival. All our boys geared up, and then we located the first breach point. I sent down a team to the third floor in response. We lost contact with them. No responses at all. Do you want us to send another team in?"

Defoe shakes his head. "Negative. Avoid contact with all Adamites. I want us to secure the docking bay before we even think about engaging them. Understood?"

"Affirmative."

They exchange a nod before Defoe swipes the screen away.

He turns to me. It's subtle, but his eyes flick briefly to my sword. A second later, he fixes his attention on the shattered moons outside the command center. I wonder if he's considering the risks of leaving me weaponless. If we do encounter Imago, the sword he originally gave me would be useless. I could not help him. Defoe decides to trust in his own abilities.

He takes one last look out the window and nods to me.

"Let's get moving."

I follow Babel's king through the halls. My sword bounces against my back with each step. I can feel the moment approaching down in the deepest part of my heart. Battles are waiting in the distance. I try to keep my hands steady. My moment is coming. I will strike a blow that echoes.

For now, I march quietly after my unknowing target.

Everyone we encounter will see Defoe first.

I am the quietest thing aboard the ship.

CHAPTER 30

OLD TRICKS

Emmett Atwater

The elevator opens again, but this time the hallways are empty. No one from either side waits to greet us. Gander suggests we keep a normal pace and slowly work our way toward the main corridor. We keep up the charade. No one says so much as a word.

It feels like the day that we finished our competition. I walked down to the escape pods that day and it was like the hallways were full of ghosts. Gander's card gets us all the way to the main corridor. Every time he swipes it, he looks just as surprised as we are that it's working.

When we finally reach it, I realize I do remember the main hallway. It's the path we took every day to get down to the Waterway. There are a few random entrances to our right, and I realize they must be the bridges that Requin and Defoe would use to watch our progress.

We start around another bend, and I recognize this section of the ship.

Our rooms are off to the right. The place where I first met Morning. Little fears snap back to life. Where is she? Where are the others? Did they survive? Have they been captured?

Those thoughts are still hammering through me when Bilal stumbles to a sudden halt. Our whole group hitches at the sight of interlopers. About fifty meters ahead. They look as surprised to see us as we are to see them. A curse hisses through my lips.

"Defoe."

He survived his flight through the forest. I note the thick padding around the base of his left arm. It's where Morning took his hand off with a clean blow. But the real surprise is the person who's striding at his side: Longwei. He actually did it. He infiltrated Babel's ranks.

Their reactions say everything. Longwei's eyes widen. Defoe's narrow.

He takes in our group, eyes tracing the details in less than a few seconds. I watch Longwei and wait for a sign. If ever there were a moment for my friend to act, this would be it. I can see the sword hanging from his back. His hand drifts up toward the handle. I feel like I'm barely breathing. Everything hangs in the balance of this moment.

"You brought prisoners," Defoe says.

I know him well enough by now. It's a probing statement. Gander doesn't realize it.

"We caught them in one of the supply shipments," he says.

"And you brought them here?"

Gander nods. "This one is from *Genesis 11*. Thought you'd want him right away."

"In direct defiance to my ship-wide orders?"

Defoe reaches for his data pad. His eyes lock on us as he swipes. There's a blast of noise in the surrounding corridor. Doors hiss down from above. One cuts the corridor in two, separating us from Longwei and Defoe. The others cut off our access to the rooms and hallways on our right.

We're trapped.

Defoe swipes again. His voice echoes out in the air above us as it casts to the whole ship.

"General High. I need two details sent to ground zero. Access through the supply freighter. I've locked all entrances. Our targets are trapped in the southeastern wing of the central corridor. Eight of them. Remove access from Kit and Holden Gander's credentials. Proceed with caution."

Longwei's eyes flick from Defoe to us. He has the drop on him. Defoe's not as strong as he used to be either. All it would take is for him to strike. He licks his lips once. Defoe turns and whispers something before marching down an adjacent tunnel.

"Longwei!" I shout.

But he follows Defoe. I almost can't believe what I'm seeing. He's saving himself. I guess he never changed at all. I look back at our crew. The Ganders are striding down the exterior corridor and testing all the entrances. It's clear, though, that their cards aren't working anymore. Jazzy jogs back in the direction we came, but returns a few seconds later.

"There's a barrier like this one," she says. "We're stuck in here."

Greenlaw transforms her nyxia into a massive blade. She

adjusts her grip and jabs the point right into the glass partition. Before it can even reach the surface, though, there's a flash of black along the length of the barrier. Her sword point stops a breath short of the wall.

"How clever of them," she says, then turns back to us. "Now what?"

I'm still processing Longwei's betrayal when I realize Bilal isn't with us.

"Bilal?" And then I'm shouting. "Bilal!"

There's a bang to our right. My heart about stops when Bilal shoves back through a swinging door I hadn't noticed and holds it open like a hotel valet. "Our escape route."

The rest of the group crosses over to where he's standing. The doorway leads into a shadowed room. Glass runs along the one wall that we can see from where we're standing.

"This is where I watched you all from," Bilal says. "When I was injured and unable to participate in the first few weeks of dueling. I came out here and watched you, cheered for you. For some reason, I remembered the doors being . . . old. They don't look like they belong, do they? No security access needed."

He swings it open wider as we all duck inside.

"Saving lives, Bilal," I say, slapping him on the shoulder as we pass.

Emergency lights glow along the baseboards. This part of the station has been powered down, but I can still see the faintest reflection of light running over the surface of the water below us. When everyone's inside, Bilal closes the door.

"There's a spiral staircase through the opposite doorway,"

he says. "It leads down to the Waterway. I never used it, but Requin and Defoe came through a few times."

Jazzy pops the door open. An unlit stairwell waits.

"Let's keep moving," Gander suggests. "Those teams will be down here in five minutes. I'm going to find the best exit point. The Waterway is its own system. Maybe we can find the right exit before they shut it all down. Bilal, are there other bridges? We'll have to cross back once we get to the right location."

I hear a little *click*. Light flutters out from Jazzy's shoulder. She leads us down the stairwell as Bilal answers, "There was one other bridge. On the opposite side."

"Might be too far," Gander says. "Are there other exits?"

Bilal nods. "Along the outer rim of the Waterway."

"So we just need to get across somehow. . . ."

Our progress brings us back out through a pair of double doors. A sudden draft of wind hits the group. We all look out into the cavernous room that hosts the Waterway. Jazzy's shoulder light lands directly on a pair of boats floating in the water ahead of us.

"Gander, figure out where we need to go," I order. "Everyone else, let's get the boat out into the water. Jazzy, you're on the eyes. Kit and Bilal, take defensive stations. The rear ones. If they're chasing us, that's where we'll need you. Craft and Diallo, can you two drive?"

"Of course we can drive," Craft cuts back. "Even if the boat looks . . . old-fashioned."

I turn and realize the only person I haven't assigned to a task is Greenlaw. And then I realize—in the panic of escape—that I just acted the captain while striding next to a queen. I throw her an awkward look, but she waves it away. "Captain the ship. This is your territory. I'll take the power position at the back. This is not the time for posturing."

I grin back as we board the ship. It takes a little effort to get it shoved away from the railings and untangled from the other boat's lines, but before long we're drifting out. I take the captain seat and feel the connections snap to life. Green-law shoves her energy into the engine. There's a brief roar before the sound completely muffles. I raise an eyebrow and whisper through our link.

"How are you doing that?"

"It's the same trick as the rifle I used outside Ravine Shel-ter," she answers. "I set aside a piece of nyxia, and I'm fun-neling all the noise into it."

"Perfect," I reply. "All right, Jazzy, scan every thirty seconds. Let's treat this like a night mission. Complete si-lence. Cloak our signal. All of that. Gander, where are we heading?"

"B-34," he answers. "It's one of the emergency entrances the divers used to get in and out during our training. There's a hatch that leads back up to the loading area for all the Genesis ships. We're underneath the H-Bridge."

There's noise overhead. A brief glow in the bridge room. Soldiers arriving and searching.

"Nice and quiet," I whisper. "Let's get moving."

The ship eases out past the docks. The silence is broken only by Jazzy's occasional whispers. She directs Diallo and Craft through the leftover obstacles of our last Waterway challenge. I don't remember this particular course because at the start of that challenge I leapt overboard and tackled

Morning into the water. As we round the first bend, I glance back. I can just make out movement in the bridge room. How long until they figure out where we went?

"Emmett . . ." Jazzy hesitates. "I think there's something . . . ahead of us. . . ."

My eyes search the darkness. It's hard to see anything in the restless shadows.

"Is it on the radar?"

I can see her rise slightly to get a better look over the railing.

"No. It's . . . I could have sworn . . ."

The collision comes without warning. There's a sharp snap of wood grinding against wood. The impact sends me stumbling out of the captain's chair. Jazzy just managed to duck back into her station at the last second. "What the hell did we hit?" I ask in a whisper.

A shadow rises. My mind flashes back to the corrupted creatures we saw on the third floor as it leaps on board. I start to reach for my boxing claws when the shadow speaks.

"Guess I'll just have to accept the fact that I'll show up before you *everywhere* we go."

I stand up in time to get leveled by Morning's hug. She buries me against the floorboards as the rest of the crew tries to process what's happening. Katsu's voice echoes over the water.

"Learn how to drive, Jazzy!"

She laughs back. "*You* ran into *us.*"

Relief thunders through me. Morning buries her face in my chest. I let myself feel safe and whole for about a breath. I know none of this is over. Not even close. There's a good chance we'll still die out here, but now the end of the story is something we'll write together. She whispers into my neck, "I wasn't going home without you. Thanks for saving me some trouble."

She smiles before helping me back to my feet. As my eyes adjust to the distance and the dark, I spy her crew: Azima. Katsu. Isadora. Roathy. Gio. Beckway. Alex . . .

. . . "Anton? You're alive?"

He nods back. "Everyone sounds so surprised."

It's hard not to notice the missing Genesis members. "Where's everyone else?"

"We got split up," Morning says. "They were heading toward *Genesis 11*. We were trying to get back to the command center, but if you're here, we might as well rendezvous with them. Do you know where you're going?"

"The exit is B-34," I answer. "Kit's dad helped us with the location."

She squints through the dark. "Kit's up here? That's how you got back up to the ship! You went to Foundry! That's so damn smart!"

Greenlaw finally leans in. "Hey! We're being *chased*. A reunion might be in order, but I highly suggest we have it *after* Babel is defeated. Get moving!"

Morning nods back. "I told you I liked her. Our ship took the most damage on that collision. Let's get everyone packed on here and get moving."

It takes about thirty seconds for her crew to load up with us. Anton's the last one over. When he realizes it's Bilal helping him across the gap, he wraps my friend in an unexpected hug.

"You're alive. Thank God you're alive."

I forgot the history between them. Bilal and Anton were put in the same room at the end of our training and told by Babel that only one could survive. Anton held himself responsible for what happened too, even though we knew it was Babel's fault. Bilal pats his back.

"I told you it would be fine, no? It is good to see you, Anton."

The crew crowds safely aboard. Shields are still up on the back end of our boat. I'm about to order us forward when lights blind in from overhead. It's like someone flipped the switch for the entire area. We squint up, and I hear the echoing sound of shattered glass come from every direction at once.

Babel marines clear out the jagged shards, set their weapons on the ledges, and take aim.

CHAPTER 31

THE TRAITORS

Emmett Atwater

"Shields up!" I shout. "Engines, Greenlaw!"

Gunfire erupts from above, but our nyxian stations answer. Black shields cover the ship as we jolt forward over the man-made river. There's another loud scrape as we brush past the abandoned vessel. Greenlaw's not bothering to mute the engines now. She guns it—putting more force in than I can ever remember feeling from Longwei. It channels back through the connected stations, and as we thunder away from the main barrage, I realize it's the only thing that keeps the shields intact.

We turn a corner, and Gander shouts through the comm.

"We're passing section C. B-34 should be on the right after the next straightaway."

Craft and Diallo guide us toward that side of the Waterway. A few more shots ring out above our group, but we slowly put distance between us and the two pursuing units as we round a corner. I'm thinking we're in the clear, when

Bilal points ahead of us. Circling the opposite direction, just rounding the bend, is a Babel-led ship. The marines are poised at the front stations.

"Cannons, Bilal!" I shout.

He doesn't hesitate. Maybe it's just the instinct of all those practice exercises. He converts his cannon, and Azima pushes aside Kit to do the same on the opposite station. Both of them take aim as Babel's ship comes out of their turn.

"Fire when ready!"

Morning's standing beside me. I realize she's counting under her breath.

"B-40, B-39, B-38 . . . Slow us down, Greenlaw! The exit is coming up."

I'm expecting the engines to cut, the way we used to do it in training. Instead, she just redirects the gathered energy. Our momentum slows, and the burst from Bilal and Azima's cannons almost triples in size. The blast shakes our entire ship and sears the air with bright light. We all stare as the Babel marines swerve. The burst of energy breezes just past their ship.

And wrecks another ship as it comes around the corner.

Our crew lets out a roar as our own flank skids against the slanted sides of the Waterway. Morning squeezes my shoulder. "You were great, but I'll take it from here." She transforms into the captain again. "Keep your shields up in case we get fire from overhead. Bilal and Azima, keep firing at that approaching ship. You're the last ones off the boat. Let's *move!*"

Greenlaw remains at her station, pumping energy into the ship, but the rest of the group leaps overboard. In the distance, Babel's ship glows with blue light. They send a volley of their own, and I flinch as it gusts overhead. Most of the Genesis crew has unloaded. Morning pushes me toward the railing, and I leap overboard, turning to help her. But she's always the captain. She forces Greenlaw and the others to leap to safety before she'll leave.

Another ball of blue light forms, and the Babel ship is closing in on our location. Morning and I sprint together into the waiting mouth of B-34. Blue light absolutely rocks the front of our ship. There are snapping boards and a con-cussive blast that sends us flying forward.

Gander slams the door shut. "They're right behind us!" he shouts. "Get climbing!"

No one needs to hear that order twice. There's a single ladder leading up to a hatched exit. Jazzy goes up first, scal-ing easily. Isadora's behind her. It's clearly an awkward ascent, but Roathy sets a hand on her lower back just in case. It's like traveling back in time, running through Ba-bel's physical gauntlet, pushing ourselves to the limit. I glance back and see Gander working to seal the doorway. Kit stands nearby, and the two exchange heated words. I can only imagine which episode Kit's comparing *this* mo-ment to.

Morning nudges me forward when my turn comes. "Go ahead. I'll enjoy the view."

I shake my head and start up. She's right behind me. Overhead, Jazzy has the hatch popped. I'm half expecting another attack. So far it's felt like there's something nasty around every corner. It takes about thirty seconds to get all the way up the ladder. Bilal's standing near the rim with

Katsu, lugging everyone up to their feet. Morning tugs at my ankle before I reach them, though.

"What are they doing?" she asks.

Her question draws my eyes back down below. Kit and Gander haven't started the climb. I'm about to yell down to them—call them lurches for wasting time—when I realize they're not planning on making the climb at all. Kit is shouting and trying to force his way to the ladder. But he's such a thin kid. Gander is strong enough to hold his son back as he shakes his head. It's not hard to figure out what's happening. His dad thinks the tides are changing again.

Gander's taking his chance with Babel.

"They're changing teams," I mutter back. "Come on."

Bilal pulls me up through the entrance. Morning's close behind. I can barely hear Kit shouting something below. "Shut the hatch," I order. "Bar it if you can. They're not coming."

As Bilal and Katsu set to work, I step past them. We're in a low-ceilinged hallway. A perfect square of white light waits in the distance. Jazzy stands about halfway down the hall with a hand up to shield her eyes from the waiting brightness. Our group regathers and resets our ranks. Morning and I stride up to the front, and we're flanked by our best fighters: Azima, Anton, and Katsu. The Imago take their places up front too. Greenlaw strides alongside Craft, who is trying his best to shove Diallo back behind our front line. Roathy and Isadora fall in behind the rest of us.

We move down the hall as a single unit. Jazzy nods when we reach her. Her view looks out at a wide loading bay. Gander mentioned it before, said it was big enough to host a football game. He was right. The ceilings are three times as high as the other hallways. It's clear that the massive room was full of supplies and ships before Babel sent all their troops down to the surface. It's almost empty now.

"I thought I saw something moving," Jazzy says. "But there's nothing now. I think we need to move fast. Gander will give up our position. They'll know we're out of the Waterway. It won't take long for Defoe to divert more troops this way."

"Where are all the Imago?" Katsu asks. "Didn't the other stations launch?"

"Defoe controls the ship," I remind him. "He might have quarantined them too."

Morning nods. "Let's move. Everyone together. Be ready to run. Or fight. Or both."

She leads us out into the bright. It takes a second to realize this is the same loading bay where Babel delivered their first big twist. Where we first learned another set of ten contestants existed. We start across the same massive loading bay that Genesis 12 waited in that day. In the distance, we can see a series of circular openings that connect to the exterior wall of the Tower Space Station. My eyes scan the room. Each opening represents a ship.

Genesis 11 waits on the far left. The place where *Genesis 12* should be docked has been sealed off. It looks like a dark wound. I lower my voice to a whisper. "One of the ships is gone."

And then there's *Genesis 13.* I glance over at Gio. I've barely noticed the kid. He stays quiet, but he's marching in rank like he's one of ours now. Morning's survival meant

Beatty's downfall. I didn't ask her about it, but I realize now that means Gio is the last one from their crew. A cold truth. Finally, on the far right side is another ship. One that undoubtedly delivered another crew.

"There's a *Genesis 14?*" Morning asks. "Seriously?"

Anton nods. "They're loose somewhere on the ship. I've met them. Not exactly friendly."

"And Parvin's group is on the *Genesis 11?*" I ask.

"Let's hope so," Morning answers.

We've made it about halfway across the massive loading bay, when there's movement ahead. A single marine appears at the entrance of the *Genesis 13.* Morning's about to sound an order, when another marine appears at the entrance to *Genesis 14,* and another at the entrance to *Genesis 11.* All three guards take up defensive stances.

"Really?" Katsu laughs. "That's the best they can do?"

But movement stirs in the shadow of each opening. Figures emerge, one by one, marching forward in formation. We all stare as the numbers continue to grow. Ten, fifteen, twenty . . .

Far too many to count. Far too many for us to fight. A full battalion fronts the entrance to each ship. I look left and right. Soldiers are appearing there too. The other exits that feed back to the Tower are being cut off. Marines fan out and slowly circle until we're surrounded. The group that we saw up on the fifth floor got here before we could. Fear and adrenaline rush through me.

"Shields," Morning orders, but even I can hear the catch in her breath as she says it. She's been able to find a way since the beginning. We always survive, and we almost always survive because of her leadership. This time it's different. There's no magic switch we can flip to get out of this one. "We make our stand *here*. We make our stand *now*."

Our crew forms a circle in the very center of the massive room. We stand, shoulders touching, all of us ready to face our enemy one last time. Only Isadora positions herself inside our ring. I can see the fear in her eyes. Not fear for Roathy or for herself. Fear for her baby. Everyone else settles into fighting stances. Greenlaw separates from the group to stand in the center as well.

"I've trained for this my whole life. If you want to survive this, let me take the lead."

Morning doesn't hesitate. "What do we do?"

Babel's forces continue to spread and circle. None of them approach. Their first goal is clearly to cut us off. Eliminate escape routes. Most of our group has summoned shields. I remember this is Greenlaw's specialty. She can take our nyxia and enhance it with a forged manipulation.

"Shields up," she commands. "I'm going to weave the manipulations into one shield."

As everyone obeys her command, I try to cling to hope. I want to believe we can defy the odds one more time. But as I look around the circle, I see more fear than fight, more concern than courage. How many times can we be pushed to the edge and fly?

Greenlaw carefully weaves our shields together, stretching and molding them, before turning back to us. "Do you know how to make the substance orbit?" she asks, looking around. Everyone nods. "Good. Keep that in the back of your mind. Focus on fighting. Hold the line no matter what. Work together. But in the back of your mind, keep pushing that energy around. I'm going to use the shield throughout the fight. Keep the inner ring clear. Got it?"

Nods all around. Morning takes a deep breath.

She makes sure to look at everyone who's standing in our circle.

"Shoulder to shoulder. Until the end."

The whole group answers with an echoing shout. Morning comes to stand beside me. She sets her shoulder intentionally next to mine and breathes the words, "I love you. Just in case. I love you."

Our eyes lock on the faces of the gathering troops.

"I love you too," I whisper back.

There's a disturbance in the ranks near the western entrance to the Tower. Soldiers hustle out of the way and I watch them hopefully. Maybe the Imago have come to save us?

But it's not a rescue party. Defoe prowls forward. Longwei walks in his shadow. Through the shared link of nyxia, I can actually feel the pulse of anger our group experiences at the sight of them. Defoe pauses at a careful and calculated distance. The marines wait for his signal.

"Welcome home," he calls. "We last spoke on Eden. I offered you the chance to choose. Give up and come with us or fight and die with *them*. You made the wrong choice, and there are consequences for that. For most of you. I'll make one final offer. We need . . . spokesmen. We are willing to spare the first three volunteers. Consider it a final peace offering. Come with us. Back our story on Earth. And we will let you live."

My eyes find Longwei. His face is controlled. He watches our coming death with complete calm. My eyes drill into him, and I'm hoping to break through, hoping to remind him of the promise he made to me. But my friend isn't there. He seems to have forgotten all of that.

"Longwei has claimed the first spot," Defoe says with a gesture. "Who will join him?"

The translucent shield around us flexes with more energy. We glance around our circle, and not one face shows even a trace of doubt. Even Gio doesn't give the offer a second thought. We will die here together before any of us walks across that line. This family has been carved in blood. We carry the ghosts of those we have lost with us. We are the promise of home and the beating hearts of our families. We are more than what Babel has tried to make us.

Defoe sees our defiance. He smiles.

"Admirable," he says before raising his voice. "Spare the last few survivors. Kill the rest."

His order echoes. Hundreds of marines start forward. Morning's shoulder presses against mine. She lifts both of her hatchets up, and there's a promise in her eyes. She intends to take down as many Babel soldiers as she can. Bilal is on my other side. I can see realization on his face. Death is coming. He stands, and it's clear he is not afraid to face it.

I take courage from both of them. Morning the warrior, Bilal the healer.

My hands flex inside my claws.

I'm ready for one final fight.

As Babel's ranks start to move forward, I see Longwei reach for his sword. Defoe does not see him. He's too busy savoring our destruction. The sword slides from Longwei's straps like a poem. It catches and throws the light in a glittering arc as he plunges it into Defoe's back.

CHAPTER 32

THE FINAL STAND

Emmett Atwater

We all see the sword tip punch through Defoe's stomach.

The approaching tide of Babel marines stumbles to a halt. Their leader gasps. A circle of blood spreads across the front of Defoe's perfect suit. Longwei slides the blade back out, and I can see a mix of victory and shock and fear. Defoe locks eyes with him, and the nyxian suit he's wearing *pulses* out. The substance strikes Longwei square in the chest, sending him sprawling away.

Defoe drops to a knee.

He's not dead. It still isn't over.

I break from our ranks. Morning shouts, reaching for me, but I slip free of her grasp and shoulder through our shield. And then I'm sprinting. I can't let Longwei die.

Defoe rises. His breathing is labored. He has enough power to summon Longwei's sword into his right hand. Even injured, he crosses the distance with cruel intention.

The marines are still frozen, as shocked by the betrayal as they are by the fact that Defoe survived it.

He lifts Longwei's sword into the air. The motion clearly causes him pain, but he channels all of that into a scream of rage. He starts to drive the blade down at the exact second I bring my shoulder ramming into his hip. I stumble through the blow and barely keep my feet. Defoe fumbles the sword as he slides back toward the line of marines. Longwei's eyes widen in shock.

"Come on!" I shout.

I grab the front of his suit and pull. Longwei springs to his feet, and we're both running. The tidal wave of marines releases again. I can hear Defoe screaming. Something lashes against my back, and the glancing blow makes me stumble. Longwei's feet are steady. He rights us. We keep running together.

Behind, the marines are closing in. I realize we're not going to make it back to the shields. Morning realizes it too. She sprints forward. "Down! Get *down*, Emmett!"

Nyxia rises around her like a summoned storm. Seven different pieces forge into one, and she manipulates all of them into a new shape. I obediently slap a hand down on Longwei's shoulder and pull us both into a skidding slide. Morning's nyxia sweeps overhead in an arch of razor-sharp blades. Metal sings against metal. I turn in time to see four pursuing marines drop, just like that.

We duck back inside the shield. Morning backpedals to join us, and her shout echoes within the confined space. "Hold the line. If Defoe can bleed, so can they. We break them now!"

Longwei drops to a knee, clutching his chest. Defoe's strike must still be doing damage.

"Bilal!" I shout. "Help him! I'll take your spot."

My friend eyes the approaching troops and makes the trade gladly. I slide into his place and lift both claws. "Tighten up!" I shout. "No gaps in the line!"

Morning's at my right hip, but Jazzy hears the call and slides over to adjust. The soldiers approach in their own staggered formation. I squint through the translucent shield. The front line of runners is wearing bulky, bone-thick armor. I've never seen anything like it outside of video games.

"We fought a group like this!" Morning shouts. "The bigger suits will try to bulldoze their way through our lines. The soldiers behind them will pour through the gaps they make."

Greenlaw calls back. "I'm adjusting the shield. This should slow them down."

The marines are fifteen meters away, ten meters, five. . . . I notice black threads weaving through our shield. I can feel them too. The substance tightening and binding and threading together as Greenlaw tweaks it. We stand as one inseparable unit. I cling to that thought as the first line of marines come into contact with our force field.

And passing through the shield staggers them.

It's like running into a wall. The marine in front of me blinks like he just got smacked. All the front-liners rock back on their heels, vulnerable. "Hit 'em hard!" Morning shouts.

We were all braced for impact. Now we take the offensive. My marine's arms shoot out as he tries to regain his balance. I sweep forward and land two jabs with my off hand. The first blow is glancing, but the second one crushes his unprotected nose. His head reels back, and I spy the narrow gap between helmet and breastplate. I bring my claws hooking around, and they bury in the side of his neck. Blood sprays as he falls to the ground.

A glance shows that Morning's already dropped both of her marines. I backpedal, eyes cutting to the left, and see that Jazzy is still trading blows with her opponent. She holds a dented shield in one hand, a short sword in the other. I slide that way as the marine slams a reinforced arm into her shield. When she stumbles, he lunges forward and doesn't see me coming.

I thrust my claws into the gap under his armpit.

A scream. He drops to a knee, and Jazzy recovers enough to land a kick that sends him spinning out of our circle. All around us there are shouts. Metal against metal. I plant my feet and reset my stance in time for the second wave of soldiers.

"Changing the manipulation," Greenlaw calls. "Take advantage of it."

I settle into my stance as the next group comes. They're smart enough to learn from the mistakes of the first. Greenlaw's first manipulation used the group's momentum against them. The second crew approaches cautiously, almost tiptoeing through the shield.

Nothing happens at first.

My next marine has a trio of scars running down his face. He shouts a war cry and charges forward, then freezes. My first jab falls well short. We both stare at each other in confusion until I notice the nyxia. Vines tangle around his shoulders and snake beneath his arms. He squirms, but Greenlaw's summoning tightens and tightens. He can barely move.

It makes my job all too easy. I strike twice, and the marine slumps. When Morning finishes her marine off, she shouts back, "Keep it up, Greenlaw! Everyone keep talking. If you're wounded or need help, call it out!"

A glance shows Bilal has Longwei back on his feet. The rest of the crew has held their ground. No casualties, and we've dropped at least twenty of Babel's soldiers. It's the third line that makes a dent. I've got my fists raised as they approach, but my marine cuts to the right. It's the kind of move a defensive lineman would pull to get to the quarterback. A stunt move.

He disappears around Jazzy's soldier and I stare at empty space for a second. My reaction comes a breath too late. Jazzy's marine forces her a step back and my marine comes sprinting through the gap on that side. I dive for him and miss. He's inside our circle. Isadora screams as she ducks out of range.

It leaves Greenlaw as his next target. The marine levels her with a bruising tackle, and our barrier blinks briefly out of existence. I shout from the ground, "Help her! Someone help her!"

Longwei and Bilal rally to her side. I shove up to my feet just in time to turn and face the sudden onrush of marines. They sense weakness; they smell blood. A spear jabs at my throat. I parry the blow, but another stabs in from the left. Soldiers press eagerly forward. It's chaos.

There's a shout behind me, but I'm too busy ducking and swinging to do a damn thing about it. A misstep has me set up to get punished by the marine on my right. Morning barely rescues me with a sideswiping hatchet. She dances past that fallen soldier and guts the other one. A spin brings her slamming back into my side.

Greenlaw's shield flickers back a second later. She's up on her feet. Her fury pulses into the shield now. Energy blasts outward with blinding light. It's a manipulation I've seen her use before, at the Ravine Shelter. The approaching soldiers are temporarily blinded. As their approach halts, we turn to focus on the soldiers who have broken into our ranks.

Anton and Alex have adopted Babel's method. Alex holds a massive nyxian shield up and suffers the hammering blows of an armored marine. Anton waits and waits before ducking forward, finding just the right spot to jam his knife. Azima's spear is a blur. She jabs and jabs, distracting two marines as Beckway and Gio work to hamstring them from behind. Katsu's actually laughing as he swings his massive ax at the nearest heavy.

I realize Craft has abandoned his place in the circle to fight off soldiers from Diallo. His nyxia wraps around them, squeezing tight, before he sweeps in to finish them off. The last marine falls, and we get exactly three seconds to recover. It feels like an eternity.

Greenlaw shouts, "Lighter gravity. Everyone jump!"

She gives the command a moment to sink in. Morning and I both turn back to face the next onslaught before planting our feet and leaping. The lighter gravity snares us upward. We're floating up to the top of our domed shield—at least two meters in the air—when Greenlaw shouts again. "I'm going to bring you down right on top of them!"

The marines shoulder through the barrier. Mine grins up at me like I'm the easiest target he's ever seen. His feet start to lift off the ground at the exact moment Greenlaw flips the switch. The heavier gravity slams down on all of us. In their bulky armor, the marines suffer it the most. Every one of them staggers to a knee, and we descend on them like demigods. They don't stand a chance. When we're clear again, Morning shouts.

"We've got this, Genesis! Shoulder to shoulder!"

Babel tries another tactic. Their newest front row of troops takes a knee. Gunfire erupts. I can see the bullets burying into the side of the shield. The whole thing holds, but little cracks start to form too. "I need a little help!" Greenlaw shouts. "Focus on the shield for a moment!"

Our group answers. I can feel our combined effort pouring into the substance. It flexes against the coming bullets. All the forming crevices and holes start to vanish. Greenlaw starts to call out another order, when a figure bursts through the side of our shield. He comes right through the gap that Craft left behind. He looks like a man possessed. Both of his fists are clenched tight. . . .

"Grenades!" I shout. "Everybody *down!*"

The man slides to his knees in the very center of our circle. His eyes close tight, and I realize we're all going to die. A permanent image of every reaction burns into my mind. Roathy has shoved forward to get between Isadora and the soldier. His hands reach out, like that will be enough to stop the blast from claiming the two people he loves the most.

Azima's arm has cocked back, spear steady, as she prepares to throw it at the man. Anton pulls Alex away by the collar. Jazzy's face is the perfect picture of calm. Katsu's smiling like this is the worst punch line he's ever heard. Most of our circle flinches away, the natural reaction.

But there are four of us who move *toward* the man.

Morning's shoulder collides with mine. We both had the same idea. Dive forward. Cover the blast. Save the others. It slows us down. The other two are closer than we are by a few steps.

I scream as Bilal and Longwei race toward the soldier.

CHAPTER 33

FIRST PLACE

Longwei Yu

It is second nature for them. The way Morning plants her back foot in preparation for that first stride. How Emmett's shoulders turn to face the danger head-on. In the straining reach of Bilal's outstretched hands. Death knocks at our door, and the sound forces all three of them to act on an unspoken promise. It is a contract each of them keeps in the quiet of their own hearts.

All three would trade their lives for any of ours.

Sacrifice has never felt natural to me, but anything can be learned, and I am an excellent student. My own back foot plants. Every muscle draws tight as I square my shoulders and launch myself into action.

My mind works in perfect harmony with my body. I mentally tear the nyxia from Greenlaw's grasp. I can sense her surprise. She didn't expect resistance from within our circle. Once I have a firm grip of the substance, shaping it to my needs takes less than a thought.

Bilal has the advantage on me. He is a step closer, but I hook his hip with my own outstretched hand. The motion pulls him back, pulls me forward. There's a blur of black as the nyxian shield tightens around me. I dive forward, wrap myself around the marine, and close my eyes.

I thought I would be afraid, but the fear never comes.

There is no room for it.

Pride roars through me like a river. It rushes over my oldest wounds and washes away the most haunting memories. It sweeps over all the scars that pushed me to leave my family and launch into space. Pride brighter than the sun. Pride in the fact that I can be the one who saves my Genesis brothers and sisters. Pride in knowing they will never forget my name.

And pride in knowing—even at the end—that I am the one who finished first.

CHAPTER 34

FALLEN

Emmett Atwater

It all happens in less than a second.

There's a pulsing ripple, but it's not from the grenades. Our nyxian shield suctions inward. The material ghosts through my body and sends a shiver down my spine. I'm thinking Greenlaw is about to do something miraculous, when the material reforms around Longwei instead. There's pure determination in his eyes as he edges past Bilal and dives on the suicidal soldier.

The shield swallows both of them.

An explosion shakes the floor.

"Longwei!" I scream. "Longwei!"

He saves us all again. I stare at the black pit where he was standing and try to take hope from his sacrifice. We all turn and face the coming waves. Our shield is gone. Babel marines are pouring forward. Wave after wave of soldiers. Defoe has slipped off through the Babel ranks. Adrenaline rushes through all of us, and Longwei's the only reason we keep our feet.

But even that isn't enough.

Our lines start to crumble. Craft breaks our circle in desperation and sprints forward into the heart of Babel's lines. Surprised soldiers fall left and right. He cuts through their ranks, causing the whole group to turn and watch, but there are too many. He's still swinging recklessly when someone hamstrings him from behind. He stumbles, and the gaps close. Our vision of him is cut off as Babel marines strike down from above.

Bilal has to restrain Diallo from following his brother. *Longwei is dead. Craft is dead. We're all going to die.* My heart is pounding. I look around and see that our entire crew is struggling to catch their breath. My hands fall to my side. The adrenaline is fading. We might be bloodied and bruised, but we will fight to the end.

Babel's next wave of soldiers prepares their approach. Morning lifts her hatchets and turns. "For Longwei!" she shouts. "Shoulder to shoulder! Hold the line!"

We echo her cry, but this time words aren't enough. I barely get my gloves up and my feet set when the first Babel marine barrels into me. I'm ripped from my feet, spinning and turning end over end. I roll away from him and see an endless chaos surrounding us. Half our circle has dented inward. Most have fallen. Morning keeps slashing and screaming. A handful of marines circle her. I try to rise, only to catch another backhand from a random soldier. It sends me to a knee.

This is the end. For all of us.

And then we hear the screams. At least they sound like screams at first. It takes a second to realize they're actually war cries. "For the Sixth! Fight for the Sixth!"

Another cry answers, "The Seventh lives to die!"

The cavalry arrives. Imago troops come pouring in from every entrance. Babel's soldiers try to turn and face them, only to get crushed. I switch into a defensive mode, turning away blows and watching as the impossible happens. Babel is falling. Even at a distance, I can see which fighters are from which rings. The Sixth drives through the heart of everything like a spike. I realize their rallying cry is not about fighting for themselves. It's about fighting for *us.* We are their honored members. We are the Sixth Ring too.

The Seventh looks far more disciplined. I hear a general barking orders. She has her troops cut off Babel's possible escape routes. Another group of Imago storms out of the entrance to the *Genesis 13.* I even spot Vandemeer leading our group of loyalists into the madness.

It's not hard to figure out the numbers. It's going to be a rout. We're going to win. Longwei saved us, and all we have to do now is *survive.* The soldiers around us snap back to life. I can see desperation now, though. Their eyes flick nervously around the room. The tides are changing.

I take my feet. A soldier approaches, and I spin past him. One thought pulses through me: I have to keep Morning alive. She's surrounded, fending off blows, backpedaling. One of her attackers takes a hatchet to the shoulder, but another brings his blade skimming across her planted leg. The blow cuts deep. Morning screams, and the soldiers crowd forward.

None of them see me coming.

My shoulder sends the first marine sprawling. I bring around a right hook for the second. All three claws rake across his chest. I land the first of two jabs and duck his sloppy riposte. An uppercut ends him. Morning's still down when the third steps past her to swing at me. Morning uses the distraction to bring a hatchet down into his foot. He stumbles back into Azima's line of sight.

She drives her spear forward to finish him.

"Genesis! To me, Genesis!" Morning's down, but still shouting commands.

Our crew pinches in tight. There's so much chaos and destruction. Imago soldiers are pouring in, and Babel's troops are breaking. We stand there, breathless, and watch it all happen. A marine or two tests the edges of our group, but we're turtled tight together. No one in, no one out. One group of Babel marines forges a path aboard the *Genesis 14.* The Imago give chase.

The rest of them surrender.

It's over in less than a few minutes.

Vandemeer makes a line for us. He brings medics with him. It takes their group a few attempts to get our crew to set weapons down. It's hard to accept the help we'd given up on. It's hard to turn off the instinct to fight. We're still reeling from the attacks, the blood, the approaching death.

But the second we set our weapons down, it's like we're too weak to stand. Almost everyone collapses. Only Bilal keeps moving. I can see the pain in his face. He was supposed to be the one who sacrificed himself to save us. He keeps working—bandaging wounds and passing canteens—like he's already trying to earn the second chance Longwei sacrificed to give us all. I glance over and see Jazzy on her back, crying. I feel like doing the same thing. My eyes flick back to the black scorch marks on the floor. I don't want to believe Longwei is gone, but without him, I know we all would have died.

Vandemeer dispatches a couple of his medics before heading my way.

He drops down to a knee and wraps me in a hug. "You survived!"

I try to smile. "I told you I'd see you again. Do me a favor and check out Morning. She's hurt."

He nods once and slides past me. She tries to convince him to help everyone else first, but he ignores it. Greenlaw doesn't rest. Like Morning, she's ready to start giving orders again. A handful of Imago soldiers come for Diallo. He's weeping as much as anyone. They pull him in and hush him as he tries to blame himself for what happened to his brother.

Survivors. That's what we are now.

And survivors have scars.

Our group's passing around canteens, trying to wrestle with the idea that it all might be over, when Jacquelyn marches out of the western entrance to the Tower. Erone trails her. Even though I'm tired and shell-shocked, my stomach turns uncomfortably. I'll always associate him with Kaya's death. I'm not the only one who takes note. Anton stands up and stabs a finger that way.

"He shouldn't be here, Jacquelyn. You didn't see what happened in the control room. He killed people who were loyal to us. He floated fifty Imago out into space. . . ."

Jacquelyn shakes her head. "It wasn't him. Defoe used some kind of device to control him. Erone was experimented on, remember? That was a part of the experiment."

Anton looks skeptical. Erone steps forward. "I tried to tell you. It was like I was trapped in a corner of my own mind. He took over *everything*. He killed Aguilar. He—" A tremor shakes through Erone. "He used me to kill my own people. There was a moment when I stumbled. And he was gone. Just like that. I tried to tell you, but you just kept running. Jacquelyn found me. We worked together to loosen Defoe's control of the ship. I'm sorry it took us so long to arrive."

Anton looks horrified now. "I didn't understand. You were speaking another language."

"That happened to us too," I say. "It was an echo from the moons' collision."

When Jacquelyn's content the conflict is settled, she nods.

"We need to keep moving."

Katsu speaks up. "Seriously? Do you see us? What's the rush?"

"Corruptions," Jacquelyn answers. "It's a faster-spreading version than what the Imago are accustomed to on-planet. It corrupts anything it touches, and it works fast. Erone and I had to override Defoe's system and open doors for our people to reach you. We tried to quarantine the corruptions at the same time, but they'd already started spreading through the Tower. We need to get on board these ships and detach from the main base as soon as possible."

I remember our brief glimpse of the third floor. The Imago who had been taken over. The green-black smoke that swirled in the air and smelled like death. The same color floating out in the darkness of space. "We saw the corruptions on the way down here," I say. "If Jazzy wasn't there, I doubt we would have made it out alive."

"So what's the plan?" Morning asks. "Who goes on what ships?"

"*Genesis 12* is lost," Jacquelyn answers. "Our people have taken *Genesis 13*. Do we have the personnel to fly all three of the remaining ships back to Earth?"

Vandemeer steps forward. "We have loyal astronauts, but not that many. I'd suggest taking two of the ships. Trying to man all three would force us to rely on personnel that stayed loyal to Babel until the very end. It would stretch our resources too."

"And *Genesis 14* isn't worth taking," Anton adds. "We never refueled it."

Everyone stares at that entrance. A squadron of Imago troops stands at attention—clearly from the Seventh Ring—awaiting orders on whether or not they should pursue the small group of Babel marines that escaped aboard *Genesis 14*. "Pull our people back," Beckway suggests. "Let the Babel survivors waste their time. Are you sure they can't make it back to Earth?"

Vandemeer nods. "Without fuel? It's impossible for them to get home."

"So we take *11* and *13*," I say. "Sounds good to me."

"Our crew boards the *Genesis 11*," Morning says firmly.

"The rest of our team should already be waiting there. The Remnant is with them too."

"Greenlaw goes with you," Jacquelyn says. "Beckway will take temporary command of *Genesis 13*. I hate to part ways with Erone again, but we agreed it would be best. Our technical expertise is more useful if it's divided between the two ships." She pauses long enough to eye the rest of our group. "I'd also feel more comfortable if some of your Genesis team agreed to go on the *Genesis 13*."

Morning shakes her head. "No more splitting up. We stay together."

"And if there's an accident?" Jacquelyn asks. "If Babel has a trap waiting? If they greet us back on Earth with offensive measures? We need emissaries who will speak on our behalf."

Gio rises. "I'll go. I'm the last one from *Genesis 13*. It will give me a chance to say goodbye."

After a second, Morning nods. "Will that work?"

"More would be better, but that will work," Jacquelyn replies. "I'll go get a team of Imago ready as well. I'd like them to go with you aboard the *Genesis 11*. Increases our chances. I think it would be best if I boarded *13*. One more human with them. And I'll need to survey the survivors." She looks over at Vandemeer. "Can the ships communicate?"

"Certainly," he answers. "We'll go ahead and get the links running."

Back in the bowels of the station, an ungodly scream echoes. A shiver runs down my spine. It's the same inhuman noise we heard on the third floor. The entire loading bay pauses to listen. When the scream fades, everyone starts moving a little quicker. No one wants to risk letting the virus spread to the main group. And Jacquelyn made it clear the monstrosities are coming. Time to move.

Jacquelyn turns to us. "Let's board the ships. Seal them off. We'll talk after we start back to Earth. Genesis, please know that what you just did . . . There is no favor you cannot ask of us."

She offers the slightest bow before turning away. I watch as she takes a moment to whisper something to Erone. I'd almost forgotten that the two of them were lovers. It's painfully obvious now as they press their foreheads together, as she rests a hand on his chest, as he breathes in the woman he thought he'd never see again. A second later, she whips around and is back to barking orders.

"Round up the prisoners! Let's get going!"

More chaos follows. It's all our group can do to stand up. Morning limps to her feet and doesn't complain when I slide her arm over my shoulder. We walk together, and the rest of our crew follows. Vandemeer is checking in with some of the Babel converts. They've all tied red bandannas around their arms. It's a small group, but they're the ones who joined us before Babel fell. The ones that we know we can trust. We've almost made it to the entrance, when Vandemeer catches us.

"There's a small problem."

I side-eye him. "Of course there is."

"Defoe," he replies. "He's not among the casualties."

"So he boarded the *Genesis 14*. Good for him. He deserves a cold death out in space."

Vandemeer shakes his head. "Defoe arrived before you, Emmett. He restored Babel's security systems and had full access to our information. Do you think he's foolish enough to board the only ship that can't get home?"

No, of course he isn't. Our surviving crew is listening closely.

"Let the Imago know," I say. "In case he boarded *13*. But I've got a pretty good feeling he's not there. He probably went home. Back to the place he feels most comfortable: *Genesis 11*."

"That was my fear," Vandemeer replies.

Something steels inside me. I want all of this to be over. I want to touch back down on Earth, hug my moms and pops, and take a hot shower that lasts forever. There's always one more thing around the corner, though. I silently promise myself this is the *last* corner, the *last* thing. We have one more chapter to write, and it ends with Defoe. It was always going to.

This time, Imago soldiers are with us. Former Babel techies and astronauts are boarding, and they're loyal to *us* now. Defoe is outnumbered and wounded and on the run. But all the logic in the world can't clear away the nervous energy knotting in my stomach.

This is Defoe.

A fallen king, his final fight.

"Let's finish what Longwei started," I say. "Let's go find the bastard."

CHAPTER 35

GENESIS 11

Emmett Atwater

We move cautiously through *Genesis 11*. Memories are waiting around every turn. We pass the rooms Kaya and I shared. We walk the same hallways we took every morning to get to breakfast. We pause along the catwalk where I first met Bilal. It all feels like it happened to someone else. Our crew looks determined to finish this game, once and for all.

"We should head to the control center," Vandemeer says. "Defoe would have gone there first." I nod once and let him escort us forward, the same way he has since I first met him. It's an effort to get Morning downstairs, but when I suggest that she head to the med unit, she almost cuts me in two with the look she throws back.

A group of fifteen or so Imago follow us. Greenlaw leads them confidently. Erone trails like a ghost. It's not hard to see how intentional Jacquelyn was in her selection. There's a mix of survivors from every ring coming with us. I walk more confidently with them in tow. It's a reminder that we don't have to face Defoe alone.

Our progress takes us in the direction of the Contact Room. I remember the times Vandy took me down to talk to my parents. The room adjacent to it was always buzzing with techies.

He pauses us in front of the same door now. "The control center."

"It's barricaded," Morning points out. "Look at the frame of the door."

She's right. There should be slight gaps, but someone's clearly sealed it off with nyxia on the other side. My fists tighten instinctually inside my boxing claws. "Defoe?" I ask.

"Whoever they are, they know we're here." Vandemeer nods to the nearest ceiling camera. "Let's find out."

He takes two steps forward and knocks.

I raise an eyebrow. "Seriously? You think he's just going to open up?"

A static *snap* cuts through the air. Our group flinches as the overheads burst with noise.

"Password, please?"

It's a voice we recognize. Morning actually laughs.

"Parvin? I knew you'd make it," she says. "Never a doubt in my mind."

"I hope you brought me someone who knows how to fly the bloody ship!"

Morning thumbs back to the Babel employees Vandemeer recruited.

"We've got pilots. We've got medics. We've got engineers. Take your pick."

The static snap cuts out. It's followed by a gasp as the

door opens, and one of the Remnant survivors pulls away their summoned nyxian barrier. Parvin grins at us.

"I'll take all of them," she says, and wraps Morning in a hug.

The others come piling forward. Noor's grinning from ear to ear. Holly offers a quiet nod, like this was just another day at the office. My eyes move past them, though, to a set of unfamiliar faces. A darker-skinned girl detaches from the others. Her hair is curled and almost golden.

I'm surprised when Anton waves at her. "Ah! My newest friends!"

Parvin gestures. "Everyone, this is Estelle. Their crew was aboard the *Genesis 14.* We found them here in the Contact Room, trying to send an emergency message home. There was some tension at first, but as you can see, we sorted everything out."

Estelle smiles at that before nodding Anton's way. "Sorry about that headlock."

"Oh! A *headlock.*" Anton smirks. "Is that what you call a headlock?"

She rolls her eyes. "You fought dirty."

"I always do," Anton snipes back. "Which reminds me, when all this is over, I'm really interested in hearing the story of how you all broke out of containment."

"Deal."

Something about the exchange puts me on edge. I wish I could laugh or smile or joke, but there's a weight in the pit of my stomach. We know this isn't over yet.

"We're looking for Defoe," I say, and the words snuff out every smile.

Parvin nods. "He came knocking too. We turned him away. All the vital areas of the ship are sealed off. I ran back through the ship's architectural plans just to make sure. Estelle and I agreed to post guards at all the possible entry points just in case. Honestly, though, he looked like hell. I was kind of hoping he'd crawl off somewhere and die."

"It was just him?" I ask.

She nods again. "We debated coming out and finishing him off, but it's Defoe. We figured it was some kind of obvious trap. Our cameras tracked him for a while, but he disabled a string of them in the eastern wing. I'd guess he's down there. Alive or dead, I'm not sure."

"The eastern wing," I repeat. "Vandemeer, do you want to oversee launch prep?"

He shakes his head. "I trust our recruits. They'll oversee things. I'm coming with you."

I nod my respect back to him. It feels right somehow. I always imagined one final showdown with Defoe, but for some reason, I imagined myself fighting him alone. I'm thankful that won't be how it ends. I'll have my family with me. And the Imago too.

"So one team goes after Defoe," Morning says. "Another team stays here to oversee the launch. Everyone needs to keep their eyes open just in case."

At her command, our group shifts and trades places. Greenlaw handpicks ten soldiers to join our detail. I'm half expecting some of our crew to say no to one final exploration. I wouldn't blame them. We've already been through enough to last us a lifetime. But only Isadora crosses into the safety of the control center. I watch as she and Roathy have a long, whispered argument.

The sight of them has me side-eyeing Morning. Her wound is bandaged up, but I know there's no way she can plant her foot or pivot or run. Protective instincts kick in.

"You know, you could always stay . . ."

She glares at me. "Boy, stop talking."

". . . stay with us. You could stay with us. That's all I was saying."

"And I need your permission?" She rolls her eyes. "I'm going."

Eventually, Roathy separates from Isadora and rejoins us. She doesn't look too happy. He keeps his voice low, and I can hear the determination in it.

"After what he did to us, I want to make sure he dies."

He holds out a fist, and I bump it.

"Let's get moving."

About twenty-deep, our group starts down through the bowels of the *Genesis 11*. I'm thinking about how massive I remember the ship being, and how hard it will be to find Defoe, when Morning spies the blood. There's a trail leading us on. The tunnel curves into a wider room that I recognize. I spy the table we sat at between every competition. Where forced friends became brothers and sisters. It's where I first sized up Longwei and argued with Jaime and laughed with Kaya, long before they became my brothers and sisters. Before Babel took each of them from us.

It's where all of this began.

Our footsteps echo.

In the distance, Defoe is waiting.

CHAPTER 36

KINGS AND QUEENS

Emmett Atwater

The debris panels on the landscape windows have been rolled away. It was through these windows that we first found out we were in space. Defoe showed us that famous view of Earth that only so many people in history have ever seen.

Now it offers us a different view.

The destruction of Magness and Glacius. The field of debris has stretched across space. All that red fire has faded, but in its place the cloud of green-black debris has grown. I can make out larger chunks of the moon floating past, but polluted swirls ghost between and around them. There's a defined trail as some of the debris gets dragged back into the planet's atmosphere. One impact might not have mattered, but thousands of them? The continents will get rocked. The tides will make life impossible. The atmosphere will choke. It will all come to an end.

Defoe stands with his back to us. As we walked down,

I kept telling myself not to underestimate him. No matter how weak he looked. No matter how close to death's door. We cross the distance, though, and it's hard to feel any fear. He has one hand pressed to the reinforced glass. It's the only thing that keeps him from collapsing. Blood pools at his feet.

I'm sure that he hears us, but he doesn't turn.

Our group stretches out in a half-moon. We cut off all the possible escape routes. Something in every expression and every stance says this is final. Either he dies or we do. When I glance over at Morning, she nods to me. If it was Requin, she'd be the one to go speak, but Defoe is ours. He guided us through our time on *Genesis 11.* He reserved his darkest sins and his worst lies for *us.*

I walk forward and call his name. "Defoe."

Hand still pressed to the glass, he struggles to glance back. The movement claws at him. He does not look like the king who brought us into space with promises of gold. Sweat runs down his forehead. His eyes are bloodshot with strain. Even the perfect posture is gone.

"Mr. Atwater," he replies. "So we arrive back where we began."

I stop walking about halfway between him and the others. At this angle, he's framed by the unfolding apocalypse. Great shards and poisonous gases and shattered light. It almost looks like it's ready to swallow him whole. But he belongs to us. I point one of my nyxian claws at him.

"Game over. You lost, Defoe."

He looks back out the window and nods. "So we have. I figured my survival would depend on who handled the negotiations. It looks as if I got a fair drawing. Emmett At-water. What do you say? Am I to be a prisoner? Will you show me that surprising mercy?"

"Nah. You don't get to go back to Earth. Journey ends here, man."

I can see in the reflection of the glass that he's smiling. "I thought so. No mercy for the king. If his empire falls, he must fall farther. It is a duty as sacred as crowns and scep-ters and all that."

Silence follows. Our group is watching and waiting. We have the numbers on him. He can't talk his way out of this. It ends in claws and blood, and he knows it.

"You trained us," I tell him. "You made us into weapons. It was your biggest mistake."

At that, Defoe turns. It's a struggle. He has to keep one hand up on the glass for support, but he turns enough to let his eyes trace through the ranks. We are the people he re-cruited. We fought past his lies and his betrayals. We dodged bullets and took down bases. But I don't think any of us will thank him for how sharp and how deadly we've become.

"You all know why you are here," he says, and the words echo back to the beginning. "Or do you? I am not sure you understand our intentions for you. We came here to start a second world. A new civilization guided by new principles. In our best-case scenario, you would have been the pillars of that new world. Our founding fathers, so to speak. Be-trayed or not, we believed you would have eventually said yes. You would have been the Genesis. History makers."

His words grind through me. I can feel my anger grow-ing as he tries to claim the high road in all of this. The more he speaks, the more animated he gets. "Each of you was chosen because you embody some characteristic we wanted in our world. It is not all that you are, but it's the *main* thing that the world sees and experiences in you. We chose you, Emmett, for your *perseverance*."

"Chose me," I repeat. "Then lied to me. Then tried to kill me. More than once."

Defoe ignores that. His eyes move around to the others.

"Jazzy for her poise. Roathy his durability. Katsu's perspective." His voice rises, and I see the same thing I saw in him on that first day: a man trying to play God. "Azima for her curiosity. Morning her leadership. Bilal's kindness. Alex's loyalty. Anton's resourcefulness. Longwei, his determination. Kaya for her—"

"Hey!" I shout. "Keep their names out of your mouth."

Defoe trails off, eyes lingering. I can almost hear the increased heart rates, the sound of tightening fists. We can take pride in who we are without Babel's stamp of approval. It was their invitation that transformed us. We've become more than we could have ever imagined back on Earth, but we have done so in spite of them.

Babel came to us as conquerors, and we've left them in ruins.

"Were we wrong?" he asks. "Look at all of you. Did we not choose proper foundations? Would this group not have been the beginning of a bright new world? The people of Earth would have slowly joined you, and you would have ruled them like kings and queens. We were right."

I shake my head. "Nah. That doesn't work for me either.

You don't get to take credit for *this*. You know what you get credit for? The abandoned marines down on Magnia. The body count on the Tower. You get credit for *those* things. You'll go down in history as the guy who lost his space station to a group of punk kids. But *this*?" I glance around, taking in the faces of my brothers and sisters. "We built this. This is our family, and you don't get to take credit for that."

There's an understanding in his eyes. He knows what happens next.

"It ends here," he says.

"It already ended," I throw back. "We won your game. You made one too many mistakes, Defoe. This is just the part where we cross your name off the scoreboard."

He smiles at that. "Mistakes were made. You're right. I never claimed perfection. But it does seem you're forgetting the first lesson I taught you, Mr. Atwater. You don't have to be perfect. You just have to be better than the other guy. For all your improvement, I am still *stronger*."

Defoe turns fully around to face us. The whole front of his suit is covered in blood. He throws both hands out, and I flinch. A nyxian shield blossoms in front of me. I don't have to look back to know Morning conjured it. I stand there, waiting for something to happen.

A second passes. Another. Defoe's face is clearly straining. His whole body contorts with the effort of what he's doing, but nothing happens. His nyxian suit doesn't transform. None of his normal weapons appear. Could he really be *this* powerless?

I almost allow myself a smile.

And then I see them. Seven massive moon shards approach the window. In all the chaos outside, it was impossible to see a pattern. It all seemed to be drifting at random, but these stones are making an unnatural line for the *Genesis 11*. A trail of green smoke highlights their path.

My eyes go wide. They're not just aimed at the ship. They're heading right for the glass behind Defoe. I realize the hand he kept pressed to the window wasn't for support.

He was summoning them.

"Goodbye, Mr. Atwater," Defoe calls.

"Shields up!" Morning shouts. "Emmett!"

She's one step ahead of me. I watch as her own shield expands and races toward the right wall to seal in that section. It's not hard to see what she wants me to do. Focus, thought, transformation. My own nyxia rises into the air. I shove it forward, careful to attach the edges to Morning's shield first, and then I channel it toward the opposite end of the room.

Behind me, the others are shouting. I can sense other nyxian shields blooming, but I know they won't get to me in time. If that black-green smoke reaches us . . .

All seven shards hit simultaneously.

My shield is still a few meters away from the wall as the reinforced glass shatters. I look up and catch Defoe's final smile. Green smoke clouds around him like an explosion. Defoe doesn't fight it. A pressurized wind whips through the room before dragging him out into space. One of the green-black stones rebounds against the window before trailing him into the void.

The cold hits us first. It snakes through the air and almost steals the breath from my lungs. A second later, my shield reaches the far wall and seals it off. The howling wind dies. Cold still hangs in the air and claws at exposed skin, but not enough to kill us. Green smoke fogs the sealed-off space.

Three stones are lodged into the window. A second stone rebounds away. My eyes widen as I watch the final two come screaming and scraping toward our shields. I raise my hands and try to focus on keeping my shield *strong.* The substance pulses in response.

And the first stone hits my side.

I'm expecting the impact to knock me back a step. It doesn't.

Instead, there's a burst of green dust. A circle forms at the center of my shield. I stare helplessly as the corrupted nyxia branches out from it like the beginnings of a spider-web. It reaches and multiplies and grows like a living thing.

It keeps growing until I hear a familiar noise. That warning *crack* that frozen ice gives just before you're about to plunge below the surface. "It's going to break!"

I whip around and almost run into Azima. She and Katsu stand a step behind me. I watch both of them draw their nyxian bands and rings into the air. There's the usual whisper as their substances transform through the air and layer over my shield. Not a second too soon.

My shield shatters. It falls in a smoking heap, and the corrupted nyxia leaps to the next target. We all watch as it repeats the process on Katsu and Azima's shield. Jacquelyn was right. It's like a virus spreading through the nyxia. "More layers!" I shout. "It has to be thicker!"

I summon my claws into a new form. Jazzy appears at

my side. Morning's joined by Alex, Anton, and Roathy on her end. Weapons and jackets and boots ghost into the air. Every piece of nyxia we can spare forms new layers. It still feels like we're losing. I can see the cloud of green mist getting thicker and stronger. The more nyxia that we add, the faster it seems to spread.

Until the Imago step forward.

They carefully stagger our ranks. One Imago stands between each of us. I can feel my arms shaking with the strain of holding the current shield. Greenlaw takes point for them. As soon as they're in position, there's a surge of energy. The pressure lifts. A strength beyond anything I've ever felt thunders out. My grip of the nyxia slips, but it doesn't feel like I've fumbled anything. Instead, it's like I've dropped into the current of a coursing river. Surprise flickers across the faces of all the gathered Genesis members. We stand in awe as the Imago wrestle control of the struggling wall away from us. And the wall strengthens.

Greenlaw leads them forward. I can see her gloves stretched out, adjusting the manipulation as the virus continues to react. The green mist hunts for an opening, any weakness, but the Imago are too strong. The wall continues its advance, and the Imago advance with it. Step by careful step, they press the corrupting gas back into space. The edges of our shield tighten until they're a perfect fit with the borders of the landscape window Defoe shattered.

Outside, the green smoke clings and claws fruitlessly. With their feet still set and their arms extended, the Imago take a synchronous breath. Their heads tilt as they consider what to do next.

Greenlaw says, "The substance isn't going to leave on its own."

Another Imago replies, "It will search for a weakness. It will cling onto the nyxia until it finds one. If it does find a weakness, it will move forward until it taints everything."

More glances are exchanged. The group of Imago seems to reach an unspoken agreement. One of the younger members steps out of line. "I will go," he says. "Send me."

A voice echoes from behind us. "Stand down."

Shock ripples through the ranks. Erone strides forward. He was supposed to be readying the ship. A familiar shiver runs the length of my spine. I can't help imagining him as he was when we first met. Bound and tortured and reaching for Kaya's necklace. The image comes and goes. He marches forward now with a clear purpose in mind.

"I will go."

I frown. They've said that twice now. Go where?

"There's balance in this," Erone says. "Lose one ship. Save another. Stand down."

He removes an epic-looking sword from his back. With less than a thought, it ghosts through the air and re-forms around him like a dark cloak. He adjusts the collar as he marches toward the shield. I realize he's put on a shroud. Like he's dressing for a funeral . . .

"Tell Jacquelyn who I was at the end."

Morning shouts for someone to stop him, but the gathered Imago part ways as Erone sprints forward. There's no hesitation as he dives headfirst through the gathered shield. We watch him vanish into the cloud of corrupted nyxia. It takes a second for his intentions to become clear.

The substance found no weakness in the wall, no place to latch on and corrupt.

Now it has a new target to chase.

Erone drifts out into space, and the mist unlatches from our barrier. The shift is subtle at first. The floating green cloud slowly transforms into a swirling tail. No one in the room makes a sound. We're all silently counting down the seconds, and we know Erone might already be dead.

But even in death, he shows his strength. We all let out a collective breath when the final green tendril disconnects from the wall. Our group stumbles forward. We form an honor guard and watch solemnly as Erone sacrifices his life for all of us. I pick my way over to Morning's side. She was either too tired or too hurt to keep standing. I drop down to the floor and wrap an arm around her, and the two of us pay our silent respects.

Erone's progress draws a bright line back to Magnia.

For a few more hours, it will be the world that it has always been. Speaker might already be dead, but I try to imagine him surviving that first fight and taking the rest of those loyal Imago soldiers onto the next Babel base. I can almost see him on the prow of some ship, surrounded by other doomed warriors, chasing his enemy until the very end.

It hits me all at once.

All that we've lost. The ghosts that we'll take home with us—Kaya and Speaker and Longwei and all of the rest. Guilt that I'm still alive while thousands of Imago are abandoned below. Relief that there are no more fights waiting around the corner. Morning leans in and kisses me on the cheek.

She laces a hand through mine as the tears come. For a long time, no one says a word.

One of the Imago is the first to move. I've never seen her before. She's young, though, clearly one of the Remnant. We all watch as she approaches the barrier and sets a steady hand against the substance. The entire wall flashes white. The brightness slowly fades to pitch-black. Our view of the planet vanishes. I wonder if maybe it was too much to look down at the end of their world. Maybe they couldn't stand the sight any longer.

But then the colors flash back to life. We watch as thousands of brushstrokes appear, coloring the wall in less than a minute. On the far-right side, both of the shattered moons. An image of Erone appears as a distant and glowing streak in the middle. The painting captures Magnia too, in all its flawless mystery. When the painting finishes, the Imago turns around.

"So we always remember. Our world as it once was."

Greenlaw steps forward and makes it a rallying cry.

"Now we set our eyes on a new world," she says. "Who will come with me?"

PART IV

HOMEWARD

CHAPTER 37

THE NEW RING

Morning Rodriguez

A single day passes.

I sleep without a hand resting on one of my hatchets. I eat food without thinking about how it will sit in my stomach if I'm chased through a forest. Emmett and I hold hands—not because the world is about to end or we are about to die, but just because we want to. Our crew comes and goes at the breakfast table. Bilal has people playing cards. Katsu tells jokes like . . . well, like Katsu.

For twenty-four hours, the world lets us pretend to be normal people.

But on the second day, I wake up and I am asked to be the captain again. Representatives are chosen from all the respective parties. Parvin could have gone on our behalf, but she was kind enough to ask me to join her as a cocaptain. *Genesis 11* chooses Emmett. Greenlaw takes her place on behalf of the Remnant. We surprise Vandemeer by asking him to represent the converted Babel squads. Finally, Estelle joins us from *Genesis 14.*

The six of us gather in the main hallway and head toward the private quarters of Marcus Defoe. It's like stepping into a library. A central desk surrounded by polished bookshelves. I try not to feel the ghost of Defoe in the room as we gather enough chairs to sit around the desk together.

The Contact Room we used was designed for communication home. Our techies are working to reestablish those channels, but until then they point us to a better alternative. Defoe's office has a direct link to the other ships. We watch a console unfold from the floor. Vid screens fill with camera angles and surveillance shots. They spin briefly to life before being replaced with an outbound call.

Jacquelyn Requin appears on the screen. She already knows about what happened to Erone, and it shows. I've never seen her look more burdened, and still she marches on to complete the necessary tasks for her people. It's the thousandth mark of courage and bravery and persistence I've counted in her favor. In my mind, she's what a true hero should be.

Our angle zooms out, and we catch a glimpse of another interior office. Jacquelyn is flanked by other representatives. I count one from every ring of Sevenset. Beckway stands in for the Seventh. The woman representing the Sixth looks familiar, but the others are random Imago faces. The fortunate souls who were chosen by the lottery to launch into space.

Gio's there too. It's sad to think that the lone survivor of the *Genesis 13* is present only to represent himself. Still, he sits straight-backed and nods his respect when he sees us.

Once everyone is settled in, Jacquelyn begins.

"None of us wants to dwell on what has happened," she says. "So I will try to make this as efficient as possible. I've arranged a series of necessary items for our agenda. I hope you'll pardon any insensitivity. I want to take a functional approach to all of this. It is best to set emotions briefly aside as we make decisions on what happens next. Agreed?"

Our crew nods in return.

"First item of business: prisoners."

A ragged sigh escapes me. Emmett sets a steadying hand on my leg like he gets it. We all just want this to be over. Jacquelyn patiently brings up the names and faces of every surviving Babel member. These are the marines who were wise enough to set down their weapons, and lucky enough to avoid the Imago onslaught at the end.

The whole goal is to prioritize prisoners. A ranking system of sorts. Our ships might be fully loaded, but the ration supplies weren't meant to sustain so many extra bodies. We didn't really think about that when we boarded. Jacquelyn's ship has almost all the prisoners. As we run through the list, Vandemeer is the most vocal participant. He flags a particularly cruel commander, but he also points out a captain who kept his battalion out of the fighting at the end.

Of the forty-four survivors, we only recognize two: the Ganders.

Emmett sits up straighter when Kit's face appears on the screen.

"Kit. He helped us launch into space. He didn't want to go back to Babel in the end. His dad forced him to do it. Greenlaw can confirm that."

She does. "I would not be here without him. The two of them guessed incorrectly at the end. I believe the father was trying to save the son. He thought Babel was his best chance."

Jacquelyn nods before marking their files. It takes a little while longer to grind through the rest of the names. It turns my stomach to see some of the faces smiling back at us. How close did some of them come to killing us? For no other reason than that was what they were ordered to do.

"Next order of business: the *Genesis 12*."

She reminds us that the ship was released into space by Erone when he was under Defoe's control. Everyone agrees that Erone will be honored, not demonized. Jacquelyn takes great care to explain his role from the beginning. The purpose of why he was captured. The brief and crucial time in which he held control of the station. There's no argument about it from us. We all saw who Erone was at the end. Both of our crews searched every nook and cranny of our ships. We looked for traces of the corrupted nyxia, and the only reason those sweeps came back clean is that Erone sacrificed his life for ours. Everyone on our ship has visited the mural by now. He ended his story a hero.

"We sent several messages," Jacquelyn reminds us. "And received no initial response. As you know, the survivors were all from the Third Ring. None of them knew how to work the tech. We were worried they were lost. Until we received an urgent signal just an hour ago."

Our entire table sits up straighter.

Jacquelyn smiles. "Apparently one of Babel's technicians

was performing standard maintenance on the ship when it was separated from the Station." She glances down at her notes. "A woman by the name of Lilja Gudmundsson. She figured out the ship had been detached and made contact with the Imago, and the ship has been in communication with us all morning!"

There's a small roar from our crew. We need all the good news we can get.

"It'll take time and effort," Jacquelyn says. "Our pilots are trying to simplify all the systems so that she can lead the Imago in navigating home. Nothing is certain, but we think they'll make it to Earth after all. Our people needed this news."

A little more celebration breaks out as Jacquelyn tries to transition us to the next topic. I can see our crew getting a little restless. All of this is necessary, but it's hard not to feel like we're walking through the bone-deep bruises of our years-long battle with Babel.

We touch briefly on the *Genesis 14*. After Jacquelyn gave the order, Imago soldiers disabled the air lock connecting it with the Tower. Our crews immediately boarded *Genesis 11* and *Genesis 13*. Reports indicate that a small contingent of Babel soldiers had cut a path through to the *Genesis 14* before we disconnected the ship. So there are Babel survivors out there, but they boarded the one ship that didn't get refueled. All of them will die out in space.

"And now we'll discuss the Imago count. . . ."

Jacquelyn starts through with the numbers from every ring. We already know that the Second had no survivors, and that Defoe floated the members of the Third. But hearing the numbers is still devastating. Space—and all the corrupted nyxia—was unkind to the other rings.

"Forty-six survivors from the First. Zero survivors from the Second. Eighteen survivors from the Third. Fifty-four survivors from the Fourth. Fourteen survivors from the Fifth. Thirty-six survivors from the Sixth. Thirty-eight survivors from the Seventh. Two hundred and six in total." She pauses meaningfully. "Out of a possible four hundred and fifty."

"The Remnant account for eighteen more survivors," Greenlaw adds. "But I would like to take a moment now to make a change. We are leaving Sevenset behind. It is vital to remove the boundaries that exist between us. We are going to a new world. Our people will be seen by that world as one inseparable unit. If we are to survive and thrive, we must embrace the idea of being one people with one common goal."

Jacquelyn considers that. "What did you have in mind?"

"A shared title," Greenlaw explains. "It is something we established among ourselves in the Remnant just a few weeks after we learned why we had been chosen. When Feoria informed us of the plan to reach across the universe and survive as a species. It didn't matter then that I was from the Third Ring or that Bally was from the Fifth. What mattered was where we were going.

"I would establish a new title for all remaining Imago. I would ask them to leave behind their old titles and instead introduce themselves in a new way. We will call ourselves the New Ring."

Jacquelyn looks up and down the rows gathered. "All in favor?"

I smile a little seeing the representative of the First Ring hesitate, but the others don't have a problem with it. Their hands rise, and it's clear that this is the first vote in favor of their new queen, the first step into an entirely new world. The Imago from the First lifts his hand after a few seconds and the matter is settled.

"It is also my duty," Greenlaw continues, "to read the seal that was given me by our two queens: Ashling and Feoria. It was one of the last official duties they took upon themselves. As I read, I would ask you to weigh the words of the two women who sacrificed themselves on our behalf. One represented Magness, the other Glacius. It was their final duty to appoint me as the Imago leader in the world to come. Let us not take their final command lightly."

I lean back now as the negotiations begin. I let my hand settle on Emmett's, and we exchange a smile. There is still more to discuss and decide and debate, but for now I'll allow myself the brief satisfaction of knowing the current responsibilities belong to someone else.

A few hours later, the meeting finally adjourns.

Emmett grins at me. "Come on. I've got a surprise for you."

I have conquered empires and battled beside queens, but his words have my stomach doing backflips. I grin back as he leads me through the halls of the ship.

"Surprises. How do you know I even *like* surprises?"

He smiles wider. "You'll like this one."

This boy. He laces his fingers through mine and I let

myself be that girl for just a few minutes. I dismiss the thoughts and questions about home. What happens there? Who are we now? How do ever go back to normal? Instead, I focus on that bottom lip and the way his hand fits mine and the quiet confidence I've admired in him since day one.

He leads us inside the command center. Parvin's there monitoring operations. She gives us a little wave before leaning back over her console. Emmett heads into the Contact Room. When I raise an eyebrow, he guides me into a comfortable chair, then pulls over his own.

We both stare at a blank screen.

"This your idea of taking me to the movies?" I finally ask. "You promised popcorn."

He smiles. "Something like that."

It takes a few seconds for the screen to load. Our earthbound communications have been offline—and everyone's been asking about when they can call home—so it's a surprise to see two people appear on the screen. A woman sits on the left. She has a quick smile. Her eyes shine with pride. The man next to her looks so much like Emmett that it steals my breath away.

"So, Morning, these are my roommates: Jeremiah and Hope."

I can feel the blush creeping up my neck. If they weren't watching so closely, I'd smack him upside the head for not giving me any warning that I'd be talking to his parents.

His dad laughs. "Roommates? Boy makes a few checks and thinks he's the landlord."

"And you know better than to call me that," his mom says. "I am your mother, child."

Emmett just grins. "All right, Moms and Pops. This is Morning."

I manage to smile, awkwardly. A very, very awkward smile.

"Not much of a talker," Mr. Atwater points out.

"Lord, he didn't tell you, did he?"

I respond with a tight shake of the head. "He said it was a surprise."

His mom rounds on his dad. Each word she speaks is punctuated with a smack to the shoulder. "Always. With. The. Surprises. Never. Asking. Nobody!"

I can't help laughing when he uses his hat as a shield. "Why you hitting me? I didn't even do anything. It was Emmett!"

"And I wonder where he got that idea from?" She gives up her attack and looks back. "Morning, it is a pleasure. Lovely to meet you. We've heard so much about you."

"We have?" Mr. Atwater asks. "When?"

Emmett buries his head in his hands. "Y'all are killing me right now."

"I'm just saying," Mr. Atwater goes on. "Haven't seen you in a second. I'm trying to figure out when your mother had all these backdoor communications about your dating life. . . ."

She throws him a look that cuts him off midsentence. I smile a little wider, because that's a look I've got in my arsenal too. "It's nice to meet you. Emmett told me about you both. He said he's bringing me up to Detroit for burgers. Told me to watch out for Uncle Larry too."

Mrs. Atwater bursts into laughter. His dad just shakes his

head. "How you going to do Uncle Larry like that, Emmett? He's not that bad."

"Not that bad?" Emmett's eyebrows hit the roof. "Okay. Next time we have a house party I better see you fielding his conversation about crickets or whatever."

Mrs. Atwater doubles over with laughter again. "I forgot about the crickets!"

"It's not right." Mr. Atwater shakes his head again, and it's clear he's searching for a new topic. I feel like I'm smiling so much my face is going to break. "So how'd you two meet?"

Emmett smiles over at me. "I played her the right song."

"And then you tackled me off of a ship," I remind him.

"Tackled her?" Mrs. Atwater almost explodes. "My son?"

"Hey, hey, hey!" Emmett cuts back in. "Context. You need the context. We were in a competition. And let me explain that she had beaten me like fifty times before that."

Mr. Atwater perks up. "Fifty? Oh. I like this girl."

Emmett's mom rolls her eyes at that, and I almost bust out laughing again. I glance over at Emmett, and it's not hard to see how much joy is on his face. He's proud to be introducing me. He's excited to see his parents again. They take a few minutes to fuss and laugh and beam at each other.

I want it all to last forever. Maybe it will. Emmett and I haven't talked too much about what happens when we get home. We've been too busy enjoying the here and now. But we did come to the pleasant realization that long-distance relationships are a lot easier when you've just earned out a contract for millions of dollars. I just gotta get used to flying, I guess. If I can fight off an army of marines for him, putting up with the lack of legroom in coach probably won't be half as bad.

For a while, Emmett asks questions about home. It doesn't take long, though, for his parents to move the conversation back to us. His dad asks the question that all our families are eventually going to ask. "It's been five minutes," he says. "And we haven't heard *anything* about this foreign planet. We have about a million questions. How did it all go? Was the mission a success?"

Of course, they don't know anything. They've received payments. Babel's updated them here and there. But for the most part, no one on Earth has any idea that we just survived an apocalypse, overthrew an empire, any of it. Emmett and I both exchange a meaningful glance. He turns back.

"Well, it's a long story. . . ."

CHAPTER 38

PREPARATION

Morning Rodriguez

A few weeks pass.

The ship finds its rhythm. It is a fine thing to wake up some mornings, toss around in bed, and curl back into sleep. There are no competitions waiting for us. No scoreboards. No fights. No coming apocalypses. Most days there's a good book to be read. Coffee or tea. Laughing with Emmett until my sides hurt. It's like relearning the one language Babel stole from us.

Today's responsibilities have me all over the ship, though. As much as we want to kick our feet up and retire to the first beach we can find back home, there is still a need for preparation. Vandemeer's crew has done most of the heavy lifting, but our group of survivors wanted to be involved in all the strategic planning. We're done letting other people tell us what to do.

I turn a corner and find myself staring into a familiar classroom. It's the *Genesis 11* version of it, but I spent weeks at a matching desk, learning as much as I could about a new planet. Now the room is full of Imago. And we're slowly teaching them about our world. I roll my eyes when I see who today's instructor is.

"And it turns out that Harry Potter is a wizard," Katsu is saying. "And he's grown up the entire time with the Dursleys thinking that he's just stuck with this punk family. . . ."

Up front, Bally raises his hand. "So what happens next? This Haggard guy found him?"

"All right, so our story picks up where it left off. Harry climbs aboard the motorcycle. . . ."

I stand there at the back and try to resist the temptation to interrupt. We rotate instructors every day. Parvin teaches them all about history. She's got a knack for it really. I could see her being a professor someday. Emmett surprised me by teaching a lesson on race relations in America. Boy is as smart as he is good-looking. It's not really fair. Bilal and Jazzy did a few combo lessons on cuisine.

The Imago put in requests at the end of the week for topics they want to know more about, and our group does their best to assign the right person for each one. Slowly, they're learning enough about our planet to feel more comfortable about the idea of starting a new life there. I think like anyone who's escaped one land and arrived in another, it'll be all about figuring out how to adapt to the new environment while holding on to the heritage they learned in another galaxy.

"So to get into the place," Katsu says, "they had to ram their cart right into the wall."

"Katsu!" I shout from the back. "Any chance you're going

to get to your assigned topic today? You're supposed to be covering a general lecture on sports."

He thinks for a second. "Quidditch is a sport!"

I roll my eyes again. "Come on, Katsu."

One of the younger Imago comes to his defense. "He's such a good storyteller, though! We're really enjoying this one. Katsu has so much imagination. To think that he is making up this story as he goes along . . ." She shakes her head. "Our storytellers could learn from him."

I scowl at Katsu. "Making it up as you go along? You didn't tell them about J. K. Rowling?"

He at least has the good grace to blush. "So . . . who wants to talk about soccer?"

Laughing, I duck back out of the room. I don't want to miss the interviews. I find myself laughing more and more as I walk, though, picturing a whole generation of Imago who think Katsu is the author of the Harry Potter series. I backtrack through the ship and make my way to the Contact Room. The main communication center is more packed with people than I've ever seen it. We're all hands on deck today for what might be one of the most important first steps. We debated the process for weeks. How do we tell the world what happened to us?

There are mountains of evidence on our side. Vandemeer and the techies have been working to put together as much video footage as possible. We've compiled testimonies from every survivor that walk a clear line through Babel's treachery. Parvin even spent a few days researching maritime salvage laws. We're as prepared as possible to make our case to the world, but it starts with a handshake, and all of us know that's the part that has to go right before everything else falls in place.

Vandemeer pulled a few strings to connect us with one of Babel's most remote contact centers in the United States. He arranged the call to Emmett's parents first, and Parvin soundly scolded him for it. Everything since then has been more strategic and cautious. It took almost a week to get in touch with a reporter on Earth who we could trust.

And today is the day we tell our story.

Greenlaw's hovering at the entrance to the Contact Room. She's wearing a very traditional Imago outfit. She might be young, but she looks fierce enough to conquer empires. I take the spot beside her, and we both watch as Vandemeer finishes his interview.

"When I realized how the company was treating their teenage employees—people who I had promised to protect—I made the decision to intervene. I started undermining operations and was eventually discovered." He holds up the hand that has a few missing fingers for the camera. "Babel tortured me for information. But what happened to me? It's nothing compared to what Babel was planning for these children. The truth *has* to come out."

As the reporter asks another question, I nudge Greenlaw's shoulder. "Ready?"

She nods once. "It will be watched by your people?"

"Billions of them," I confirm. "It's the first interview with an alien species."

"Do you think they will like us?"

It's a hard question. Humanity is so impossible to predict. But we've been careful to curate the *right* story. We picked out seven different people for the interviews. Jazzy and Bilal from *Genesis 11,* Alex and Parvin from *Genesis 12.* Vandemeer volunteered, and the other two were crew members that had worked with Babel for decades. We didn't even have to really sell the story. All we're doing is figuring out which pieces of it put the brightest light on Babel's corruption. And we're hoping the Imago become fan favorites in the process. We need the rest of the world to see you the way we do: desperate partners hoping to survive extinction.

"Our world likes underdogs," I say.

Greenlaw takes a deep breath. "Let us hope so."

Vandemeer is done. Techies flutter around the room. It takes them a minute to reset everything before waving Greenlaw inside. She takes her seat, adjusts her posture, and I know that I'm looking at a queen. Anyone else might fail, but she's going to lead their people into what might be the strangest time in their history, and she will lead them well.

The interview begins.

"So I'm here with the representative queen of the Imago people. You heard that right. For the first time in history, we are going to broadcast a direct dialogue with an alien species. This is the moment that has—for so many centuries— captured our imaginations. Every flight to the moon. Every mission to Mars. Our people have listened and searched and waited. Finally, there's a voice talking back to us. It is my great honor to take this massive step into the future with you.

"Greenlaw. First, let me express my sympathy on behalf of everyone on Earth for what has happened to your world.

It is unimaginable. Our hearts and thoughts go out to your people. Clearly, though, you have made the first necessary step toward survival. You're heading to Earth as we speak. If you could tell our people one thing about the Imago, what would it be?"

Greenlaw sits a little taller in her seat. I'm worried for just a second that maybe the spotlight is too bright, that maybe her age will finally show. And then she begins.

"We are—first and foremost—survivors. I would tell you that two hundred of our people are coming to your world, and each one of them has counted the cost. There are names and faces that we will never forget. How many died so that we might live? Every breath we take is a gift. Every new sunrise is the same. So I would tell you that we are not walking into your world alone. We will always be a people who remember. And because we remember those who came before us, we have the confidence to stride into whatever future awaits."

I can't help smiling.

I have a feeling Earth is going to *love* this queen.

CHAPTER 39

BOUNTY

———————

Anton Stepanov

It feels like Christmas in July. Or out in space. Whatever.

I can't help grinning as the entire Genesis team starts to gather at our appointed time and location. I've had this surprise in mind ever since we successfully boarded the *Genesis 11*. It wasn't exactly easy to find time for proper celebration, what with all the dying, but I feel like a few weeks into our journey home provided plenty of time for mourning. These ghosts will never fully leave us. It's time to take a step forward, into a brighter and better world.

Alex walked down with me. Being back at his side is its own reward. If all I got out of this was a trip to Bogotá and a lifetime of feeling this honest comfort, it would have been worth it. But why take just icing when you can have the cake too?

Azima's the first to show. She drags Jazzy along with her and throws a huge smile in our direction. "Quick," she says.

"Before everyone gets here. Tell us what's going on. I love being in on the secret. It's more fun that way!"

I smirk at her. "You have to wait like everyone else."

She rolls her eyes as another group rounds the corner. Parvin, Noor, and Holly come strolling in together. The three of them have tried to stay busy. It's a different way to handle grief. Busy hands to distract themselves from all the memories and loss.

Bilal and Roathy turn the corner next, Isadora following a step behind. She's getting closer to her due date, and we're all starting to make bets on when it will happen. Emmett and Morning come in on their heels. Our fearless captains have spent the last few days playing together like a couple of kids, and they deserve that much after all they've done for us.

It's hard to fight away the reminders of people who *won't* be coming around the corner. Ida and Longwei. Omar and Jaime. Loche and Brett. I never met Kaya, but each of their names feels like a wound that's having trouble healing. Even losing one of them would have been far too high a cost.

The last person to arrive is Katsu. He comes yawning into the room.

"Where are your shoes, man?" Emmett asks.

He looks down at mismatched socks. "Does this mandatory field trip require shoes?"

I shrug. "I suppose not. And it isn't mandatory. But the group had a discussion, and everyone agreed if we left you out, you'd spend the rest of the journey complaining about it."

Katsu nods at that. "Probably true."

"All right," I say. "Follow the leader, little ducklings."

I start marching them down. Only Alex knows where we're heading. I got bored and showed it to him a few days before. He agreed that the rest of the crew should know. A few discussions need to happen, but that's not why I'm taking them down. I just want to celebrate. I want us all to enjoy a taste of why we came in the first place. The whole group buzzes with questions.

"Anton, are you taking us to see your stamp collection?" Katsu calls.

Noor laughs at that. "We all know Anton would collect knives."

"Or skulls!" I call back. "Nothing like a good skull!"

Alex shakes his head, a little smile playing over his lips. Some of the other crew members actually groan. "There better not be skulls," Noor says. "Why do you have to make it so creepy?"

We turn another corner. I swipe a borrowed identification card. It takes us into a transition room. I wait for everyone to funnel inside before swiping again. The room activates. Air brushes in from all sides, sweeping in as a cleansing agent. Everyone perks up.

"All right." I clap both hands together. "As you all know, we had a small agreement with Babel. I dare say that they violated a few clauses. But now that we have stolen their ships and removed their tyrannical leaders and have started our journey home like proper space pirates, I thought it was more than past time to count up our bounty."

Azima leans forward. "Bounty? What bounty?"

"Glad you asked," I say, crossing the room. "It's not really enough for Babel to honor their contracts. And we're really not even sure they'll do that. In fact, I have a sneaking suspicion their stock is about to fall drastically in our world. Hard to balance accounts when you lose a planet, I suppose. Given their precarious situation, I think it makes sense to start our own venture."

I pause for effect. Alex smacks my shoulder. "Come on, man! Just show them already!"

Reaching out, I swipe my card on the opposite door. I turn back and can't help grinning wildly at the people who have become my friends, my family. "We dreamed about going home like kings and queens. I won't point out that you *rudely* had that fun discussion without me back at Foundry. But I'd like to propose having it again. Especially now that all of this belongs to us."

The doors open. The lights inside flicker on, and the crew gets their first view of Babel's supply bay. It took some digging, but I figured out our entire haul had been stored aboard the *Genesis 11*. It was an afterthought then. I was more focused on survival, but even in desperate times, it doesn't hurt to remember where you buried the gold.

The whole crew slides forward like bandits into a vault. There are a few gasps. I know they climbed to the top of the silo to get a look at it the first time, but they could only see the first layer. Here it's kept in stack upon beautiful stack. Billions of dollars. And it all belongs to us.

I watch them, and it's almost like a movie. The kids who stumble on the hidden treasure and aren't really sure what to do with all of it. I like to think we're smarter than the kids in those movies, though. I think all of us have a pretty good idea of what we would do.

What we *will* do.

"Hey, Emmett," I call out. "Remind me, who drilled down into the ground for this?"

He smiles. "We did."

"Yeah? And, Azima, who built those conveyor shafts to get it out?"

She looks delighted by the game. "I'm pretty sure that was us."

"Noor. Any chance you know who manipulated each and every one of these nyxian pieces into these pristine bars so they could sit in these pristine rows?"

She laughs. "If I'm not mistaken, that was us too."

I pause long enough to make eye contact with each of them.

"We dug down into the earth. We built the shafts. We worked the drills. We did this. Our hands in the ground. Our lives on the line. I'd say that all of this belongs to us."

There's a roar from our group. The excitement builds and echoes. We're not the same desperate kids we were at the beginning, back when our payday depended on the good faith of crooks. We control our fate now. We captain this ship.

And we decide what happens next.

"Hey, Anton," Emmett calls. "You never got to say what you'd do with your money."

I smile wide and shrug. "I could use a few more knives."

CHAPTER 40

FAMILY

Emmett Atwater

We start using all the words we were afraid to use.

Home.

Family.

Freedom.

Victory.

It takes time to feel comfortable with the way they sound on our lips. I have a hard time convincing myself most days that all of this is really over, or that it ever happened in the first place. It's not hard to figure out that—when we do get back home—no one will really understand. We'll tell our story to everyone. The truth will bury Babel, finally and fully. But we have scars that the rest of the world won't see. Scars that can only be understood by the people whose ghosts have the same names as ours. We are bound in ways even we can't begin to explain.

We will return to our corners of Earth. But now I have a home in Palestine. I have a flat in Bogotá and a farm in

Russia. I can catch a flight to Memphis or Nairobi or San Jose. There are homes waiting for me in all those places. Brothers and sisters who will open their doors and give me a place to rest if I need it. We will never be strangers, because we have shared more than even blood can boast.

I start spending more time at meals. Instead of ducking back into my room, the way I would have in the beginning, I linger and talk with whoever is there. Most nights some of the Remnant join us. The first seeds of friendship that will carry over into the new world. On other nights, it's just the Genesis crew, and I find myself wanting to learn everything I can about this forever family. A small part of me knows I'm trying to make up for the things I never asked Longwei or Jaime or Kaya.

Someone stole chairs from one of the comfort pods and brought them over to where the Imago mural decorates the wall. Dinner finishes, and tonight, Bilal decides to make tea. He summons the stragglers—myself and Morning and Anton—over to the stolen chairs. Smiling, he shoves steaming mugs into our waiting hands. We all sit, sipping our drinks, quietly honoring the dead. Anton sets down his tea. It clatters, and I realize he already drank the whole cup.

He nods to Bilal. "Not half-bad."

Bilal stares over. "You finished it?"

"What?" Anton frowns. "It's a compliment."

I'm still blowing on mine to try and cool it down.

Morning laughs. "Where's Alex tonight?"

"Down in the Rabbit Room. Wants to stay in shape."

Morning nods. "He's not the only one. Jazzy's been going regularly. So has Noor."

Our group has grown restless, and I get it. We launched into space and it's been bang-bang ever since. I can't remember a twenty-four-hour stretch that wasn't laced with adrenaline. Some of the others can't handle that quiet. Organized runs in the Rabbit Room. A regular soccer match started by Alex. Even Noor's successful commandeering of all the baking equipment in the kitchen.

Anything to stay busy. The one place I haven't seen anyone go is the pit.

"Surprised he doesn't drag you down there," Morning is saying.

Anton grins and taps his temple. "I'm staying fit up here. Breaking a mental sweat."

Footsteps sound behind us. My eyes rest on Morning, the way she reaches instinctively for the hatchets that aren't hanging at her hip. It took me a few days to convince her not to wear them, that we were safe. I wonder if we'll ever hear footsteps behind us and feel safe again.

I turn to see Roathy and Isadora making their way to us. She's deep into her third trimester now. The baby will be born in space. When someone pointed that out to Isadora, she lifted a single eyebrow and said, "Good. She'll always have a fun fact to share on the first day of school."

I smile in greeting at the two of them. "You come for Bilal's famous tea?"

"No," Roathy replies bluntly. Isadora actually elbows him, and he realizes how it must have sounded. He nods apologetically to Bilal. "I'm sure it's fine. We came for you, Emmett."

Once those words would have sent a chill down my spine. Now I'm just curious.

"Look, I told you before," I say. "I'm not delivering the baby."

Roathy grins. "I was just kidding about that."

Isadora shakes her head. "You are such *boys*. We came to say thank you. It has been hard to swallow my pride and admit my mistake. I treated you horribly, and yet you're the one who spared Roathy. And you're also the one who brought him back to me. We've spent the last few days trying to figure out how to say we're sorry, how to thank you for what you've done."

I shrug, a little embarrassed. "You don't owe me a thing."

"That's where we disagree," she says firmly. "And there is very little we can give you that you don't already have. What do you think of the name Emmanuelle?"

I stare back at her. "I mean. It's a pretty name I guess?"

Morning laughs. "You are *such* a boy. Think. Emmanuelle. Does that sound familiar to you at all? Like—I don't know—maybe the name Emmett?"

"Oh." And then my eyes bug wide. "Wait? You serious?"

Isadora shrugs. "It's a good name. Ida Emmanuelle."

Roathy throws me the biggest smile I've ever seen from him. Morning actually has to reach out and shake me by the shoulder to loosen a response from my slack lips.

"It's perfect. Means the world to me."

There's a satisfaction on Isadora's face. It's like a final debt has been paid. Roathy nods, and the two of them set back off through the nearest hallway. I hear Isadora say something about a foot rub as they go. Morning sets a hand on mine. I turn back to the others, still stunned.

"Those two almost killed me. Several times."

"And now they're naming a kid after you," Morning says.

I grin. "Little Em. Can't tell me nothing now."

She laughs at that. "All right. Bedtime for me." I watch as she sets her half-empty cup on the floor before standing. She leans down low enough to kiss my forehead, whispering as she does. "Feel free to come tuck me in." And then to the others. "Good night, boys."

Anton shoves to his feet. "Tea has me buzzing. I'm going to go find Alex."

Bilal and I both nod to him. We settle back into our chairs, and it's just the two of us. Time stretches back and spins my memory to the beginning. I stood up on the catwalks above and looked down. There was a table full of competitors waiting. I remember sizing them up and thinking through strategies. I came into all of this with clenched fists and so much hunger.

Hunger to prove myself. Hunger to be the best. Hunger to go home a king.

Those things came true, but not in the way I imagined they would. I did prove myself, but as a brother and a teammate and a survivor. *Best* wasn't a label I ever earned, but it's one I could use for *us* now, this unbreakable family. And I will go home a king, just not the kind of king Babel wanted. Bilal was there on that first day. He introduced himself on that catwalk. His kindness forged a permanent path into the heart of the cutthroat competitor I wanted to be. Looking back on all of it, I realize that version of me never stood a chance.

I glance over. "What you thinking about, man?"

"I was thinking about Longwei."

I haven't said his name out loud. Not since he died. We never got the chance to talk to him about what happened. He went chasing after Defoe, and the next time I saw him was in space. There's no way to count how much he sacrificed or gave us. No way to know what he did to sway the tides. I only have the sight of him striking Defoe at the exact right moment, and that last glimpse of him diving on top of a grenade to save us.

"He asked me to teach him," I say. "He wanted me to teach him how to be good."

Bilal smiles. "He was good. It took time, but he showed us how good of a heart he had. I wasn't thinking about that, though. I was thinking—and it almost feels disrespectful—but I was thinking about how satisfied he must have been at the end."

I frown. "Satisfied?"

"Think about it. He finished first."

Bilal's smile stretches into a laugh, and I can't help grinning. He starts to laugh even louder, and it's contagious. The two of us crack up so much that I spill tea down one sleeve. It feels so good to laugh, so good to remember the lost as people, not as symbols.

He recovers enough to say, "He won, and I will never forget him for it. Maybe you understand more than the others. I was so *close*. I was prepared to die, if it meant saving any of you. And now it's even harder, I think, knowing that he beat me by less than a second. I was *right* there, Emmett. I watched it all happen. Now it's like Longwei is walking around inside my head. I can't—I can't tell if that's a bad thing?"

I smile and nod. "Kaya's still walking around mine. Every now and again she'll tell me something. I'll hear it in her voice and everything. She has all these clever strategies and her instincts are always right. I don't think it's a bad thing because I don't want to forget her. I don't want to forget Jaime, or Speaker, or Longwei. I'm going to keep them with me for as long as I can."

He nods decisively at that and raises his cup for a toast.

"To not forgetting."

I tilt mine to his.

"To not forgetting."

CHAPTER 41

EARTH

───────────

Emmett Atwater

It still takes us months to get home, but they are months I will cherish for the rest of my life. We find slices of heaven in a place that tried to drag us through hell. In honor of Pops, I organize the first intergalactic football game. We keep it to two-hand touch, because three plays in we figure out the Imago know how to truck stick with the best of them. The last thing we need is for someone to survive the apocalypse only to get taken out in a game of pickup football. In the least surprising news ever, Morning can apparently run routes like Odell Beckham III.

Alex and Anton start planning our future family reunion, and the discussion about the location gets as heated as an Olympics committee. Katsu insists that we already agreed to a sexy party in the middle of the ocean. Noor insists that she's not attending *any* party that Katsu calls sexy. Eventually we narrow it down to Nairobi and Dublin. Holly's argument centers around a list of pubs longer than most grocery lists. Azima counters with coffee, hookah, and lions.

Dublin wins by a vote.

About a week later, Vandemeer helps deliver Isadora's baby. Ida Emmanuelle becomes the brightest, most hopeful light aboard the ship. We spend most of that week referring to each other as Uncle Emmett and Aunt Jazzy and the God-father (Anton, of course).

Greenlaw offers to perform the Imago ritual that will implant a pattern of nyxia in the baby's skin. We're all sur-prised when Isadora decides to accept. She gestures to the tattoo on the back of her neck: the familiar eight with its crooked crown. "Can you make it look like this?"

Greenlaw smiles. "I can certainly try."

That raises a few curious eyebrows. Thankfully we can always count on Azima to ask the questions we're too shy to ask. "Why an eight? I've been trying to figure it out since we boarded."

Isadora smiles. "It's not an eight. It's an infinity symbol. I got it when I was thirteen. It was a promise I made to my-self, because the world promised me nothing. I was given no options. I was offered no way forward. The tattoo was a re-minder that infinite possibilities were waiting for me, even if most days that felt untrue. For little Ida, it will be true. It will not be something she has to imagine."

The words sound like prophecy. I know that's why I came in the first place. Not just to change my life, but to change future generations. I wanted a world where the last name Atwater could mean whatever we wanted it to mean. Pops told me to break the chains.

I did, and then some.

It feels good to walk headfirst into all those possibilities. This whole time, the Imago and Babel have referred to us by the name Genesis. And for the first time I feel like the shoe really fits.

The final day arrives.

It starts like most days. My arms around Morning. The strange sensation of having slept without fear. Slipping out of the room noiselessly and bringing back a coffee for her. The way she sits up in bed and smiles over the rim of her mug, a smile that is as much mine as it is hers. I smile back and try to figure out how to make all of this last forever. I take a warm shower. She sits in bed and flips through a few of her favorite poetry books.

And then the day diverges from the rest.

Morning eyes herself in the mirror briefly before nodding. "Ready?"

We march down together. Back in our original suits. We've taken time on the way home, though, to carefully alter each one. The Babel insignias on the upper arms and chest have been removed. Babel will not share the glory of this day with us.

Downstairs, the Genesis crews are gathered. So are the Remnant. Greenlaw has the Imago dressed in their finest, standing in proper formation. I note their matching necklaces. The same Imago artist who created the mural came up with them. It's a thin plate of nyxia dangling from an even thinner chain. Every few seconds, the emblem etched on the material changes. She explained that they'll cycle through for months, flashing the name of every Imago left behind on Magnia. It's an astonishing tribute.

Our massive mess hall has two landscape windows. One shows the mural. There is already an agreement to preserve the painting. It will be a good starting point for any history lesson we would teach on their people. The other landscape window is empty, though. Morning and I march through the gathered ranks and take our places. The debris panels are still down, so we're left staring at a blank wall. Morning steps out in front of the group and turns a smile our way.

"I thought this is something we should witness together," she begins. "For the Imago, this is a new beginning. One that has come at a great cost. We know you are the reason we could safely return. We made our stand, but it was your soldiers who defeated Babel. We will not forget that. You have our loyalty. You have the loyalty of the astronauts and civilians who have joined our side. We will argue for you. We will fight for you. We will honor the agreement."

Greenlaw makes a gesture. Her entire squad mimics it. A sign of respect.

"The New Ring salutes you," she says.

"And to our crew," Morning says, turning to us. Her eyes run through our ranks. I know she feels the weight of every loss under her command, but in this moment, she allows herself pride. She steps free of the guilt and the burdens because she can see that she made a difference. "You deserve this moment too. I wasn't sure we would ever get to see Earth again. I can say without a *doubt* that we're here because of the part that each of you played. Welcome home."

She reaches back and presses a button on the nearest data pad before hustling back to take her place beside me. The debris shields roll slowly away . . .

. . . and Earth waits in the distance.

There's an audible gasp from the Imago. I'm not sure what they were expecting, but the gasps transform into delighted laughter. Morning reaches for my hand. I hold on tightly to her and try to smile as the tears come. Bilal is on my left. He sets a hand on my shoulder to keep himself steady. His face is full of indescribable joy. Alex has an affectionate arm wrapped around Anton's neck. He kisses Anton's forehead and wipes away tears. Jazzy has actually collapsed to her knees. Azima has both hands on her friend's shoulders as they reintroduce themselves to the world we left behind.

Isadora looks down on Earth like a queen. Roathy stands with her, holding their princess of a daughter tightly between them. Parvin looks solemn and serious, even as Noor shakes her by the shoulders and shouts with excitement. Holly's the only one to stumble forward and set a hand on the glass. I can see her tracing rivers and oceans with one finger, trying to figure out where home is.

Katsu catches my eye and shrugs. "Looks smaller than I remember."

We all laugh at that. Morning takes advantage of the distraction. She pulls me down by the collar and sneaks a kiss. We stand there for what feels like an hour, trying to process the idea of home and what happens next. Morning kisses me again—on the back of the hand this time—before stepping out in front of everyone.

She stands unafraid, unbowed, unbroken. We watch as she lifts one fist.

"Shoulder to shoulder!"

Our answering roar is loud enough to wake the dead. I get a brief glimpse of all the ghosts standing in the room with us. Kaya squeezes in beside me like she's been there the whole time. Longwei kneels by the window with a rare smile on his face. Jaime hangs casually back, like seeing home again isn't the biggest deal in the world. And then reality echoes.

Morning and the others are with me.

Earth waits.

We descend like conquerors.

ACKNOWLEDGMENTS

I'm still processing the idea of being *done*. This trilogy has taken me through every rise and valley imaginable. The first book offered all the thunderous excitement one might expect from a debut novel. I was honored and terrified in equal measure as I began my journey into the world of publishing. Book two was an equally predictable experience. I joined so many of my colleagues in struggling to write a fitting sequel. The third book, however, was uncomplicated. The whole thing swept into being like a strike of lightning.

I honestly believe I have *you* to thank for that, dear reader. There is something magical about the experience of communal joy. It's one thing to watch a funny movie by ourselves, but watch that same movie with five friends who share a similar sense of humor? That movie suddenly becomes hilarious. You're exchanging looks and belly-laughing and nudging one another. I felt that same experience as I worked through this trilogy. From the very first moment that I set *Nyxia* in the hands of readers, I had the sense that others were joining me on a long and meaningful road. Every week, new travelers joined our party, until we were all walking along, building momentum, promising with each step to reach the end. I cannot thank you enough for joining me on this journey.

My heartfelt thanks to Emily Easton at Crown BFYR. I also believe book three's edits were so much smoother because I'd learned to hear your voice along the way. If edits were easier, it was because I had you chipping away at things long before you'd even read the first draft. Many thanks to Josh Redlich and Samantha Gentry for all their brilliant, behind-the-scenes efforts. If you adored any of my covers (how could you not?), then please join me in thanking Regina Flath for luring in readers with those magnetic cover designs.

I would never have been in this position without the hard work of Kristin Nelson and the entire team at Nelson Literary Agency. As one would suspect from a secret society of wizards, they took my fledgling project, cast a few spells, and launched my career like it was no big deal at all.

There are several authors who have, one way or another, pushed me to be a far better writer. A big thanks to Marie Lu, V. E. Schwab, Nic Stone, Vic James, K. D. Edwards, Jason Hough, Kwame Mbalia, Brendan Reichs, and Jay Coles. I'd especially like to thank Tomi Adeyemi for her incredible enthusiasm as she read this series. The bold-faced reactions of our peers always act as buoys when we need them the most.

I am once more indebted to my wife, Katie. I could not have asked for a more patient and loving person to stand beside in life. Thank you for always listening, even if all my characters from all my stories have slowly merged into one giant fan-fiction piece for you.

Finally, I wrote this one for my baby boy, Henry. I have had the unique blessing of a smiling, laughing baby as I attempt to start my career as an author. One day, you'll read this, buddy, and I hope I can somehow express what a gift you are to us. On the days that this work could have been the hardest, I knew I had your smile waiting for me at home. It was so much easier to find purpose and push through, and you're a big part of that.

What a thing. Thank you again for sticking with me until the end.

God bless,
Scott Reintgen

ABOUT THE AUTHOR

SCOTT REINTGEN is the author of the Nyxia Triad. He has spent his career as a teacher of English and creative writing in diverse urban communities in North Carolina. The hardest lesson he learned in the classroom was that inspiration isn't equally accessible for everyone. So he set out to write a novel for the front-row sleepers and back-row dreamers in his classes. He hopes that his former students see themselves, vibrant and on the page, in characters like Emmett.

ITSPRONOUNCEDRANKIN.COM